KAIJU CORPS

MATTHEW DENNION

SEVERED PRESS
HOBART TASMANIA

KAIJU CORPS

WWW.SEVEREDPRESS.COM

ISBN: 978-1-925597-36-3

This book is written with fond memories of the Tokusatsu Television shows and movies that I loved as a kid, and to my sister who indulged my brother and me by letting us watch those movies without arguing over TV time!

PROLOGUE

Endless emptiness surrounded the Signal as it made its way through the vast abyss of space. The Signal had no understanding or concern of things such as life, time, or distance. The Signal simply continued to hurtle through the cosmos, looking for the next planet that had sufficient technology to receive it. Once the Signal had found a planet that had the required level of technology to upload itself into, the Signal would cascade over the planet and insert itself into that planet's systems. Then it would continue its journey through space. While the Signal itself would continue its never-ending journey, the part of itself that it uploaded into the planet's technological systems would carry out its programming and then return home.

The Signal had reached hundreds of planets. Each of those planets carried sentient lifeforms on it prior to the Signal arriving. After the Signal had uploaded itself into a planet's technology, the planet's resources and populations were decimated, leaving only a sufficient amount of each to maintain a breeding population.

The ever-widening Signal was quickly approaching a solar system. The Signal passed over the small planet of Pluto, the frozen rock known as Uranus, the ringed planet Saturn, and the gaseous giant Jupiter. The Signal cascaded over the red planet known as Mars and then it headed for the one planet in the solar system that had the sufficient level of technology required to upload itself into. The Signal made contact with the planet's satellites where it quickly began reprogramming them. The Signal then continued toward the planet itself where it began to infiltrate the databases of every computer system on the planet. It would be several days before any of the planet's inhabitants would notice what was occurring to their systems, but by that point, it would be far too late for the population of the planet to act. The fate of the planet's population was sealed. Within three months, two-thirds of the living organisms on the planet would be deceased, and most of the remaining third would be sent into space on the long journey back to where the Signal had originated from. A small breeding population of the remaining organisms would be kept alive to ensure a steady supply of the resources they provided.

CHAPTER 1

Catskill Mountains Horsemen Facility

The warm water from the shower poured down Nick's body as the steam filled his bathroom. Nick took a series of deep breaths and once he had slowed his heart rate, he sat down. He had just completed another training exercise, and as usual, the training had taken a lot out of him both physically and mentally. The warm shower helped his body to relax as his bones and muscles shifted back into their original positions. Nick focused on the sound of the falling water and he used the steady white noise to calm his mind. He kept quietly repeating, "I am Nick. I am a human being. I am in control of myself." Nick repeated those words for over ten minutes before he finally let other thoughts enter his mind. His *Instructors* had taught him that reminding himself that he was a human with a name was crucial to his ability to maintain a sense of self and a normal life.

Nick laughed sarcastically to himself, "A normal life. As if that was ever an option for me." He could feel his back muscles twitch beneath his skin and he knew that it meant he needed to calm himself down. He took a series of deep breaths and thought back to his decompression training. His Instructors had taught him that focusing on his life and the things that were important to him as a human would help him retain control of himself. Nick closed his eyes and he tried to think about what a normal life meant in regards to him and the other three members of the Kaiju Corps.

Nick thought back on what was defined as *his life* by the Instructors. Nick and his fellow Kaiju Corps members were genetically engineered by a group of individuals who called themselves *The Horsemen*, as in the Four Horsemen of the Apocalypse mentioned in the Bible. The Horsemen are a group that is composed of some of the greatest scientific minds in the world. They come from nearly every country on the planet and yet they answer to no single nation. The Horsemen know that the extinction of the human race is an inevitability. One way or another, the time would come when humanity would cease to exist, as did all species of living things. What the Horsemen tried to do was to limit the causes of the extinction and to prolong humanity's existence for as long as possible. There were potential extinction level threats that the Horsemen could influence subtly like Global Warming or overpopulation. There were some threats that there was nothing they could do about, like the potential of the super volcano under Yellow Stone National Park erupting and covering the earth in a planet-wide cloud of ash.

Then there were the threats that could only be addressed through force, such as power-mad dictators armed with weapons of mass destruction or the threat of extraterrestrial invasion. In order to deal with these possible threats, the Horsemen had created the Kaiju Corps. The Horsemen gathered human embryos and subjected them to genetic modification. The embryos were infused with steroids, hormones, both extinct and living animal DNA, as well as controlled doses of radiation. After years of failed attempts, the Horsemen were finally able to have four of the embryos grow into infants. The modifications that were done to these infants would give them the ability to protect the world from even the direst physical threats. The infants that were engineered by the Horsemen would have the ability to turn into the gigantic creatures that the film industry had dubbed kaiju.

Nick was one of those infants. When he was young, he always had the sense that there was someone else inside of his body. Like all of his fellow Kaiju Corps members, Nick had amazing physical skills when he was an adolescent. He could run at the speed of an Olympic track star and he was strong enough to bench press a car. It wasn't until Nick reached puberty that his other-self first emerged. Nick's Instructors had made him fully aware of what would one day happen to him. That he would eventually find that he had the ability to turn into a giant monster. When it first happened, Nick was only fourteen years old. He vividly remembered the pain that accompanied his first change. He felt as though his bones and muscles were forcing their way out of his skin. He can still remember the first time that he felt the pain of his skin ripping apart as the kaiju within him tore through his body.

Nick looked down to see everything around him shrinking as he grew to an enormous size. He would later be told that his kaiju-self had grown to a size of nearly two hundred feet tall.

As he watched everything around him shrinking, Nick noticed that it wasn't just his size that was changing. The entire structure of his body was morphing into something new. Nick looked at his hands to see long green claws covered in scales. He turned his thick and powerful arm over to see a long fin-like appendage that stretched from his wrist to his forearm. He then noticed that his shoulders and chest were covered in a thick caprice that resembled the back of a crocodile. He looked further down his body to see that scales covered the lower half of his torso and thighs. Both of his knees had short but thick horns protruding out from them. He moved his foot and he noticed that what had once been five toes had merged into three thick digits. One digit extended out from the base of his foot while the other two had shifted to the sides of his feet to support the weight of his massive body. Nick recalled trying to speak only to hear an earthshaking roar emerge from his mouth.

Nick walked over to the side of the installation, and it was there that he first saw his face. His face had merged into something like a combination of a lizard and a fish. His jaw now protruded forward and he opened his mouth to see long serrated teeth. His eyes had been elongated and stretched further back on the side of his head. His hair was gone and it was replaced by a fin that ran from between his eyes to the back of his head. When Nick saw his reflection, his mind was overwhelmed with rage. He can remember staring at the wall of the installation as a painful burning sensation began to form in his throat. A second later, a huge fireball erupted from Nick's mouth and exploded against the wall. From that point on, he could only remember snapshot memories of his first transformation. He could remember vague images of a small town and people running away from him. His next memory was of the cool and calming ocean.

When Nick regained his senses, he was aboard a large yacht owned by the Horsemen. Nick can remember waking up and seeing one of the Instructors sitting next to him. The Instructor leaned forward, held out his hand, and said, "Hello, Nick. I am one of your Instructors and my name is Timothy." Timothy had explained to Nick what had occurred after he had seen his reflection in the side of the installation. "When you saw your kaiju-self, you became overwhelmed with rage. It seems that in your kaiju form, you have the ability to project bursts of flames with temperatures reaching those of volcanic magma. You burned and smashed through the installation. You then destroyed several towns before the military attacked you and drove you out to sea. They followed you for as long as they could, but your kaiju-self was able to move faster than even their fastest ships, and when you dove beneath the water, their planes lost sight of you."

Nick can remember shaking with fear when he heard the news. He recalled looking at Timothy. "Did… did anyone die as a result of what I did?"

Timothy placed his hand on Nick's shoulder. "Several hundred people died, but none of those deaths are your fault." Nick began to tear up, and for the first time, one of Nick's Instructors hugged him. "Those deaths are my fault, Nick. Mine and the rest of the Instructors. We should have been better prepared for what would happen when you changed. We should have worked with you more on being psychologically prepared for what would happen when you first became a kaiju. We failed you, Nick. We failed you and all of those people that died." Timothy pulled away and looked Nick in the eye. "I can't bring those people back to life or remove the pain that you feel over their deaths. What I can do is promise you that going forward, we are going to learn from this tragedy and use what we have learned to save billions of lives."

Timothy let go of Nick then he picked up the television remote. He turned it on to show a CNN news feed. The television was running footage of the devastation that Nick had left in his wake. The ticker at the bottom of the screen kept running a line that said, *Leviathan causes havoc in Asia.* Timothy gestured to the screen. "As I said, this is a horrible tragedy but we can take something from it."

Nick shook his head as his eyes filled with tears. "What can we possibly take from this?"

Timothy walked up to the screen and pointed to the ticker. "Your kaiju-self is going to need a name and this news station has just given it to you. The world is now aware of the existence of Leviathan."

As painful as the memory of Nick's first transformation was, he always thought about it when he needed to consider the high points in his life. This was a high point for him because up until then, none of his Instructors had told him their names. They were simply referred to as *Instructor*. They had also been indifferent to Nick. The Instructors were not callous or neglectful to Nick; they had simply carried out their duties without offering much encouragement or emotional support. When Nick had met Timothy, he immediately knew that he had found someone he could confide in. From that day on, Timothy was there for Nick after each and every one of his transformations. He was also there for Nick on a personal level. He helped Nick with other life skills, such as learning to drive a car, shaving, and how to better interact with the other members of the Kaiju Corps outside of training. Timothy quickly became the father that Nick had never had and never knew he was missing. With Timothy's help, Nick quickly learned how to retain his human intelligence when he was in his kaiju form.

Nick opened his eyes and then stood up in the shower. He stretched his neck from side to side as he thought about the other people in his life that brought him joy. Nick rolled his shoulders to loosen them up as he focused on the only other people on Earth that he felt close to. Those people were the other infants who had been modified like him. They were the people who would join him in forming the Kaiju Corps.

The first person who came to mind was Nick's best friend and the man whom he considered to be his brother, Jerome. As the only two male members of the Kaiju Corps, Nick and Jerome shared a special bond. Nick stood about six feet tall and he was of Caucasian descent while Jerome was of African descent and stood over six foot six. Due to the fact that they had both undergone the same enhancements as embryos, they shared similar physical abilities. As the two male members of their small group, they shared a special bond. They were born at the same time, they were raised together, and they saw each other as brothers.

When they were young, they often played together without the restrictions that were placed on their interactions with the females. Before Nick had met Timothy, Jerome was the only person in existence that Nick looked at as a source of emotional support. Nick and Jerome understood each other in a way that no one else could. They could relate to each other as children, and now that they were each in their early twenties, they could relate to each other as young men. Even more than the bond they shared as friends and brothers, they shared a closer bond of having the shared experience of having an other-self that was a giant monster.

While they shared the ability to morph into a kaiju, there were dramatic differences in their experiences as monsters both physically and mentally. While Nick became the scaled Leviathan, a reptilian creature that was at home in the water, Jerome changed into the winged creature that was a master of the skies. Nick recalled that shortly after his initial transformation, Jerome came to see him. Jerome was eager to learn from Nick how he had forced himself to transform into Leviathan. Nick tried to explain to Jerome that he truly had no idea how the transformation had first occurred. Nick can specifically recall telling Jerome that it, "Just sort of happened."

In the weeks following Nick's transformation, Jerome had pushed himself hard trying to transform into a kaiju. Nick recalled how Jerome would push himself to the point of physical exhaustion in hopes that it would trigger his initial transformation. Nick could still see Jerome sitting in the large hangars of various installations where he would meditate for hours on end in an attempt to transform himself. When the transformation finally occurred for Jerome, he handled it far differently than Nick had. Nick could recall Jerome's initial transformation with complete clarity. Jerome was attempting to pick up a six-ton forklift. The weight was twice the maximum limit that Jerome had previously lifted. He was straining to move the forklift when his skin began to split as feathers protruded through it. Jerome quickly began growing in size as feathers continued to sprout across his body and massive wings grew out of his shoulder blades.

Nick watched in awe as Jerome grew and lifted the forklift off the ground as if it was a child's toy. When Jerome had finished transforming, he stood at roughly one hundred and eighty feet tall. Jerome still had the body structure of a human with a torso, powerful arms, and two thick legs. His body was covered in feathers and the wings that had grown out of his back looked similar to the wings of an eagle. They extended out from his shoulders and the tips of his wings ended parallel to his calves. Jerome's feet and hands ended in sharp raptor-like talons. His face had taken on the visage of a hawk and his head was wreathed with long pointed horns.

While Nick could recall every detail of how Jerome had appeared physically, it was Jerome's mental state that stuck with Nick. Nick had lost his mind after his first transformation, but Jerome was in total control of his kaiju-self. While Nick had been scared and terrified of his kaiju-self, Jerome immediately accepted who he was, and instead of seeing himself as horrific like Nick did, Jerome saw himself as a majestic and noble creature. Jerome was able to move his new body around with ease. The massive beast that was the kaiju-self of Jerome gestured for the large doors of the hangar that he was in to be opened. The Instructors complied with the kaiju's request. Jerome's kaiju-self walked out of the hangar and then he stretched his wings to their full capacity. He flapped them several times and then he took off into the air. He would return several hours later amongst several reports of a giant flying monster. When Jerome's kaiju-self landed, he immediately started to change back into his human form. Jerome walked into the hangar to find Nick and the Instructors waiting for him. Jerome looked around at everyone in the hangar and he only said one thing, "Garudasaurus. From this point on, my kaiju-self shall be referred to as Garudasaurus. In honor of the god, Garuda, and the mighty dinosaurs that had once ruled this planet." Jerome then calmly exited the hangar and headed for his quarters.

It was obvious to Nick, and to the Instructors, that another change had occurred to Jerome in addition to becoming a kaiju. Jerome had clearly established that he was the person to be the field leader of the Kaiju Corps.

Jerome was met by an Instructor named Thomas who served the same role for him as Timothy did for Nick. The difference was where Nick needed support in dealing with his change, Jerome needed guidance in how to be a leader.

Nick turned around in the shower and arched his back. He was two-thirds of the way through his de-escalation process. His mind was focusing on the good things in his world that made life worth living. Thinking of his first meeting with Timothy gave Nick a sense of support and security. Recalling his relationship with Jerome and his brother's ability to control his kaiju-self helped to give Nick a sense of both pride and inner strength.

The third step of recalling the good things in his life centered around his thoughts regarding the two female members of the Kaiju Corps, Miki and Michelle. Nick was starting to focus on them when an alarm blared throughout the installation. Nick wasn't sure what the alarm signified, but it was quickly followed by the announcement, "This is a level one alarm. All members of the Horsemen are to report to the conference room! Kaiju Corps members are to report to the Hangar 18 in one hour."

Nick shook his head and turned off the shower. He had nearly gotten his body to a stage where he felt as if he was completely human and now he feared that he would not only have to stop the process, but he was afraid that he would need to change into Leviathan again. Nick feared that for the first time in history, the Kaiju Corps would be officially activated.

CHAPTER 2

The cold and dark was crushing her as she continued to push her way through the hard rocks and dirt that surrounded her. Miki reached up and tore another chunk of earth out of her way, causing even more soil to fall into her face as she made her way up in an attempt to escape. A moment ago, she had been in a secure underground bunker in the Pocono Mountains. The next thing that she was aware of was that she felt the need to escape and destroy. Miki found that her head had nearly reached the ceiling of the warehouse-like bunker. As she reached up for the ceiling, she noticed two long and thin lizard-like claws where her hands should have been. She tried to scream but all that emanated from her mouth was a hissing sound. She hissed and then ripped through the ceiling that confined her. As dirt poured into the hole she created, she started increasing the size of the opening in the ceiling until she was able to crawl into where she now found herself buried beneath the ground.

Miki kept digging her way up until she felt her face force its way into the open air. A moment later, she managed to pull her entire body into the sunlight. As soon as she had pulled her head out of the ground, she threw it from side to side and hissed at the sky. She looked around to see that she was surrounded by what appeared to be tiny fir trees. She heard shouting to her right, and instinctively, she tried to run from it. As she fled, she became aware of the odd manner in which she was moving. Her head and neck seemed to be swaying from side to side as she moved. She swung her head to the right, and she was amazed at how far back she could turn her neck. She was even more amazed when she saw a long serpentine body with two small thin sets of legs attached to them. Miki continued to extend her neck and to examine her body as she tried to comprehend what she had become. Her first was thought was *snake*. Miki had thought that she had transformed into a giant snake.

She tried to orient herself to where she was, but the hissing sound and the screaming below her made it nearly impossible for her to concentrate. She was filled with rage at all of the noise, and when she turned her head to see where the screaming was coming from, she saw a tiny man and woman standing below her. The young couple was standing next to the campsite where they had slept the previous night. Miki tried to tell them to be quiet so that she could think, but once more, the only sound that came out of her mouth was a terrible hissing noise. The young couple turned and began running toward a lake. When Miki saw the lake in the distance, she felt compelled to head for it as well.

She began to slither toward the lake, and as she moved toward the water, she crushed a winding path through the forest. The couple that was running away from her heard her heading for them, and they had the good sense to take a ninety-degree turn and move out of Miki's path. Miki ignored the couple as she made her way to the water that seemed to call to her. When she reached the water's edge, she stopped for a brief moment and she looked down at her reflection. She had expected to see the flat round face of a snake, but instead, she saw a long snout with whiskers poking out of it staring back at her. It was at that point that she realized she had not changed into a giant snake. With her thin rear and hind legs and her long, whiskered snout, she more closely resembled a Chinese Dragon than she did a snake.

Miki stared down at the alluring water for a moment and then she gracefully slipped below its surface. The lake was not very large, and Miki's nearly two-hundred-foot-long body was able to swim the circumference of it in less than two minutes. The relatively small size of the lake was of no concern to Miki; she simply felt more at peace with her new body when she was submerged in the water. She continued to swim circles around the lake while the two campers that she had scared ran back to the nearest town's police department, screaming about a lake monster.

Two hours later, the local police department, along with half of the town, arrived at the lake armed with everything from shotguns to dynamite. The lake water was crystal clear and everyone who stood around it could see Miki's dragon form as she swam by them. The town sheriff grabbed a microphone and called for everyone to open fire. Miki remembered hearing an explosion as she felt harmless but annoying projectiles bounce off her thick hide. She swam to the surface of the lake, and when her snout rose out of the water, people either screamed and ran or started shooting at her eyes. Even the bullets that struck her eyes were not able to injure her, but the part of Miki's brain that was still maintaining her human consciousness was enraged that these people were attacking her for simply going for a swim. Miki saw a flash of red before her eyes, and then the next thing that she remembered was waking up naked in her human form along the shore of the lake. She sat up to see the crushed and mutilated bodies of the town's people surrounding her. Her mind quickly came to the realization that she had caused the deaths of all of these people. A wave a panic ran through Miki's body as she stood up to see that entire shoreline of the lake was covered in bodies.

Miki awoke screaming in her bed as the memory of her first transformation had once more returned to haunt her dreams. It had been five years she had first morphed into her kaiju-self, and still, she was disturbed by what she had become and what she had done.

She walked over to the bathroom that was part her quarters and she splashed cold water on her face as she tried to calm herself down from the nightmare that she experienced on an all too frequent basis. She looked in the mirror at herself to see the pretty face of a thin and athletic twenty-year-old woman staring back her. Her hair had grown longer than she liked it to be. Miki usually cut her hair when it reached her shoulders, but now, it was draped over her shoulders and down her back. She started brushing her hair, then she sighed as she continued to recall the events that had occurred after her first transformation.

The Instructors had learned after the first time that Nick had changed how emotionally and psychologically devastating the first transformation from a human into a kaiju could be. In response to this, the Horsemen had the Instructors move the members of the Kaiju Corps to remote underground locations in hopes of containing them in case they were overwhelmed by the shock of when they first became a kaiju. This plan had failed miserably in Miki's case. When she first changed into a kaiju, she had not only burrowed out of the underground bunker, but she had also been attacked by the local law enforcement agencies, and in attempting to defend herself, she had killed several dozen people.

Dozens of people had died before Miki finally reverted back to her human form. In response to the disaster, the Instructors quickly destroyed the bunker, removing any evidence of where the kaiju had come from. Miki herself was placed on a train and whisked away from the Poconos. She was looking out the window when an Instructor sat down next to her with a cell phone in her hands.

The Instructor began reading information off her phone. "Miki, you are a member of the Kaiju Corps. You are fifteen years old and the human part of your DNA is of Japanese origin."

Miki nodded in reply, not fully aware if the Instructor was asking her questions or simply stating facts.

The Instructor smiled. "My name is Clarissa, and I will be your personal Instructor from now on." She placed her arm around the teenager. "Would you like to talk about what happened?" Miki remembered breaking down in tears as she hugged Clarissa, and as she was reliving this memory and looking at herself in the mirror, she saw a tear run down the side of her check.

Clarissa whispered into her ear, "It's not your fault, dear. It's not your fault." Miki knew that these were the same words that Nick had heard when he first underwent the change. She shook her head and sobbed into Clarissa's breast, "What are they calling me?"

Clarissa hugged her tightly. "Chagon. It's a blend of the two words Chinese and Dragon."

She filled her hands with water again and splashed it over her face when she heard the alarm sound in her quarters followed by the order to go Hangar 18. Miki took a deep breath as she realized what Hangar 18 meant. She took one last look in the mirror as she fought back her emotions and composed herself. She stared directly into the reflection of her own eyes as she spoke to herself, "Hangar 18, this is it. This is no drill. The Kaiju Corps is being activated. We are going to war."

CHAPTER 3

Deep in the Atlantic Ocean, the submarine *USS Venture* was cruising along the ocean floor. The sub was moving at top speed as it made its way along the coast from Philadelphia to Norfolk. The submarine had crossed roughly half the distance of its journey when a huge set of eyes snapped open in the darkness behind the vessel. A massive beast lifted itself off the ocean floor and began swimming toward the sub. The monster swam closer to the surface of the water, and when it did so, it was illuminated by the sunlight that had managed to pierce the darkness. The sun reflected brightly off the glistening white fur that covered a body with a form similar to that of a polar bear but less bulky and more elongated. The creature also had a face that was akin to a polar bear with long powerful jaws and a short black nose. While the kaiju had many similarities to the endangered bear, there were also marked differences. The most notable features were the two bull-like horns that protruded from the sides of its head. Additionally, the monster also had a long, thick, fur-covered tail that ended in a series of spikes like the ancient *Stegosaurus*.

The kaiju moved through the water with a velocity that far surpassed the speed of the submarine she was pursuing. The creature was over two hundred and fifty feet long from head to tail, but it was able to move through the water with the agility of a river otter. The monster was known as Bearadon and she was the fourth member of the Kaiju Corps. In her human form, she was known as Michelle. She was a twenty-three-year-old woman whose genes had originated from Apache ancestors. Her human appearance reflected her Apache heritage. She had beautiful brown skin, long raven-colored hair, and stunning hazel eyes. She was an intense young woman who had devoted herself totally to the cause of being a member of the Kaiju Corps and defending the human race. Michelle had not been raised as an Apache. She and all of the members of the Kaiju Corps had the same diversified upbringing that came from being taught and raised by the greatest minds around the world, all from different cultures. While Michelle had not been raised as an Apache, she was still aware of how her ancestors and other Native America tribes were decimated and nearly driven to the point of extinction when they came into contact with Europeans. Michelle took this tragedy to heart, and she vowed that she would do all that she could to ensure that no other large-scale genocide occurred while she was walking the earth.

Her focus on her training and her determination to protect her world allowed her to be able to make a seamless transition from human to kaiju without incident. Just as Jerome was able to control his kaiju-self when he first transformed, Michelle also maintained complete control of herself when she first became Bearadon. Like the other members of the Kaiju Corps, Michelle was assigned a personal Instructor. Her name was Susan, and while it was her responsibility to offer Michelle emotional guidance, the two of them were never close due to Michelle's desire to be independent. While the other Instructors acted as mentors and surrogate parents to their assigned members, Michelle mainly treated Susan as her liaison to the inner circle of the Horsemen. Susan continually tried to be an emotional outlet for the young woman, but Michelle always opted to keep her relationship with the Instructor professional.

Michelle's work ethic and her determination to succeed in her missions had at first led to the idea that she would be the field leader of the Kaiju Corps. As the Instructors studied her more closely, they began to realize that she lacked several of the key attributes that were required to lead a team. While Michelle had excellent instincts for tracking and battling in her kaiju form, she had extremely poor interpersonal skills.

Michelle often saw the other members of the Kaiju Corps as extra baggage that hampered her from successfully completing her mission rather than teammates who could help her complete it. It was these traits that led the Instructors to designate Jerome/Garudasaurus as the leader of the Kaiju Corps. This fact didn't matter to Michelle when she was first informed of it, nor did it have any bearing on her current training mission, as she continued to make her way toward the remote-controlled submarine that she was supposed to destroy.

She was closing in on the vessel when she noticed that it altered its course from moving in a straight line and dove to the ocean floor. Bearadon snarled as she realized that the Instructors who were controlling the submarine must have realized that she was stalking them, and as such, they dove to the sea bed in an attempt to lose her. The act was futile, as she was still fully capable of tracking the submarine and catching it, but it galled her that she had been noticed by the people controlling the crewless vessel. She changed her course in pursuit of the submarine when, to her surprise, it turned around and started moving toward her.

Bearadon was confused by this motion. She had performed this drill several times before and each time that she did, the submarine had done its best to avoid her. Yet in this instance, it appeared as if the sub was turning around to attack her. Bearadon increased her already considerable speed as she charged toward the strangely behaving submarine.

Bearadon had closed roughly half the distance between herself and the sub when she saw two torpedoes streaking toward her. The lithe kaiju streamlined her body and rolled, causing the projectiles to streak past her and explode in the water behind her. Bearadon was fairly sure that her thick hide was capable of withstanding the force of the exploding torpedoes, but she had no desire to find out during what was supposed to be a routine training exercise. She quickly swam up to the submarine, reached out with her powerful claws, and with a single swipe, she sliced the aquatic drone to pieces.

Bearadon's attack was surgical in its precision. She had struck the ship in such a way that it would not explode but rather the drone simply filled with water and then sink to the bottom of the ocean. Bearadon's mind was a mix of both anger and confusion. She needed to return to base so that she could confer with the Instructors as to why they had so drastically changed their tactics in the approach to this mission. The mammalian kaiju swam in a tight circle and then she started heading back to shore. For both security purposes and for their own protection, she and the other three members of the Kaiju Corps were constantly being moved around the world from one hidden location to the next. The facility that the team was currently housed in was the Horsemen's primary facility in the Catskill Mountains.

Bearadon was swimming back to shore when she received a radio transmission through the communication relay implanted within her ear, "Bearadon, we have a level one alarm. Please return to the Catskill station and report to Hangar 18." Bearadon growled as she continued to push through the water. The Instructors had run numerous drills claiming that there was a level one emergency over the past few years, but they had never conducted a drill that started in Hangar 18.

Despite the fact that the Kaiju Corps moved all around the world, they never felt like they left home. This was mainly due to the fact that no matter where they went, each and every facility that they were sent to was set up exactly the same. Not just in terms of the ways the facilities were constructed by everything down to the artwork on the walls and even the personal belongings of the team members were exactly the same in every facility that they were sent to. Miki had a thing for snow globes. She had at least a dozen snow globes, and in each facility around the world, she had the same dozen in each of her quarters. Having the facilities set up in the same manner not only helped to keep each facility running as efficiently as possible, but it also helped to create some sense of normalcy and consistency for the Kaiju Corps and the Instructors who traveled with them.

One of the most consistent rules of their travel was that no matter what facility they were in did they ever enter Hangar 18. Each and every facility that they lived and worked from was constructed as if it were an underground air base. Every facility had twenty large hangers where the team members had the space to change into their kaiju forms and train. In each of these facilities, Hangar 18 was off limits. The Instructors had never explained why this was the case, and Michelle and the other members of the Kaiju Corps had often discussed amongst themselves that Hangar 18 must be reserved for actual emergencies. With the drone submarine acting out of its normal operational pattern and the order to report to Hangar 18, Bearadon was sure that a real emergency had presented itself. That alone would have been enough to concern her, but the fact that it was designated as a level one emergency terrified her. Level one emergencies represented potential extinction-level threats. Bearadon growled again as she continued to push herself as hard as she could to return to the Catskill installation.

CHAPTER 4

Detroit, Michigan

It was almost ten in the morning as Brian Linke continued to work furiously on his computer at the Ford motor car assembly plant. Brian was the head computer programmer for the site, and when he arrived at work a little over an hour ago, he was met by several of the floor workers who had shocked looks on their faces. The floor workers had informed Brian that when they arrived at work and started the automated assembly line, it was not working properly. The robotic arms that constructed the cars piece by piece were not assembling the cars in the fashion that they usually did. The workers had shut down and rebooted the assembly line several times but each time that the assembly line was reactivated, it simply continued to not follow its protocols. After the assembly line had moved forward for roughly half an hour, putting all types of odd parts together, the line stopped moving, and whatever the system was putting together started to look far different and far larger than any car or truck.

Brian looked at the assembly line, and he was shocked to see what appeared to be a skeletal structure composed of car parts starting to form as the mechanical arms of the assembly line continued to build the mystery machine. Brian ran up to his office overlooking the assembly line floor where he had direct access to the plant's mainframe. It took Brian several attempts to log onto his computer, and after he was able to access his PC, it took nearly twenty minutes for the computer to connect to the factory's mainframe.

As soon as Brian was able to access the mainframe and see the commands running through the assembly line system, he was immediately able to determine that it had been hacked. The level of intrusion that had occurred to the assembly line program was far greater than anything Brian had ever seen. Brian had graduated in the top third of his class from MIT. He knew what he was doing when it came to securing a computer network. When he had first been hired at Ford a few months ago, he had installed state-of-the-art firewalls into the factory's system, and while no system was completely secure, he couldn't understand how the person who had hacked the system had managed to do it so completely. The firewalls that he had erected were not just circumvented, they were completely destroyed!

He was even more shocked by the fact that whoever had shattered his firewalls had completely taken over the system! Even more astounding was that they had reprogrammed it to the point where the assembly had not only stopped making cars, but they had entered commands to have the robotic arms construct something that physically they should not have been able to make!

Brian's mind was racing. The level of incursion that had occurred to the system was something new that no one had ever seen before. This was not just the type of thing where he would have to inform the heads of the company of what had occurred, but he would also have to inform the NSA and the FBI cyber division. What Brian was looking at could only have been the work of some new tech terrorist or a foreign nation. Brian was doing his best not to panic at the magnitude of what was occurring. Instead, he focused on taking as much data as he could on the hack in order to pass it on to the authorities.

He looked over his computer at the construct which was quickly forming on the assembly line. The skeletal structure that was being constructed out of car parts was growing to an enormous size. The arms of the assembly line were starting to add layers onto the frame they had constructed, and it was then that Brian realized what the assembly line was building. Brian was watching the construction of some form of giant robot. He shook his head in disbelief then he swallowed the saliva that was building up in his mouth as a metaphor to himself for swallowing his fear. He once again tried to focus on obtaining data.

Brian looked toward the floor workers who were still watching the assembly line construct the robot. The floor workers clearly had no idea of the severity of the situation before them. Brian decided to keep the men in the dark as to the complexity of what was occurring because if they knew what was truly happening, it was likely that they would panic. Brian needed as much information as he could to send to NSA and the FBI and panicking workers would not be able to help him.

He called out to the men, "I need measurements of the size the thing that the line is making as well as your best observations of what that thing is composed of."

Two men quickly grabbed measuring tape. They placed the tape at the end of what was starting to look like a foot. They ran out the tape as far as it would go, made a mark, and then repeated the process. While two of the men were measuring the robot, the rest of the crew circled around the assembly line and took notes of what they could see of the machine that was now almost as large as the line itself. Brian watched as the assembly line's robotic arms lifted several of the onboard computers that were installed into the company's newest cars and placed them in the robot's chest.

The workers who were measuring the robot yelled out from next to a huge head that the assembly line's robotic arms had just placed on the construct's shoulders, "This freaking thing is two hundred and nineteen feet tall!" He then used the measuring tape to check the width of the robot. After marking and moving his tape measure a second time, he yelled out to Brian, "This thing also measures seventy-two feet wide." The man's eyes looked up from the robot's back to its chest. Then he yelled at Brian, "I don't think I can measure its depth without the cherry picker."

Brian nodded in reply as one of the workers starting yelling up to him what he could make out of the robot's composition, "It looks like most of the frame is made out of steel with aluminum composing the rest of its body. It has several exhaust ports at the bottom of its feet and the line keeps putting more and more onboard computers into its chest." The man looked overhead as the assembly line arms lifted several tires into the robot's chest and began placing them around the onboard computer system. He shook his head and then yelled again, "Now it's putting tires in there? Just what in the hell is the assembly line doing?"

Brian ignored the man's question as he entered the data he had into the computer and quickly used his tablet to take a picture of what was a nearly complete giant robot. He took a quick look at the picture he had taken. The robot had an overall humanoid form with a head, torso, arms, legs, and feet. The robot was a multitude of colors, as if whoever was constructing the machine was more concerned with getting the robot together quickly as opposed to having it appear ascetically pleasing. Brian had been hoping that whoever had taken over the assembly line was just some sort of really smart teenager who had hacked the system and was using it to make a copy of his favorite Power Rangers Zord. As Brian looked at the robot, it was clear that the automaton was no joke.

Brian saw a large canister being lifted off the factory floor that was also placed within in the robot's chest. He yelled to the men on the floor, "Was that one of the liquid nitrogen canisters that we are going to test on the new cars?" A man on the floor quickly replied that it was indeed one of the canisters. Brian became even more concerned at seeing the liquid nitrogen being loaded into the robot. The chemical was being used by the military, car manufacturers, and locomotive builders as a potential clean source of energy. The liquid nitrogen vehicles would be able to power themselves far longer than even a fully charged electric plug-in car. In fact, some estimates suggested the car could operate for up to six months on only a single canister.

Brian compiled all of his information into a single file and then he attempted to email it to the NSA and the FBI. He hit the send button on his email, but his screen flashed a warning indicating that his file had not been sent. Brian tried to send the file again only to have the server rebuff his request a second time. He was trying to figure out what to do next when the robot's hand slid off the assembly line and clanged loudly on the concrete floor. Then, like the Frankenstein Monster in the old Universal Movies, the robot's hand lifted itself into the air. The floor workers stared in awe as the robot sat up and turned its head toward them. Brian watched in horror as the mech lifted its giant metal hand into the air and then brought it crashing down on at least a dozen workers whose bodies were crushed into a mixed puddle of blood, bones, and organs. The remaining floor workers screamed and began rushing for the exit. The robot then stood up, causing its head and shoulders to smash through the roof of the building.

The robot then started walking forward. Its thick metal chest cut through the roof of the building as easily as a human's chest would cut through water in a pool. As the robot walked, it crushed people beneath the massive weight of its feet while others were pinned to the floor by the chunks of roof debris that fell upon them. Brian looked behind him to see people from the offices connected to the factory running in to see what was going on. He jumped out of his chair and pulled the fire alarm in hopes that he would get some people out of the building before they were crushed to death.

Brian grabbed his tablet as he ran to the nearest exit. He reached the door at the exact moment that the robot smashed through the south wall of the factory floor. Brian screamed and tears filled his eyes as he watched dozens more people crushed to death beneath the robot's feet. He was shaking his head, and in his mind, he was asking God why this was happening when he heard a ping on his computer. He looked down to see that he had received an email from some group called the Horsemen. He opened the email and read a message that would change his life.

We are the Horsemen. Most of the computer and internet services that we rely on have been permanently corrupted or shut down. We are maintaining a small bit of communications through a Dark Web that we have created which is temporarily secure. Use this link to connect to it and to keep us aware of the robot's position. Help is on the way.

Brian couldn't believe everything that was happening. First a giant robot, and now an email from some group called the Horsemen! These Horsemen obviously had some pretty impressive programming skills if they were able to bypass whatever was keeping him from reaching the NSA. For all that Brian knew, these people were the ones who had high-jacked his system and had used it to make the robot. Brian heard a loud crash then he looked at where the south wall of the plant used to be. Through the now-crushed wall, he saw the robot plowing through buildings as if they were made of cardboard and killing hundreds of people in the process.

Brian didn't know who the Horsemen were. Maybe they were the people who were controlling the robot and maybe they weren't.

The only thing that he did know is that people were dying, and if there was anything that he could do to save some of their lives, he was going to try and do it. He figured if nothing else, that he would at least have a clear conscious knowing that he accepted an offer to try and help save lives. Brian connected his tablet to the link that the Horsemen had provided and then he began to type in as much information as he could about what the robot was doing and where it was in the city.

He was about to run after the robot when he heard the sound of the assembly line turning on again behind him. He spun around to see the arms of the assembly line gathering more car parts and fusing them together. Brian quickly typed a message to the mysterious Horsemen.

The assembly line is building another robot!

Brian dashed out of the building before the new robot was completed. He stayed a safe distance behind the first robot and he followed its path of destruction through the city. He saw a group of people run out of the building in front of the robot and Brian expected to see the robot step on them but instead the robot did something completely unexpected. It bent down and sprayed a white mist over the people that Brian was able to recognize as liquid nitrogen. Brian watched as the people that the robot sprayed were instantly frozen solid. The robot then reached down, picked up the frozen people, and loaded them into a compartment in its back. Brian quickly typed into his computer.

The robots are not just using the liquid nitrogen to power themselves! They are killing some of the people here, but they appear to be freezing other people and storing them for later usage. Whatever help is coming, please hurry!

CHAPTER 5

Catskill Mountains Horsemen Facility

Nick was totally exhausted as he made his way through the hallway toward Hangar 18. It took a lot out of him to change into his Leviathan form and then back into a human. He had nearly completed the process when the alarm went off and sent a surge of adrenaline running through his system. The surge nearly triggered the change into Leviathan, and it took all of Nick's will power and energy to keep the change from occurring within his quarters. He needed to meditate for several minutes to get his body under control. When Nick was finally in total control of his body, he started making his way toward the ominous Hangar 18.

When he entered the hangar, he saw Jerome and Miki already standing in one of the few illuminated spots inside of the empty structure. Hangar 18 looked like any typical aircraft hangar with the exception that it was four times larger than any other hangar in the world. While Nick had never been in this hangar, he a good idea of what capabilities the hangar possessed. He assumed that like all of the other hangars in the Horsemen's facilities, the walls and the ceilings also doubled as monitors where the Instructors could upload news feeds and information from around the world. During previous training missions, the Kaiju Corps had met in hangars like this one, and when they were ready, the Instructors would show them their current mission on one of the walls or the ceiling. Usually though, the entire hangar was at least lit up when they entered it. The fact that only a few lights were on in the hangar only added to the tension that Nick was feeling for being called into actual action.

Nick saw his friends staring at him and gesturing for him to come over to them. He nodded and then jogged over to Jerome and Miki.

Jerome had a look of mixed excitement and apprehension on his face. He shrugged and smiled as he took a step toward Nick. "Hangar 18. Whatever is happening, it's real, and it's serious."

Nick gave a nervous laugh. "Any idea about what's going on?

Jerome shook his head. "No, the television in my room isn't working and the computer systems have all been blocked out."

Nick looked around the room. "Where is Michelle? She is usually the first to show up for a drill. I figured she would have run here the minute that they said Hangar 18 over the intercom."

Miki walked over to them. Nick noticed that she had her arms wrapped around her body almost as if she was hugging herself. She was shaking and Nick could see that she was scared by the thought of whatever was going to happen. She tried to smile. "Michelle is still out on a training mission. She is on her way back, but I get the feeling that we are going to have to start this mission without her."

Nick knew what was bothering Miki. All of them had been trained since birth to be warriors and to be ready to face threats beyond the scope of what the mind could conceive. They were the Kaiju Corps. They were the giants who would protect civilization from potential apocalyptic events. They were soldiers who were ready to do their duty, but they were also soldiers who had never seen real combat. Like any soldiers preparing for their first actual mission, they were beyond nervous. Especially because unlike typical soldiers, they had no idea where they were going or what they were going to fight. This feeling was further exasperated by the fact that Michelle/Bearadon was not with them. Jerome was their leader and they trusted him in that role, but Michelle was the backbone of their group. During their training exercises, there were times when all three of them felt fear or a lack of confidence in their abilities, but Michelle never showed any of these emotions. Michelle was not the type of person to give a rousing speech or to crack a joke to break the tension, but when they needed strength from one of their teammates, they could always look to her. Michelle's aura of fearlessness was even more exemplified when she was in her Bearadon form. Nick, Jerome, and Miki were all ready to perform their duties as best they could, but without

Michelle with them, they were missing the support that her demeanor provided.

Nick found it hard to take his eyes off Miki. He was struggling internally with the feelings that he had for her. His life was far from normal, but he knew that he was attracted to Miki. What he didn't know was that if it was appropriate for him to have these feelings. The Instructors had always spoken of Jerome in terms of being his brother, and he knew that Miki and Michelle were encouraged to look at each other as sisters, despite the fact that none of the four of them shared any genetic background.

What was never clearly defined was the relationship between the males and females. They were always taught that they were teammates and soldiers, but otherwise, their relationship was never discussed. At one point, Nick had tried to approach Timothy to discuss these feelings that he was developing toward Miki. In all of the times that Nick had approached Timothy with personal questions, it was the only time that he declined to discuss the situation with him. As Nick was standing in Hangar 18 and awaiting the first real mission of his life, part of him regretted never talking to Miki about his feelings because now there was no guarantee that he would ever have the chance to again.

More of the lights in the hangar started to switch on and illuminate the room, forcing Nick's thoughts away from Miki and back to his surroundings. The other hangars that the Kaiju Corps team members had seen were predominantly empty. They had observation decks and the occasional small transport or forklift, but this hangar was full of weapons and aircraft that they had never seen before. As the lights came on, five or six aircraft came into view that looked like large black triangles.

Nick shook his head in surprise when he saw them. The Horsemen kept Nick and the other members of the team unaware of the other projects that they were working on outside of the Kaiju Corps. Nick had taken up an interest in fringe elements of science and science fiction during his free time. He knew that he had been created to battle potential threats such as alien invasion, and he looked up UFO sightings in his free time to get a better idea of what he might be facing some day. In addition to helping him gather potential intelligence on a threat, it also helped him to feel more normal. For one thing, he was engaging in activities that many other people did on a regular basis, and while the Instructors monitored everything he did on the internet, they allowed him to engage in conversation in UFO forums, as the people in those groups were likely not to be taken seriously by the majority of the population anyway.

During his conversations with these groups, one type of UFO that was frequently a topic of discussion was the black triangles. One of the prevailing theories in the UFO community was that these UFOs were actually man-made crafts that some people referred to as TR-3Bs. Not that he would be allowed to say it on any of his forums, but Nick could now confirm that the black triangles were not only real, they were a top-secret project.

As more lights came on, huge cannons and other futuristic-looking weapons came into view. Nick could see something that looked like a giant megaphone that he could only guess was some manner of sonic weapon. A huge door opened on the opposite side of the hangar and teams of workers began rolling in large bell-shaped objects that had what looked like Tesla Coils wrapped around them. Nick could actually see the electricity moving around the coils.

Jerome and Miki were slowly drifting toward the TR-3Bs when the ceiling projector turned on and revealed the faces of several Instructors including Timothy, Clarissa, and Thomas. Michelle's personal Instructor Susan was noticeable by her absence.

Nick, Jerome, and Miki all stopped moving and looked up at their Instructors. Nick felt his stomach tighten even more as the moment approached where he would receive his first mission and go to off to fight some world-threatening horror.

Timothy cleared his throat and then addressed the group. "Kaiju Corps, as I am sure you know, the time that we have dreaded has come to pass. Your team is being activated in an attempt to secure some manner of future for the human race." Timothy brought up a quick feed of a satellite in space. "Approximately three hours ago, an alien Signal hit Earth's satellites and immediately overtook their programming. This Signal used our satellites to relay itself to virtually every computer system across the planet. In a matter of less than an hour, this Signal was able to overtake nearly every personal and commercial computer system on Earth. Military and National Security firewalls are still currently holding, but we expect them to fail within the next twenty-four hours. The Earth's military forces will be totally shut down before they even have a chance to respond to this threat. We are reasonably sure that our systems will be able to hold out against this Signal for several days, which will allow us a brief window in which to mount a defense strategy."

Timothy took a deep breath. "This is the type of threat that you have been created for and trained to fight. However, this is not the type of war in which we imagined that you would engage in." Timothy started to tear up. "We had hoped that the Kaiju Corps would be able to fight to save our civilization, but sadly, that is no longer an option." The view on the screen changed to show four giant robots that were constructed from car parts laying waste to the city of Detroit. Nick saw a street full of people trying to run away from one of the robots. The robot turned away from the building it was destroying and began walking over the crowd of people, crushing them beneath its feet.

Timothy continued to talk even as the robots continued to raze the city to the ground and crush people to death. "Detroit is only the first of what will be many casualties. The main function of this Signal is to override all of the planet's manufacturing and electronic resources and then divert them to create these giant robots. We are getting reports of other factories slowly being taken over where their assembly lines are creating giant robots as well. Within the next five hours, robots like the ones in Detroit will canvas the entire globe. These robots are destroying most of the population as well as freezing and collecting some people. Based on their current mode of operation, we suspect that these robots will kill off roughly seventy-five percent of the human population. Once our civilization falls, they will start collecting and freezing other examples of animal and plant life. These frozen specimens will be sent back to the planet that the Signal originated from. The rest of the human population and other sources of protein and chlorophyll will be bred in manageable numbers and then regularly frozen and shipped back to the Signal's home planet as well."

Miki's eyes widened in horror. "They are not just here to destroy us. They are turning us into a farm."

Timothy shook his head. "As far as we know, protein and chlorophyll are only produced here on Earth. It's likely that there are other Earth-like planets which also produce these resources, but they are scarce. Sending out a Signal which could corrupt another planet's technology and then create collection units which could send those resources back to the home planet is a very efficient way to assure that the civilization which sent out the Signal has a never-ending supply of resources. The only good news in this situation is that whoever sent out the Signal wants our resources and it wants us. That means even though the Signal will soon have control over our nuclear and biological weapons, it won't use them against us because doing so would also destroy the resources that the Signal's creators covet."

Jerome yelled up at the screen, "Break us up! Send each of us to a different part of the world! We can fight these robots off in our kaiju forms. We can turn the tide of the war!"

Timothy shook his head. "This is the end of our civilization and our way of life as we know it. The Signal will produce the giant robots in numbers and at a rate that you could never possibly match. Splitting you up is not the best way to address this issue. There are already four robots in Detroit and likely more by the time we reach the city. You will need to work as a team in order to not only defeat the robots but to survive. You must defeat the robots, and you must survive because you three and Michelle are the keys to a second future for the human race."

Timothy moved the projection of his hand so that he was pointing at the weapon with the Tesla Coil wrapped around it. "This is an EMP bomb. We are currently working as hard as we can to develop these weapons in mass for the purpose of dropping them on our own cities. The intel that we are receiving from Detroit suggests that the Signal is constructing robots with rubber shielding inside of them to protect them from an EMP, but these bombs will stop the creation of any more robots by knocking out the electrical systems of each city that we bomb. This will, of course, shut down everything in the cities that we bomb. Power, water, electricity, medical supplies, and transportation will all grind to a halt. Between cutting off the power and water, people will be forced to flee the cities or to hide in the most remote recess such as sewers and subway tunnels. Under those conditions, only the strongest and most intelligent people will survive."

The screen suddenly changed to show images of wars in Vietnam, Iraq, and Afghanistan. As the images moved across the ceiling of the hangar, Timothy began filling in the Kaiju Corps on the parameters of their mission. "The history of warfare on this planet has taught us two things. The first is that a war against a population of insurgent guerilla fighters can never truly be won. If the insurgency remains resolute in its cause, the war will eventually reach the point where the attacking force finds that the cost of fighting the war outweigh the benefits."

The images of the war faded and the faces of the Instructors returned to the screen. "Insurgencies are particularly successful when they have leaders who can rally and inspire them. You will be these leaders. Through our EMP bombs, we will end the production of these robots and you three and Michelle will lead humanity in the revolt against them."

A map of North America came onto the screen. "You will target areas near bodies of water as they will provide the most-needed resources for humanity to survive. We have designated two areas in the United States on which you should focus your efforts. Start from Detroit, fight the robots off there, then move to cities like Chicago, Toronto, Cleveland, and Buffalo. Use the Great Lakes as the first outpost from which the next generation of humanity will originate from. The major natural obstacle that humans will face near the Great Lakes is the cold. It will be a difficult first winter as humanity regains its footing. Many people will die as winter sets in without power, but the strongest and most resourceful people will survive. Once you have secured the Great Lakes, move along the Saint Lawrence River to the East Coast and secure areas along the coastline. Clear the coast from New York City to Atlanta. When America was first colonized, settlers used this land because of fertile soil, abundant rivers, and access to the ocean. The next wave of humanity will use this area for the same purposes. This part of the operation could take years, if not decades. Even if you are able to defeat the robots that are currently attacking these areas, you will be under constant threat from robots moving from other cities and attacking the human population that has escaped them. That is why it is vital that we are successful in using our EMP bombs to stop the production of new robots. If you are dealing with a finite number of robots, this becomes a war of attrition rather than humanity's last stand against an army that is able to renew its numbers daily."

Timothy took the images off the screen and his image looked down at Jerome, Miki, and Nick. "If you are able to reach the point that the robots are no longer attacking the remaining free humans because their numbers have dwindled, you can then focus on attacking the farms that they create and look to free the humans that are captured there." Timothy took a deep breath. "Again though, I reiterate, reaching the point of attacking the farms could be a part of the plan that is decades from now and that opportunity will only arise if the first parts of our plan are successful."

Jerome had an intense look on his face as he was doing his best to remember every detail of their rough plan as he could. Nick was shaking his head in disbelief while Miki did her best to remain stoic and avoid breaking down into tears. It was Nick who finally asked the question that they were all thinking. "The way that you are making this sound, it almost seems as if you won't be there to see this war through with us. What will your role be in this conflict?"

A solemn look appeared on Timothy's face. "We and all of the Horsemen will be staying at our facilities and working as hard as we can to create and deploy as many of the EMPs as possible. Unless we stop the production of the robots, you will never be able to win this war. We are also faced with the inevitability that within a two-week period, the Signal will break our firewalls and find our locations. Currently, the reports that we have indicate that the robots are being created from car manufactures, construction vehicles, and commercial airlines plane pieces. These robots are deadly enough, but once the military firewalls fall, the robots will begin to be constructed out of tanks, jets, and combat helicopters. This second generation of robots will be even more dangerous for you to face than the first. The third generation of robots will likely be created in the engineering factories that make our space shuttles and probes. The Signal will use these drones to send the people they are freezing back to its planet of origin. These probes will likely be launched from locations that humans already utilize to send probes and shuttles into space. Our primary concern should be to save people who are still alive, but any launches that we can stop would be a benefit to us. If the civilization that sent out the Signal is not receiving any supplies from Earth, then they would have no reason to send anything or anyone to check on their operation here."

Timothy moved his hand again so that his image on the screen pointed to the weapons on the hangar floor. "We built all of the weapons that you see before you. All of the Horsemen's facilities have manufacturing capabilities on site. Once our firewalls fail, the Signal will be able to create a fourth generation of robots using the technology that we possess. This potential fourth generation of robots would then possess the most powerful weapons on the planet. If that were to occur, the chances of the robots overcoming any form of insurgency that we would create would greatly increase."

Timothy turned his head so that his face was no longer on the screen as he delivered the next piece of information to the Kaiju Corps. "Susan and I will work as long as we can on constructing new EMP bombs. Clarissa will work on coordinating our attack and deploying the EMPs around the world as efficiently as possible. Thomas will lead a think tank that will work to find alternative methods that we can utilize to combat the threat as well. We need you to understand, however, that prior to the moment that it appears the firewalls are about to fail, the Horsemen facilities around the world will erase any information we have on our weapons and then they will self-destruct. That moment could arrive at any time. There is a high probability that we will have to enact the Horsemen self-destruct sequence. Once the self-destruct sequence is activated, it will travel via closed circuit connection around the world in seconds, destroying every Horsemen facility on the planet simultaneously along with everyone inside of them."

At hearing this information, Miki finally broke down into tears. She had been trained to be soldier, but like all soldiers, she was still human. She shouted at the monitor, "You are going to send us to fight for a doomed world and then you are going to just leave us? You are the only family that we have ever known! If we are not fighting to protect you, then what are we fighting for? You want us to lead people and to inspire them to fight, but who are we fighting for? We won't have anyone!"

Clarissa stepped in front of Timothy so that her face was taking up most of the projection. "Miki, I love you. We all love you. Just as we are the only parents you have ever known, you are the only children that we have ever known. We do not want to die and we do not want to leave you, but more than anything, we want to give the three of you and Michelle a chance at surviving. Any parent would gladly give their lives for their children and we will do the same for you." Clarissa started to tear up. "We are so proud of the young men and women that you have grown into. We have total confidence that you will be exemplary soldiers in the war to save humanity. Most importantly, you will not be alone. You will have each other. That is why you cannot split up and address these threats separately. You will not only need each other's physical support in battle, but you will also need the emotional support that you can provide for one another in the times in between battles."

Timothy shifted his body back in front of Clarissa. "Every moment that we continue talking, more people are dying in Detroit. We could have briefed you on the flight out, but there was something that we needed to do first."

The screen on the ceiling went blank and a door opened on the wall across from where the Kaiju Corps members were standing. Timothy, Clarissa, and Thomas all walked out of it. Nick, Jerome, and Miki all ran over to meet their personal Instructors. Hugs were exchanged as well as words of pride and love between the Instructors and their students. After a quick but highly emotional goodbye, the members of the Kaiju Corps boarded one of the TR-3Bs. As the super jet took off into the sky, Nick and Miki took one last look at the facility. While they were in the air, a report came over the radio that another giant robot attack was occurring in New York City.

Miki shook her head. "I always guessed that one day we would have to fight. I was ready for it, but I wasn't ready to lose everything that we had. I wasn't ready to lose our homes and our loved ones."

Nick reached out and pulled Miki toward him. He hugged her as she placed her head into his shoulder. He wanted to say something reassuring to her. He wanted to say some line that would inspire her, but his mind was a total blank. He squeezed her tight and all that he could think to whisper into her ear was, "I know. I know."

CHAPTER 6

The Hudson River, New York City

Bearadon was making her way up the river and back toward the Catskill Mountains. She was several miles outside of New York City when she saw smoke and dust rising from the city. Her first thought was that another terrorist attack had occurred and that was why she was being called into Hangar 18.

As she came closer to the city, she could hear the sounds of buildings crumbling to the streets below. Her acute sense of smell was assaulted by the stench of what could only have been streets literally filled with blood. Bearadon began to wonder if perhaps she and the other members of the Kaiju Corps were going to be sent after the people who had caused this horror as a form of retaliation. From the amount of dead people that it smelled like were littering the streets, she truly hoped that she would be sent after the people who had done this so that she could personally make them pay for their actions.

Bearadon had just reached the outer limits of New York when she lifted her long white neck out of the water and peered into the city to get a better look at what had happened. She was shocked when she saw a large robot that appeared to have been constructed from various construction vehicles destroying several buildings. Assuming that she had found the threat, she had been in called in to address, the kaiju decided to forgo returning to base first and put an end to this threat here and now.

She placed her two colossal white paws on the shores of the Hudson River and then she roared a challenge at the strange giant robot. The robot ignored Bearadon's challenge and simply continued to demolish the buildings around it. Bearadon walked out of the river on all fours, and then she started making her way toward the robot.

As she was walking toward the robot, she heard one of the Instructors give her a command through the radio inside in her ear, "Bearadon, do not engage the hostiles. These robots are part of a worldwide attack. An alien Signal has taken over most of Earth's technology. The Signal is using our tech to create giant robots which are wiping out the human population. We are trying to organize our efforts to create safe zones for a small percentage of the population. The other members of the Kaiju Corps are heading toward Detroit to engage hostiles there. We have plans to send the entire team to New York after we secure the Great Lakes. Report back to base so that you can rendezvous with the other members of your team!"

If she were in her human form, Michelle would have told the Instructor to go to hell. There were people dying right in front of her and saving them from threats like a giant robot was exactly what she was bred and trained for her entire life. Bearadon roared in defiance of both the robot and the Instructor who had told her to leave millions of people to die at the hands of this soulless construct. The kaiju broke into a sprint as she charged the robot. While she was down on all fours, Bearadon was roughly half the height of the mech she was running toward. When Bearadon reached the robot, she drove her horns into its waist. The impact caused the giant mech to tumble backward onto the pile of rubble from the building it had just destroyed. Bearadon climbed on top of the fallen robot and pinned it to the ground beneath her massive weight. The glistening white kaiju lifted her right paw into the air, unsheathed her claws, and then raked them across the robot's face. Bearadon's claws cut through the steel that composed robot's head as if it were made of paper. The robot was lifting its hands up to try and push Bearadon off itself when the kaiju slashed it across the face with her left claw, destroying what was left of the mech's head.

Bearadon was roaring at her defeated opponent when another set of metal arms that also appeared to be composed of construction vehicles wrapped around her waist and then threw her to the ground. Bearadon rolled with the momentum of the throw. She rolled over three complete times before she was able to regain her momentum and return to her four-legged stance. She roared at this robot and was just about to charge him when the hands of the decapitated robot behind her clamped onto her tail and pulled her backward.

Bearadon was shocked by the fact that the decapitated robot was still able to attack her. She thought to herself that the robot was not a living thing and that unlike an animal, the systems that operated it were not in its head but more likely in its well-protected chest. She was trying to break free of the headless robot's hold when the other robot stepped closer to her and then kicked her in the jaw, snapping her teeth shut. The robot that was in front of Bearadon continued to deliver punches and kicks the kaiju's face and chest with the precision and cold disregard of the machine that it was. The headless robot that had gripped Bearadon's tail continued to hold the monster in place to prevent her from escaping.

With each blow, Bearadon could feel her head being rocked from side to side. Despite the pain and disorientation that she was experiencing, the kaiju knew that she would not live much longer if this assault continued. Bearadon blocked out the pain and focused on where and when the kicks and punches were coming from. After absorbing several more blows, she had timed the robot's attacks. When the robot was about to deliver its next kick, Bearadon shifted her head back so that the mech's leg missed her face. Through bloody eyes, Bearadon saw the robot's leg moving passed her face. She then quickly reached out with her teeth and closed her jaws around the robot's leg. The kaiju then shifted her body to the right and pulled on the robot's leg. The move sent the robot crashing into the headless mech that was holding onto her tail. When the two robots collided, the headless mech was knocked off balance, and as a result, it lost its grip on Bearadon's tail.

The badly beaten Bearadon stumbled forward. While her body was worn down, Bearadon's iron will kept her from collapsing due to exhaustion. Bearadon turned around roared, spewing a mixture of blood and saliva into the air. The kaiju then lumbered back over toward the two robots, and when she reached them, she spun around and buried her spiked tail into the chest of the headless robot. It took her two tries to pull her spikes from out of the robot's chest. She decided that the robot's chest must be filled with something like rubber or foam. Whatever was shielding the robot's central processing unit, Bearadon decided that she needed to find an easier way to attack its insides. When the robot reached down to grab her, she saw her opening. Bearadon leapt out of the reach of the headless robot and then she threw her body into the second mech, hitting the machine's leg and causing it to fall over once again.

As Bearadon turned back toward the headless robot, it punched her in the jaw. As soon as the kaiju felt the blow, she instinctively took a step backward. When the headless robot attempted to punch her for a second time, Bearadon dodged the blow and then clamped her jaws down on its arm. She pulled the robot to the ground so that it was lying flat on its chest. Bearadon then turned around to face the second robot who had regained its feet. As Bearadon was facing the robot in front of her, she thrust her spiked tail into the empty hole where the decapitated robot's head had once been. When she felt her spikes dig into the wires and circuit boards of the robot, she thrashed her tail around as violently as she could until the headless mech stopped moving.

With the robot behind her inactive, Bearadon shifted her attention to the robot standing in front of her. When the mech tried to strike her, the surprisingly lithe kaiju leapt to the side of the robot and then behind it. The robot was off balance from its attack and it was still pitched forward as Bearadon leapt onto its back. The kaiju's weight sent the robot crashing face first into the ground. With the robot pinned helplessly beneath her, Bearadon began to tear into its back. The kaiju tore off a layer of steel to find the robot's torso filled with tires. Bearadon thrust her claws into the robot's torso and then she tore out the tires to reveal the circuitry beneath it. The monster thrust her bloody jaws into the wires and circuit boards in front of her. Sparks leapt out of the robot's back and landed on the kaiju's snout as she ripped the mech's programming out.

The robot's body jittered for a few seconds as the last of the power drained from its body. A bloody and exhausted Bearadon looked around to see two destroyed robots, and in the distance, she could see countless people pouring into subway stations. The woman inside of the monster was pleased that she had been able to save these people even though the Instructors had suggested leaving them to their deaths.

She was crawling off the defeated robot when there was a sudden explosion to her right. She swung her head around to see a third robot walking through buildings, destroying them as it strode toward her.

She heard a voice in her ear as one of the Instructors relayed a message to her. "Bearadon, there is a construction vehicle manufacturing plant six blocks to the west of your current position! It's churning out a new robot every thirty-seven minutes. You need to either retreat now or defeat this robot and take out the plant before it can make another robot." There was silence for a moment before the Instructor started speaking again, "I am looking at your vitals right now. I doubt that you can defeat this robot. I suggest retreat. The robot's programming seems primarily focused on killing humans. I think that if you run, the robot may not pursue you. Retreating now is the best course of action!"

Bearadon once more roared in defiance of the suggestion. There were still millions of people who needed to reach safety. She was going to continue to cover their escape even if she died in the process. The kaiju lowered her tired head and charged the new robot. When she was within a few steps of the mech, she leapt in the air. She hoped that by bringing her weight down onto the mech that she could pin it to the ground and then tear it apart as she had done with the other robots. She had almost reached the robot when it shifted its back leg behind itself.

The mech caught Bearadon in mid-air and a small measure of concern crept into the kaiju's mind as she realized that the robots were learning with each battle they fought. For each robot that she destroyed, the next one would be cautious of not perishing in the same manner. Bearadon had no sooner finished this thought than the robot lifted her over its head and slammed her into the street. With the kaiju lying on the ground in front of it, the robot kicked Bearadon in her ribs. The kaiju groaned and then rolled away from the robot before it could kick her a second time. She looked up and saw the river only a few blocks ahead of her. She was injured and near the point of exhaustion. She knew that she needed to end the battle quickly and then destroy the manufacturing plant.

The robot was walking up toward Bearadon when she swung her tail around and embedded her spikes in the mech's left leg. The kaiju then pulled her tail back as hard as she could, causing the robot's leg to extend beyond its reach. The robot's arms flailed wildly as it tried to regain its balance. The mech fell onto its back, and when it hit the ground, Bearadon enacted her plan. The kaiju began to walk forward, dragging the robot behind her. Even in her kaiju form, the weight of the mech was immense and the fact that she was sure her ribs were cracked didn't help her efforts. Despite the pain that was ripping through her body, Bearadon slowly dragged the robot toward the river. The robot kept trying to pull her spiked tail from its leg, but Bearadon was dauntless in her efforts to pull the robot into the river.

Step by agonizing step, Bearadon drew the robot closer to the river until she finally felt her body slip into its cool embrace. She dragged the robot in behind her and then she pulled her tail out of its leg. As she suspected it might, the robot stood up in the river, unfazed by the water. She figured that the Signal who created the robots on a planet that is seventy-five percent water would make sure the thing had a waterproof outer casing. As the mech was rising out of the water, it lifted its hands over its head and then brought them crashing down on Bearadon's shoulders. The blow drove the kaiju underwater.

As her face hit the riverbed, the kaiju growled and thought to herself, "If its outer casing is waterproof, I will just have to tear it off until the river reaches something electronic."

Bearadon gathered the last of her energy and then she exploded out of the water. There was a blur of steel hands and white claws, horns, and teeth as the robot and the kaiju viciously attacked each other. Bearadon was taking a lot of blows from the robot but with each scratch and bite, she saw more steel and tires come off the robot's body. The frenzied exchange lasted for three minutes before Bearadon finally inflicted enough damage on the robot to let the river reach its insides. Sparks and smoke flew into the air as the water short-circuited the giant mech.

With this third robot defeated, Bearadon once more swam over to the river's edge. She laid down on the side of the river and she was drifting off into unconsciousness when she heard the

Instructors' voice in her ear, "Bearadon, you only have five minutes to reach the plant and destroy it before another robot is constructed!"

Bearadon forced her battered body off the ground then slowly walked over toward the construction vehicle plant. When she looked in through the shattered roof of the plant, she saw the form of another nearly completed robot looking up at her. The mech was not yet operational, but it was obvious that it soon would be. Rather than attacking the sturdy form of the robot, the kaiju destroyed the computers and machines that were building it. Once all of the machinery around the inactive mech stopped moving, the battered kaiju finally collapsed. Before she lost consciousness, Bearadon looked out through a smashed wall at the city of New York to see thousands of people still pouring into the subway tunnels and running toward the bridge. She thought to herself, "I saved those people too." The mighty Bearadon then finally fell asleep.

The Instructor who had been aiding Bearadon tried several times to rouse the sleeping kaiju, but he soon realized that his efforts were in vain. He decided that Bearadon would be safe until they were able to send out a TR-3B for her. He then relayed the results of her battle to the rest of the Kaiju Corps who were on their way to Detroit.

CHAPTER 7

Detroit, Michigan

Brian Linke was hiding in a subway tunnel as he continued to type everything that he saw into his computer. The situation in Detroit had gone from scary to absolutely terrifying! While there had originally been one robot attacking the city, the number of giant robots had grown to six. The last one that had been constructed also looked and was behaving differently than the others. The first five robots all had the same general appearance. They were constructed from different types of cars and car parts, but for the most part, they had a mainly human appearance. They had a head, arms, legs, feet, and a torso. The first five robots were all doing the same thing. They were destroying the city and grabbing a few survivors which they were storing somewhere inside of their bodies.

The sixth robot was something different altogether. It was still created from car parts like the other robots, but its appearance was far from human. Brian stared at the sixth robot as he did the best that he could to type out a description of it for the mysterious Horsemen.

The sixth robot is vastly different from the other five. It is quadrupedal in design. Its body is low to the ground with what looks like long, thick, and metallic jaws that stretch out from its face. It has a long tail that ends in what I can only describe as a double-headed battle-axe. The only thing that I can compare the sixth robot to is something like a giant alligator or crocodile. While the other robots are destroying Detroit and capturing or killing people, the alligator is just sitting in the middle of the city. It almost looks like the alligator is waiting for something.

Captain Todd Granderson was piloting the TR-3B that was flying Jerome, Nick, and Miki to Detroit. He had been in the employment of the Horsemen for over ten years. He had done things during his time as a pilot that resulted in the deaths of people, sometimes even innocent people. The TR-3Bs had the ability to drop fire bombs on buildings that could make it appear as if a hotel had caught on fire from a mundane cause such as a gas leak. Captain Granderson knew of at least three times when he had burned an entire building simply to kill a group of four to five terrorists who were staying there. He owned the deaths of the innocent people who had died as a result of his missions. Captain Granderson prayed for the souls of the people that the Horsemen had designated as collateral damage. While the deaths of those innocent people stayed with him, he never once regretted any of his missions. The leader of the TR-3B squadron, Captain Larry Richards, had taught Granderson that if one of his missions required him to kill innocent people in order to eliminate mass murders that his actions were justified with the reasoning that the dozens of innocent people who died were only a tiny fraction compared to the number of lives that would be saved as a result of his actions.

Today, however, that logic was hard for Granderson to rationalize. In addition to delivering Garudasaurus, Leviathan, and Chagon to Detroit to fight the robots there, he was also going to drop an EMP on the city. He knew the repercussions of what his actions meant this time. Dropping the EMP would effectively sign the death warrants of over half the population in the city. Those who were in hospitals, the elderly, the very young, pretty much anyone who needed an easily accessible source of power would die. Then as food and medical supplies dwindled, more people would die. He kept telling himself that taking out the power, and stopping the creation of new robots, would give the Kaiju Corps, and therefore the human race, a fighting chance. Still, the sheer number of deaths that would be on his head was difficult for him to accept. In the long run, he was a soldier and he would follow his orders. He would also spend the rest of his life praying for the people whose lives he was about to end. The TR-3B was roughly three minutes from reaching Detroit when he received a message from the computer programmer who was on the ground in the city and providing information.

Granderson turned back toward Jerome. "Sir, we have an incoming transmission from our man in the city. I am patching it through to you now. We are two minutes to target."

Jerome thanked the pilot then he looked at the information from the battle site and relayed it to Nick and Miki. "It looks like we have six robots in total in the city. Five of them are operating as the robots in New York did that were destroyed by Bearadon. The sixth one has an alligator-like appearance and it is simply standing in the middle of the city."

Nick shrugged. "Why would the Signal make an alligator robot that is just standing in the middle of the city?"

Jerome shook his head. "My best guess is that the robots are in contact with each other. That would mean the robots in Detroit are aware that Bearadon stopped their attack in New York." Jerome shrugged. "That would explain the alligator. Crocodilians are some of the most successful, dangerous, and powerful creatures in the history of the Earth. If the robots checked Earth's history for types of creatures that would be successful in a close-quarters battle, alligators and crocodiles would be at the top of the list. The reason that the alligator is not attacking the city is because it is waiting to fight off any resistance that may appear. In this case, it's waiting for us."

Jerome knew that given this new revelation that they would need to change their attack plan. He first tried to contact the Horsemen through his earpiece, but all that he could hear was static. He turned to Nick. "My earpiece is not working what about yours?"

Nick put his finger to his ear. "Horsemen, come in, this Nick." The young man listened, but all that he heard in return was static. He looked at Jerome. "Same as you; static."

Jerome shrugged. "The Signal is still trying to break through the Horsemen's firewalls. It's possible that some of the firewalls have already failed. Our earpieces may not be a viable communication method anymore." He yelled to Granderson, "Captain, I want you to circle once before we attack. We need know to exactly where the robots are in the city. Once we know where they are positioned, we can determine how best to attack them."

Captain Granderson nodded in reply as the city came into view. He yelled back to Jerome, "Passing over the city now, sir. I can relay the external camera information to the craft's screens now."

The very walls of the TR-3B seemed to disappear. In reality, the walls were simply relaying the camera feed from the hull so that from the perspective of the Kaiju Corps they were seeing everything below them as if they themselves were flying above it. The team members looked down at the robots and the death and devastation that they had caused. Nearly half of the city had been reduced to rubble. Smoke, ash, and dust were hovering around street level. The areas of the streets that the team could see were caked red with blood, bones, and internal organs. The sight was beyond horrific.

Miki had to swallow hard to prevent herself from vomiting. She shook her head. "My God. I can't believe what it looks like down there. It's worse than the interior of a slaughterhouse. Is this what it looks like all over the world? Is humanity going to come to an end in a war that results in a river of blood and gore?"

Nick walked over to Miki and grabbed her hand. Their fingers interlocked and he sighed. "We knew it would be like this. That we are fighting robots and not living beings. They have no regard for human lives. We are soldiers. We fight for a cause. Those robots are soulless exterminators. They are trying to complete their mission as quickly and as efficiently as possible."

Jerome took in everything that he saw as his strategic mind quickly formed what he hoped was an efficient attack plan. He began yelling out orders to his team, "Captain Granderson, I want you to contact the programmer on the ground and tell him to head to ground zero as soon as you drop that EMP bomb. Tell him when he sees the flash that he is to run back to the factory where this all started! He has seen these robots up close and he has been studying them from the start without panicking! He may have information that can be helpful to us! Once you have him, try to use the TR-3B to contact the Horsemen through the TR-3B's communication system. Then help me in fighting the robots that are attacking the people who are trying to flee the city."

Jerome then moved his hand over the city pointing to the humanoid robots who were destroying it. "It looks like each of the robots is more or less composed of car parts from the same type of cars. That will help us to designate them."

Jerome was still looking at the city below him as he shouted out the next part of his plan, "The three robots that we are going to designate as Focus, Mustang, and Taurus are spread out along the outskirts of the city. I can move the fastest. I will take on these three robots. If we can take them out, it will open up some streets for people to run out of the city. Chagon, you take the two robots in the middle of the city. We are designating them as Transit and Super Duty. Stay low to the ground and to try and avoid detection for as long as possible. Use your stealth and try to engage them one at a time. I will keep an eye on you. If you need help, I will fly in and assist."

Jerome turned to Nick. "It's obvious from here that extra time and materials were put into that alligator. It's got more than two times as much armor as any of the humanoid robots and it's built to fight kaiju." Jerome placed his hand on his best friend's shoulder. "Leviathan is the most physically powerful of any of us. I need you to fight what I am calling Robogator head on. Don't hold back. Let the beast loose. Do you understand?"

Nick nodded silently in reply. Inwardly, he was concerned about what would happen if he didn't hold back. Since he had first transformed into a kaiju and went on a rampage, he had gained a considerable amount of control over his kaiju-self, but it took a good deal of restraint on Nick's part to maintain that control. He found that he was best able to control his kaiju-self by only transforming into Leviathan for short periods of time. He also found that it helped him to maintain control if he tried to reign in Leviathan's destructive urges. He knew that this was a different situation than those he had trained for. Nick had worked on using his Leviathan form to operate in a surgical fashion by maintaining control of himself in case he needed to operate in close proximity to the people that he was trying to save. If he was engaging the battle robot in the middle of a destroyed city, then there would be no one alive in the immediate area. If there was ever a time that he could let Leviathan cut loose and tear into an opponent, this was that opportunity. Nick was fully confident that Leviathan could defeat the battle bot, but what concerned him more was if he could calm himself down after he had defeated it.

Jerome gave Nick a quick hug because he knew what he was asking of his brother, and he also knew that Nick was up to the challenge. Jerome released Nick then he turned around and called out to the pilot, "Captain Granderson, did you send out that message to the programmer?"

"Yes, sir!"

Jerome started taking off his clothes and Nick and Miki followed his lead. When they were completely naked, he yelled to Captain Granderson. "All right, drop that bomb then open the bay doors and let us loose!"

Captain Granderson brought the TR-3B low over Detroit and then dropped the EMP bomb on the city. There was a bright blue flash that cascaded over what remained of the skyline. None of the buildings in the city were physically damaged but every electrical system within fifteen miles of downtown Detroit was fried, including the factory that had nearly completed construction on a second robotic alligator. After he had dropped the EMP, Captain Granderson circled around and opened the bay doors to the TR-3B. The Kaiju Corps were standing at the bay door and their bodies were already shifting and growing as they started the transformation from human to giant monster.

Jerome half-shouted, half-roared, "Let's do this!" Then he, Miki, and Nick jumped out of the TR-3B to engage the robotic murders below.

CHAPTER 8

When the team had jumped out of the aircraft at roughly one thousand feet above the city, they were almost directly on top of Transit and Super Duty. Miki was three-quarters of the way through her transformation when the robots came into view. When she hit the ground, she had fully transformed into Chagon. Her Chinese dragon-like form caused her belly to slither across the ground and the hundreds of crushed bodies that littered the streets. As she crawled across the streets, she could feel the remains of each and every person that Transit and Super Duty had heartlessly crushed. Nick was right. The robots were cold, unfeeling machines. She, however, was a living creature with powerful emotions. Emotions that could be used to help push her body to their limits and passed them. In her kaiju form, the emotion that most dominated her thoughts was anger. Anger was both a visceral and primal emotion, and it was what drove all of the team members when they were in their kaiju forms. The kaiju were aggressive creatures that were prone to violence, and as Chagon felt her body sliding through the dead, her anger grew to a fever pitch.

Chagon's blood-covered body slithered over rubble and through dust as she made her way toward Super Duty. The robot was destroying an office building when Chagon slithered next to its foot. Chagon moved like lightning as she crawled up Super Duty and wrapped her serpentine body around its legs. Super Duty moved its arms to try and grab its attacker, but the kaiju's reflexes were too quick for the robot to counter. Chagon continued to wrap her body around the robot as she made her way toward its face. Super Duty's arms were pinned at its sides as Chagon finished positioning her body around the robot. Chagon's body was completely wrapped around the robot's torso as she swung her head around to stare into its face. If there was even the slightest chance that the robot felt fear, she wanted to see it in the mech's eyes as she ended its existence.

Chagon began to constrict her body, and Super Duty's armored body squealed as she crushed it like a tin can. The robot's head popped off its body as hundreds of tires and computer parts forced their way out of the upper part of the robot. In a matter of seconds, the battle was over. Chagon had attacked her target and crushed it before Super Duty even had a chance to respond. As Super Duty's body crumbled and she fell to the ground with the scrap metal that was left, Chagon took some small solace in the fact that if the robot did experience pain or fear, she inflicted as much of both as she could on it.

Chagon landed on top of the crushed body of Super Duty. The kaiju freed herself from the debris and then she immediately swung her head in the direction she had last seen Transit. Chagon quickly realized that she was not the only giant who possessed both speed and stealth as Transit's metal hand grabbed her just under her head.

Garudasaurus soared over the decimated city. He was doing his best to remain unemotional for the sake of the soldiers under his command and the citizens that they were trying to save. Chagon and Leviathan were fighting in the middle of the city. Most of the civilians in that part of the city were already dead. That fact allowed Chagon and Leviathan to attack the robots with all of the ferocity and anger that they had pent up within them. He, however, would be engaging robots who were still attacking the people of Detroit. Garudasaurus could not simply attack the robots in a blind rage. He would need to be cognizant of where he was in relation to the people who were trying to escape the city so that he did not inadvertently crush them while he battled the robots.

As Garudasaurus flew over the outskirts of Detroit, he could see the hundreds of thousands of people who were still alive and trying their best to escape the city. In their panicked state, the citizens of Detroit had become a mob that was stampeding away from the danger behind them.

Garudasaurus watched as the mob of people trampled those who fell to the ground in front of them. The robots had roused the people to such a state that the citizens of Detroit were unwittingly assisting in the extermination of their own kind. Garudasaurus was faced with a double-edged sword as he was preparing to fly into a position where the panicked mass could see him. Up until this point, the only experience that the public had with kaiju was when Chagon and Leviathan had first transformed and attacked humans. Garudasaurus had no doubt that when the fleeing people first saw him that he would only add to their terror as thoughts of those attacks mingled with the horror of the giant robots pursuing them.

Still, the initial burst of panic was an unavoidable consequence of the action that was needed for the greater good. The people of Earth needed to realize that he and the other members of the Kaiju Corps were here to protect them. If they were going to come to that realization, they would need to see the kaiju fighting off the robots on their behalf. Garudasaurus knew that when he flew over the mob of people trying to leave the city that he was going to inadvertently cause the deaths of more people at the hands of the mob. He also knew two other things. The first was that he would have the mob's attention and that they would see him fighting the robots and hopefully realize he was here to help. The second thing that he knew was that with no form of electronic communication on the planet outside of the Horsemen that he would have to repeat this scene in every city that they engaged the robots in. There would be no news report or social media feed that the kaiju were fighting to save the human race. Garudasaurus and his team would have to convince the world one city at a time.

The winged kaiju pushed his doubts aside, and he flew a wide low arc over the fleeing people below him. As he expected, the mob screamed at the sight of him and many of them near the front of the mass of people tried to turn around and run from him only to be pushed to the ground by those behind them and trampled to death. At the back of the evacuating mob, Garudasaurus could see Taurus walking into the sea of people and crushing them like ants beneath his colossal metal feet. Garudasaurus screeched as he fixed his eyes on the robot, and as his call echoed over the citizens of Detroit, they stopped running, and as one, they turned their heads around to see Garudasaurus slam into Taurus's torso.

Garudasaurus hit Taurus with enough force that he was able to push the giant robot several blocks away from the fleeing citizens. The kaiju saw the mob turn and look at him as he collided with the mech. He hoped that seeing him engage the mech was a first step in winning over their trust. Garudasaurus took one moment to look behind him to see how much distance he put between Taurus and the people it was attacking. The brief second that Garudasaurus had turned his head allowed Taurus to initiate a counter attack. The giant robot grabbed Garudasaurus by the shoulders and threw the kaiju to the ground. Garudasaurus's face slammed into the blood-soaked streets of the city. The kaiju was lifting his face out of the remains of slain humans when Taurus's foot came crashing down on the back of his head. The blow drove Garudasaurus's face right through the street so that when the kaiju opened his eyes, he found himself staring at the city's sewer system. The kaiju was surprised as dozens of people who were hiding in the sewers screamed at the sight of his massive beak smashing through the street above them. Their screams invigorated the kaiju as he realized that if he failed here, the people he was staring at would be dead within seconds.

Garudasaurus rolled onto his back to see Taurus's foot coming down toward him again. The kaiju's hands reached out and grabbed the metal foot as it was still coming down. Garudasaurus found that his strength was far greater than the robot's, as he was able to stop the mech's foot with relatively little effort. Garudasaurus pushed back on the foot which caused Taurus to lose its balance and stumble backward. The robot took a few steps backwards to regain its balance, and in that time, Garudasaurus was able to return to a standing position.

Garudasaurus clenched his clawed hands into a fist and then he delivered a stiff right jab to the robot's face. The jab shook Taurus's entire body, and before the robot could retaliate, Garudasaurus threw a left hook into its side that punctured its outer armor. Garudasaurus had driven his claw right into the robot, and as he opened it inside of Taurus's torso, he could feel tires and computer parts shifting around his fingers.

Taurus's hand shot out and grabbed Garudasaurus by the neck. The robot began to squeeze the kaiju's throat in an attempt to strangle him. Garudasaurus's neck muscles tightened as his air supply was suddenly cut off. The kaiju knew that both he and the robot had each other in a death grip. It was a matter of if Garudasaurus could do enough damage to the robot's CPU to render it inert before it was able to choke the life out of him that would determine the victor of this battle. Garudasaurus began clawing and tearing at everything that his claw could reach inside of Taurus while the robot continued to apply pressure to his neck. Garudasaurus continued to tear at the mech's insides as his legs became weak and he fell to one knee.

The kaiju could see the world around him becoming dark as his lungs threatened to burst from the lack of oxygen. Garudasaurus glared at the robot, and though he had no air in his lungs with which to create sound, the kaiju tried to screech at the mech in defiance. As Garudasaurus opened his beak and let out the soundless screech, he thrust his claw farther into the robot where he grabbed whatever he could. He then yanked his claw back out of the robot's chest with a handful of circuit boards and wires. As he pulled the robot's insides from within its body, Garudasaurus could feel Taurus's grip loosening. The robot's hands slid away from the kaiju's neck and then it fell to the ground, defeated.

Garudasaurus took several deep breaths then he looked to his right to see Mustang wading through another group of fleeing people. The kaiju realized that he had to be quicker and more efficient as he engaged the next two mechs if he was going to save as many people as possible. Garudasaurus leapt into the air and unfolded his wings, allowing them to fill with wind. The kaiju screeched and flapped his wings several times to gain altitude then he streaked toward Mustang like a living missile.

Leviathan's huge and thickly muscled body crashed down into the streets of Detroit with the force of a small meteor. A shockwave erupted from the impact point of his landing, sending dust, debris, and corpses flying into the air. Leviathan was walking through the dust cloud he had created when he saw a shining metal form close to the ground moving through the cloud toward him. As the dust continued to settle, Leviathan could make out the form of Robogator moving toward him at a much greater speed than he would have thought possible. Robogator was still several blocks away from Leviathan when the reptilian kaiju reared his head back and then thrust it forward, spewing a plume of flames from his mouth that engulfed not only Robogator but everything on either side of the street for five blocks. The five-block radius instantly turned into an inferno as Leviathan continued to spew flames from his mouth for a sustained twenty seconds.

Leviathan was still unleashing his flames when Robogator emerged from the fires around the kaiju's feet and sank its metal teeth into the monster's left thigh. Leviathan roared in pain as Robogator's teeth fell just short of embedding themselves into his thigh bone. The kaiju lifted his fists into the air, and then he brought them crashing down into the back of the robotic alligator. While the blow shook the mech's body, it did not force it to release its grip. Robogator started to roll his body to the side, which not only dug its teeth deeper into Leviathan's leg, but it also caused the kaiju to lose his balance.

Leviathan quickly repositioned his right leg to keep himself from falling over then he once again started to deliver strikes to Robogator's face. Leviathan delivered blow after blow, but despite his efforts, that robot refused to release its grip. Leviathan roared when the mech's teeth gouged farther across his leg as Robogator once again attempted to roll over and pull him to the ground. Leviathan fought to keep his balance as he considered the fact that his enemy felt no pain. He realized that he was not going to be able to force the mech to release his leg because it was taking a beating. He was going to have to pull the robot's teeth out of his leg if he was going to free himself.

Leviathan reached out and he placed his right hand on Robogator's upper jaw and his left hand on the mech's lower jaw. The kaiju roared in both pain and anger as he pulled on the robot's vice-like jaws. Both the kaiju's arms and the mech's jaws were shaking as the test of strength continued. With each passing second, Leviathan was forcing Robogator's mouth farther open. When he had pulled the robot's jaws open wide enough, Leviathan quickly pulled his leg out from in between Robogator's teeth. Leviathan then used his good leg to kick the mech in the face with such force that it dented the robot's lower jaw and knocked out several of its metal teeth.

Undaunted by the damage to its face, Robogator spun around and swung its battle-axe-shaped tail into Leviathan's injured leg. Leviathan roared with pain and fell to one knee when the metal appendage struck his open wounds. The kaiju was in a crouched position as he opened his mouth and unleashed a wave of flames that engulfed the robot. As before, Robogator walked through the inferno unaffected by the scoring fire. Robogator emerged from the flames, opened his jaws wide, and then sprang at Leviathan's face. Leviathan was able to throw his hands up and grab the robot's jaws, but Robogator's momentum pushed Leviathan flat onto his back.

Robogator positioned his body on top of Leviathan's chest. The robot's jaws were still wide open with one of the kaiju's hands on both its upper and lower jaws. The kaiju was staring directly into the mouth of the robotic nightmare as it slowly pushed its way closer to his head. Leviathan could feel his unique physiology quickly healing the wound in his leg. He needed his arms to keep Robogator's teeth off his face long enough for his leg to heal so that he could counter this attack. Leviathan's arm shook, and he could feel a burning sensation building inside of them as he strained to keep the robot from killing him. The kaiju could feel his leg sewing itself back together, and just before his arms were about to falter from fatigue, he wrapped his legs around Robogator's body and then he rolled to his right.

Robogator was now laying belly up with the enormous weight of Leviathan pinning it to the ground. Leviathan placed his left forearm on Robogator's lower jaw and then pushed the mech's mouth shut and forced its head to the ground. With the robot's dangerous jaws nullified, the kaiju used his right arm to attack the mech. Leviathan grabbed Robogator's left front leg with his hand, and then with a roar, the kaiju tore the limb off the robot's body. The robot struggled to free itself as Leviathan unsheathed his claws and began tearing at the opening where the removed limb had been. Leviathan tore chunks of metal away from the opening he had created until he had made a hole in the robot's side large enough for him to stick his hand into it.

Leviathan reached into the robot's interior and he pulled out handful after handful of tires, computer parts, wires, and pistons until Robogator finally stopped struggling. The kaiju roared in triumph. He then turned to see Chagon wrapping her long body around the arm of the hand that Transit was using to strangle her.

Chagon wrapped her slender body in a tight coil around Transit's arm. The kaiju then constricted her body and crushed Transit's arm as if it were an empty soda can. Both Chagon and Transit's crushed arm fell to the ground at the feet of the giant robot. Transit picked up his right foot to step on Chagon, but the kaiju easily slithered away from the blow by moving toward the robot's left leg. Chagon wrapped her body around Transit's left leg and crushed it as easily as she had the robot's arm. With the remains of the leg still within her embrace, Chagon pulled on the damaged limb and yanked it off its body.

The crippled Transit was trying in vain to stand up as Chagon slithered up to the hole in the robot's body from where she had removed its leg. The robot was helpless to defend itself as Chagon crawled inside of it. Once she had pushed her head into Transit, Chagon found herself surrounded by the layer of tires that the robots used to protect themselves from EMPs. The dragon-like kaiju pushed her way through the tires until she found the computer system within Transit's chest. The kaiju opened her mouth and then closed her long jaws on the computers, instantly shutting down the robot. Chagon could feel a blistering cold just beneath her body. She shifted her gaze down to see hundreds of humans frozen solid and stored in a compartment that was attached to the robot's back. She slid her forked tongue over the top of the container, and to her horror, she found that the people within the frozen pod were still alive. She doubted that even without EMPs wiping out the bulk of Earth's technology that the Horsemen had the ability to successful unfreeze the captured humans without killing them. As the implications of what it meant that these people were still alive sank into Chagon's mind, she roared in anguish and began crawling back out of the robot's body.

As Chagon was pulling herself out of the robot, she imagined what it would be like to be one of the frozen people. They would be sent on what could be a century's long voyage through space. The Horsemen were certain that anything being shipped back to the planet the Signal had originated from was being utilized as a food source. Even in her kaiju form, she shuddered at the thought of the aliens who sent out the Signal eating their food alive. The idea of a human running terrified from a giant robot one moment and then finding themselves in a situation where an alien was going to devour them the next, was beyond comprehension. Chagon made a silent vow to herself that she would do anything that she could to prevent the robots from sending the people they had captured into space.

Chagon crawled out of Transit's body to see Leviathan walking over to her. Behind Leviathan, she saw the TR-3B landing near the factory where the robots had first been constructed. Leviathan looked at Chagon then he shifted his gaze toward the outskirts of the city. Leviathan could see Garudasaurus battling Mustang, so he gestured toward Focus who was still capturing people and storing them within its body.

Chagon roared in agreement with Leviathan's suggestion to attack Focus and save more people from being frozen. The two kaiju then started heading toward Focus. They had worked on an attack plan for the two of them to engage a single adversary several times during their training sessions, and Chagon thought that this would be an excellent opportunity to utilize that plan. Chagon slithered in front of Leviathan and then laid down, indicating the plan that she wanted to put into action. Leviathan looked down at the serpentine kaiju and then he roared his approval of her plan. Chagon hissed in reply then she lifted her body off the ground and slithered ahead of her teammate.

Brian Linke saw what he could only describe as a UFO landing at the spot where he had gone to work this morning to deal with what was reported to be a virus in the system. With the city of Detroit around him in ruins, giant monsters fighting massive robots, and countless people dead it was quickly becoming obvious that this was much more than a simple virus being placed in a car manufacturer's system. A ramp opened up on the side of the UFO, and Brian ran up into it as the messages he had received from the Horsemen had instructed him to do. When he entered the aircraft, he saw only a single pilot. Brian yelled to man, "Are you part of the military? Did you drop the EMP on the city?"

The pilot shook his head. "The military's computers and weaponry fell to the alien Signal roughly thirty minutes ago. My name is Captain Todd Granderson, and yes, I did drop the EMP bomb. I am with Horsemen and now, so are you. We are trying to save enough human lives to form a resistance to fight against these robots and the aliens who created them." Captain Granderson turned around. "Civilization, as we know it, has come to an end, but the human race can still carry on if we can save enough people."

Brian was overwhelmed by what the pilot had told him, and yet he only needed to look at the decimated city he called home for confirmation of the pilot's claims. Brian pushed his fears and doubts aside for the moment. "All right, what can I do?"

Captain Granderson looked to the front of the ship. "For now, sit down. We need to get back into this fight and help out the Kaiju Corps. The Horsemen have the most sophisticated computers in the world. They figure that their firewalls can hold up against the Signal for a little while longer. They are busy trying to churn out as many EMPs as possible right now, but they have a task for you. Once this battle is over, you need to figure out how to get this TR-3B and the twenty-four other ships like it shielded from the Signal. The Horsemen say that you are pretty good with computers and I hope that you are, because a big part of the future of our species now depends on your computer skills."

Brian took a deep breath as the information he was given sank into his mind. He was still trying to process it when he saw the majestic form of Garudasaurus flying toward a robot that was made from mustang parts. Brian looked at the ship he was in, and he quickly realized that it was composed of hardware and software that he had never seen before. He was close to losing it with everything that was going on, but he knew that if he could find something to work on that it would help him from having an emotional breakdown. He yelled to the pilot, "Is there a way that I can see a schematic of the craft so that I can start to understand what I am working on?"

The pilot yelled out, "Ship, bring up an interior schematic of TR-3B-1 on the right passenger wall and then arm weapons systems."

The schematics of the ship flashed onto the wall next to Brian. His knowledge of computer systems and engineering was almost completely out of its depth as he looked at the TR-3B's layout. He took a deep breath and began looking for some kind of a starting point that he could understand.

Captain Granderson looked through his forward visual feed to see Garudasaurus hovering at Mustang's eye level and tearing at the robot's head and torso with his claws and talons. Mustang was attempting to grab the kaiju and pull him to the ground, but so far, Garudasaurus was managing to quickly strike the robot, move out of its range, and then strike again. Captain Granderson was aware that Garudasaurus was attacking in this method because only a few hundred feet behind the kaiju was a wave of several thousand people trying to evacuate the city. Garudasaurus was doing his best to prevent Mustang from capturing those people while at the same trying not to inadvertently hurt the people he was trying to protect.

As soon as Captain Granderson had assessed the situation, he knew his best plan of attack. He flew the TR-3B behind the hovering Garudasaurus and then he lowered the craft into a hovering position lower than that of the kaiju and parallel to Mustang's legs. Captain Granderson armed his heavy caliber machine guns and then fired them at Mustang's legs. The bright orange bullets shredded the car parts that composed the robot's legs to pieces. With the robot's base obliterated, Garudasaurus was easily able to push Mustang onto its back. The robot fell onto the rubble of a decimated building with its arms thrown out at its side. Garudasaurus flew down and dug his talons into Mustang's arms, pinning them to the ground. Garudasaurus then reached down with his claws and began tearing apart Mustang's chest. Captain Granderson watched as tires and computer parts flew into the sky. Once Garudasaurus had completely destroyed the robot, Captain Granderson turned to his left to see the thousands of people who Mustang was chasing moving away from the city. Captain Granderson smiled to himself as he thought that there were several thousand people more that he could count as lives he saved against the number of lives that he had ended.

Chagon moved as quickly as she could, slithering over rubble, bodies, and debris as she tried to reach Focus. The giant robot had made its way to outskirts of Detroit where another wave of people had gathered as they tried to flee the carnage that was occurring within the city. Focus was crushing most of the people below it with its giant feet, but it was also scooping up a few people and depositing them within its back. Chagon was fully aware that with each passing second, dozens of people were dying. It only took Chagon thirty seconds to reach Focus from where she had first started moving toward it, but in her mind, those thirty seconds were measured against the lives of over three hundred people.

When she reached Focus, she wrapped the lower part of her body around the robot's leg, stopping its forward progress. She then lifted the upper part of her body in front of the robot's face and hissed at it. Focus was lifting up its hands to grab Chagon when Leviathan's claws tore through the front of its chest. Leviathan dug his claws into opposite sides of the robot's chest, and then with a roar, he tore the mech in half. Chagon slumped to the ground where she was showered by falling tires, circuit boards, and frozen bodies.

With the last of the mech's defeated, Chagon started the transformation back into her human form. As she was shrinking in size, the frozen bodies of the people Focus had captured became much easier for her to distinguish. When she had fully returned to her human form, she was completely naked and still covered in the blood of all of the corpses she had crawled over as Chagon. She knelt down next to the frozen body of a girl who was roughly her age. When she looked at the girl, she could see the terror that the young woman had felt as the robot grabbed her literally frozen on her face. Miki bent down over the girl and she started to cry.

Leviathan was still enraged from the battle and he was stomping around the ruined city and roaring as he sought another opponent on which to vent his endless anger. Leviathan turned around and he saw the lithe form of Miki kneeling over the frozen body and crying. When he saw Miki, the anger inside of Leviathan began to subside. The kaiju slowed his breathing and calmed his mind. As he let go of the anger that fueled his kaiju form, Leviathan began to shrink in size as he turned back into Nick. When he had fully transformed back into his human form, Nick began walking over toward Miki. On his way toward Miki, he walked through the crushed remains of a laundry mat. He quickly looked through the wreckage where he found a relatively clean blanket and a pair of sweat pants. He slid the pants on himself and then he walked over to Miki and draped the blanket over her naked body.

He placed his arm over Miki's shoulder and held her tight. It was the second time today that he was holding her as she cried. Nick had known Miki his entire life. He knew that she was a soldier and that she was not prone to emotional breakdowns, but given the magnitude of what they had seen today, he couldn't blame her for reacting the way that she was. He wanted to say more to her, but he needed to keep a portion of his focus on completing his transformation back into a human. Miki meant a lot to Nick. He was starting to realize that she meant far more to him than she knew.

Garudasaurus and the TR-3B landed near Nick and Miki. Garudasaurus transformed himself back into Jerome and then he walked over to his teammates. He knelt down silently next to them and then he said a quick prayer for all the people who had died in Detroit.

When Jerome had finished praying, Miki wiped her eyes clean and looked at her friend and leader. "Thank you, Jerome." She turned her head toward Nick. "Thank you too, Nick."

Nick nodded in reply then he looked to Jerome. "What do we do next?"

Jerome stood up and looked toward the TR-3B. "We get on the ship, we clean ourselves up, and then get an update from headquarters on how the EMP bombings are progressing. After we talk to headquarters, we go get Michelle. The Robogator was proof that these robots see us as a threat and that they are trying to adapt to us. My guess is that we will be seeing more robots built specifically for combat. We need our team to be at full strength for our next battle and we need to get to Michelle before those battle robots find her."

CHAPTER 9

Horsemen Facility

Clarissa was working feverishly to coordinate the flow of information from what remained of the outside world. The Horsemen were lucky to have found Brian Linke in Detroit to feed them information from the field, and now they were working hard to scour what was left of the internet to find more people like him. Clarissa had managed to contact several computer programmers around the Great Lakes. She patched these programmers into the Horsemen's secure network. She was using these people to relay the information to the remaining population of the area to gather in the wilderness around the Great Lakes. She was also using these people to help inform the remaining population that the Kaiju Corps were fighting to save humanity. If the Kaiju Corps were able to survive long enough to meet back up with the survivors, they needed the survivors to see them as protectors and saviors rather than as monsters.

The Instructor was also using whatever information that was at her disposal to coordinate the TR-3B EMP bombing runs that were taking place on cities around the world. Most importantly, she had been in contact with a programmer in New York City who had witnessed Bearadon's battle. It seemed that after Bearadon had fought her way through the robots and took out one of the manufacturing plants that was creating them, she had collapsed from exhaustion. The programmer was able to give Michelle's exact location to Clarissa. Clarissa then sent Michelle's location to a TR-3B pilot who was scheduled to drop an EMP bomb on New York City. After he delivered his payload, the pilot was to pick up Michelle and then rendezvous with the rest of the Kaiju Corps.

Clarissa quickly reviewed the progress the Horsemen were making dropping EMP bombs on cities around the world. It seemed that even with every one of their TR-3Bs in the air all over the world that they had only managed to drop EMPs on roughly fifteen percent of the world's cities. That number, combined with the amount of manufacturing plants in rural and suburban areas, meant that giant robots were still being produced at an alarming rate. The current numbers suggested that there were as many as three hundred robots that were already created and gathering people all over the planet. What was even more concerning was that the number of robots on the planet was still growing. Additionally, there were reports of larger robots of various descriptions that were simply sitting in the middle of the cities. She was reviewing this information in her mind when she saw an incoming transmission from Jerome.

Clarissa shifted the transmission to the main screen in front of her. "Jerome, what's the update from Detroit?"

Jerome took a deep breath. "Most of the population of the city is dead. We were able to destroy the robots there and allow several hundred thousand people to escape the city. As you suggested that they might, the survivors seemed to be making their way along the side of the lake. Hopefully, once they get over the initial shock of what has occurred, they can be some of the people who form the insurgency." Jerome took a step closer to the screen. "There was also a different kind of robot with the ones that were capturing and killing people. It was a giant Robogator that seemed to be specifically constructed for the purpose of battling us. It is my belief that the Signal will create more robots that are specifically designed to engage us and protect their catch and kill robots. I feel that we need Bearadon before we engage in our next mission in case we run into more of these battle robots. Do you have an update on her status?"

Clarissa nodded. "As you know, it seems that that the radios within your ears are down. However, with the help of people on the ground in New York, we were able to find Michelle. I have a TR-3B on the way to drop an EMP on the city and retrieve her. I also concur with your assessment of the robots that are being constructed to oppose you. The other Horsemen facilities around the world are reporting non-humanoid robots that are appearing in the center of cities and simply sitting there."

Clarissa pulled up a feed to the EMP lab to see Timothy working with a group of other Instructors on EMP bombs. She called out to her fellow Instructor, "Timothy, what's the status of our EMP production?"

Timothy wiped the sweat from his brow. "We have just finished construction of ten more bombs. We are creating the bombs almost as fast as the TR-3Bs can deploy them and return to base, but I don't think that's nearly fast enough to counteract this threat."

Clarissa nodded. "It's not. We have dropped EMPs on roughly half of the cities around the Great Lakes. Even in the cities that we have bombed, there are still up to six robots in them killing and collecting people. New York City is the only city outside of the lakes that we are bombing and that is mainly so that we can retrieve Bearadon. For now, we need to focus on using the Kaiju Corps to secure the area around the Great Lakes. As we discussed, once we have secured that area, we will drop our remaining EMPs on the cities along the Eastern United States. New York will soon be secure and then we can move onto Philadelphia, Baltimore, Washington, and Atlanta."

Jerome shook his head. "It's such a huge undertaking, and even with it, we are only addressing a small portion of the US population let alone the rest of the world."

Miki stood up behind Jerome and she addressed the Instructors, "You said that the third generation of robots would be built to send the people they have frozen back into space. Do you have any idea of where these space-bound transport robots will be created and where they will launch from?"

Clarissa looked toward Miki as she answered, "They will likely use the resources that we already have in place. Cape Canaveral in Florida is a likely spot for them to start from or perhaps Dombravosky in Russia."

Miki shouted, "We have to expand our East Coast parameters to include Cape Canaveral. We can't let the people that the robots have frozen be sent back to the Signal's home planet!"

Clarissa shook her head in confusion. "Miki, those people are already dead. We need to focus on the people that we can save."

A wave of anger washed over Miki's face. "No, they are not dead! They are in some kind of suspended animation! I could sense them when I was inside one of the robots! We can't let them be shot into space and then wake up on some alien planet where they are going to be used as food."

Clarissa's voice took on a softer tone. "Miki, I understand how you feel, but even if we were able to stop them from launching into space, we don't have the technology to successfully unfreeze those people without killing them."

Miki screamed, "It would be better for them to die here unaware of what is happening rather than to have them reanimated on some other planet!"

Jerome subtly reached over and grabbed Miki's hand. He squeezed it, and she understood that he wanted her to back off the argument for the moment. She was still concerned about the fate of the people the robots had frozen, but she trusted and respected Jerome, so she took a deep breath and let him take over the conversation. Jerome looked first at the Instructors and then at his teammates. "I concur with Clarissa. We need to focus our efforts on saving the people who are still alive and free. Once we have secured the Great Lakes and the East Coast, we can start focusing on the farms and then the supply chain the robots will be making back to their home planet."

Clarissa nodded. "All right, your next target is Chicago. Michelle will be meeting you ..." A wave of static flashed across the screen, and it took several seconds for the video feed to return. When Clarissa was able to see both the team in the TR-3B and Timothy, she started talking again, "Sorry about that. Our firewalls are doing everything they can to hold back the Signal as long as possible, but the strain on the system is causing temporary breakdowns like that. As I was saying, Michelle will be meeting you in Chicago."

The feed flashed again for a brief moment, and when it returned, Jerome took a step closer to the screen. "Are the firewalls still holding out against the Signal as effectively as you thought they would?"

Clarissa did her best to portray an aura of confidence as she responded to the soldier's question. "It looks as if our initial estimate of the firewalls holding for two weeks may have been overly optimistic. Current projections suggest that we may only be able to hold out another five days before the Signal completely overtakes our system." She could see the look of concern on the faces of the Kaiju Corps members. Clarissa smiled at them. "Don't worry, we can do a lot of damage to the robots in five days."

Jerome nodded. "What about the TR-3Bs? Will they be corrupted?"

Clarissa bit her lip. "As far as we can tell from this end, we think that the TR-3Bs will be corrupted at the same time our system here falters." She moved to her left so that she could see behind Jerome. "Is Mr. Linke there with you? We were hoping that with his expertise he might be able to give us a clearer picture of the status of the TR-3Bs system."

Brian stepped up to the screen. "Ma'am, I apologize for not knowing your system better, but from what I can tell after looking at the schematics of the TR-3B and its system functionality, I would suggest that the firewalls for this vehicle have less than twenty-four hours before they fail."

Clarissa's shoulders slumped. "If the Signal takes over the TR-3Bs, one of our main weapons to attack the robots with will be under the Signal's control. Is there anything that you can do to extend the amount of time that we can operate the TR-3Bs?"

Brian nodded. "Yes, as far as I can tell from what I am seeing here, if we cut off the feed from outside sources such as satellite, radio, and internet feed, the TR-3B would operate in a closed system that will be beyond the ability of the Signal to reach."

Clarissa sighed. "You are talking about cutting off all communication between the TR-3Bs with each other and with their home bases?"

"Yes, ma'am. I know that my suggestion is not optimal, but it would still allow us to have access to these craft as both transportation and weapons."

Clarissa shrugged. "Sadly, I agree with you. We will keep the TR-3Bs online and in communication with each other until Michelle rendezvous with your team."

Jerome nodded. "Understood, we will contact you prior to cutting communications to see where we stand." Jerome then turned away from the screen as it cut off. He saw Miki staring at him, and he knew exactly what she was thinking. He walked over to Miki and grabbed her hands in his as he looked her in the eyes. "I promise you we will not let the robots leave the Earth with any of their victims."

Miki nodded in reply. "Thank you, Jerome."

Back in the Horsemen headquarters within the Catskill Mountains, Clarissa was still working on coordinating TR-3B bombing runs when she heard the door to the control room open, and she turned around to see Timothy walking toward her. She shook her head as Timothy made his way across the room. "I know what you are going to say. We will still have one more opportunity to speak to them before we totally lose communications. The longer they go without being aware of the next phase of the human survival plan, the longer they will be able to concentrate on what they have to do right now, which is itself a tremendous undertaking."

Timothy shrugged. "I know what they are facing right now. It's more than any four people should be burdened with, but we don't know that we will get the chance to talk to them again. What if the firewalls fail and we have to destroy the facility before we talk to them?" Timothy walked over closer to Clarissa. "You and I know Miki and Nick. There is a good chance that they reach the next phase of the plan on their own, but what about Jerome and Michelle? We need all four of them working toward the next phase of the plan if humanity has any hope of surviving this cataclysm."

Clarissa shook her head. "I agree with you that we will have to discuss the next phase of the plan with them the next time we talk to them, but the implications of that phase are not something they are ready for. We also need Jerome's and Michelle's personal Instructors with us when we discuss that stage of the plan with them. They will need their personal Instructor's support as they realize what they have to do and what it will do to them both physically and emotionally. Right now, they are preparing to secure another city. Let them get through that battle at least before we saddle them with even greater concerns."

Timothy turned and started walking away from Clarissa. "I hope that we have the chance to talk to them again. Our latest projections suggest that the Signal is attacking our firewalls with increased tenacity. We are not simply dealing with a computer virus. We are trying to keep out an artificial intelligence that was created by a civilization far more advanced than our own. The Horsemen programmers are working around the clock updating our firewalls, but their efforts are about as effective as using their fingers to plug holes in a dam. Their latest projections suggest that we have a day or two at best before our system is corrupted. Before that happens, we need to have the TR-3Bs disconnected from external communications, we need to destroy this facility, and we need to be sure that the Kaiju Corps members are ready to carry out the next phase of the plan."

Timothy walked out of the room and returned to his work station as Clarissa stared silently at her computer monitor, debating on whether or not she should inform the Kaiju Corps of their true role in the future of humanity's defense against the robots.

CHAPTER 10

There was a sound like thunder and Michelle awoke to find herself lying naked in the debris of the building she had destroyed when she was Bearadon. She stood, and unconcerned with her nakedness, she walked out into the abandoned streets of New York. She looked to the west of the city to see a bright blue light cascading over that section of the city. She whispered, "EMP." She was still looking at the blue cascade when she saw a dark black triangle moving in front of it. She immediately deduced that the craft had been sent by the Horsemen. She tried to use the tiny radio embedded in her ear to contact the craft, but all that she heard was static.

Michelle switched off her earpiece and moved into an open area of the street so that the pilot would be able to find her with minimal effort. She watched as the TR-3B slowed down as it approached the area where she had battled the robots. The triangular craft was moving slowly over the city when the pilot saw Michelle below him. Michelle waited as the TR-3B slowly floated down from the sky and landed silently in the middle of the deserted city. A door opened as a ramp came down from it to allow Michelle to gain access to the ship. She quickly walked up the ramp and entered the TR-3B.

When she entered the craft, she saw a duffel bag sitting near the entrance. Michelle recognized it as one of her bags no doubt with clothes, food, and water inside of it. Michelle grabbed the bag and walked up to the cockpit. The pilot turned around to see the still-naked beautiful young women walking toward him. He swerved his chair around as he said to her, "Ma'am, my name is Captain Rondell Okafur. There are clothes for you in the duffel."

Michelle dropped the bag next to the pilot then she bent down to open it up as she addressed the pilot in a pointed tone of voice. "The world as we know it is coming to an end due to an invasion of giant robots. I think that any uncomfortableness that you might feel due to my lack of clothing can be overlooked for the moment in favor of you updating me as quickly as possible about where our next destination is as we are heading toward it. Now, start heading toward our next target. I don't want to have to waste time undressing when we reach it if there are lives that need saving simply because you can't handle having a fellow soldier naked next to you."

Okafur continued to stare straight ahead as the TR-3B rose into the air. "Yes, ma'am. Our next target is Chicago with a brief fly over Buffalo. We are going to drop an EMP bomb on Buffalo and then head to Chicago where you will meet up with the rest of the Kaiju Corps. Your team is then to make your way along the Great Lakes, clearing cities of giant robots so that humanity can escape to the wilderness and then later form an insurgency resistance. From there, you are to move to the US East Coast and clear out cities there, forming a second sanctuary and outpost for humanity."

Michelle reached into her duffle bag and pulled out an apple. She took a bite out of the apple as the TR-3B shot like a rocket through the sky toward Buffalo. With the speed of the TR-3B, the flight between the two cities would take less than five minutes. During the trip, Michelle sat behind the pilot so as not to distract him with her lack of clothing. Captain Okafur informed Michelle of the Horsemen's plan to combat the threat with continued EMP bombings around the world. The reality that the robots were being massed produced faster than the TR-3Bs could drop EMPs and stop the production was disheartening for Michelle to hear. Okafur also informed her of the battle in Detroit with the other Kaiju Corps members and how the Signal created the Robogator to battle her friends after witnessing her fight the original set of robots.

Michelle had just finished downing a bottle of water when the city of Buffalo came into view. Through the skyscrapers, she could see at least two large humanoid robots that appeared to be constructed out of locomotive parts. Each of the robots was made from thick black steel. Just by looking at them, she could see that these robots were far heavier and denser than the robots she had fought in New York City. In the center of the city was a robot that was also constructed out of engine pieces, but while the other two robots had a humanoid appearance, this robot resembled a giant mechanical ape.

Michelle walked up next to the pilot and pointed at the visual of the city. "The one in the middle of the city, the Apetrain robot. That has to be the battle robot for Buffalo, right?"

Captain Okafur kept his eyes forward and replied, "Yes, ma'am. Initial scans are showing that the two humanoid robots come from two different locomotive manufacturing plants. The Horsemen are designating them as such. The humanoid robot on the east end of the city is GE and the humanoid robot in the west end of the city is designated Colmar."

Michelle could see waves of people trying to escape the robots. She turned away from the pilot and she began walking toward the door of the craft. "Drop the EMP. If the robots don't deactivate from the blast, then I want you to circle around the city and drop me right on top of the robot designated GE."

Okafur took a quick look back at Michelle. "Ma'am, I have orders to drop the EMP on the city and then to deliver you to Chicago to help with the battle there. Based on population numbers, Chicago has been designated as a higher priority than Buffalo."

Michelle screamed at the pilot, "There are hundreds of thousands of people down there! I am not going to let them die simply because they live in a smaller city than the one the other members of the Kaiju Corps are heading to! They can handle whatever is in Chicago, and I can handle the threat here! Now drop the EMP and stop the production of more giant robots! After you do that, I am changing into Bearadon whether you open the door in front of me or not!"

Okafur grumbled, "Yes, ma'am," in reply. He then flew low over the city and dropped the EMP on Buffalo.

Buffalo was blanketed in the blue energy of the explosion as every electrical apparatus in the city shut down with the notable exception of the three robots. The people who were fleeing the city were caught off guard by the blast. When the blue light exploded out of what looked like a UFO, even the people who were running directly in front of the robot designated GE were compelled to turn their heads and look at the explosion behind them. The brief second that they turned around cost them their lives, as it slowed their forward progress to the point where GE trampled them to death.

Michelle watched as GE crushed the people in front of it. She half-growled to the pilot as she yelled at him, "Get over GE right now, and open the door!" At hearing the change in Michelle's voice, the pilot quickly turned around to see thick white fur sprouting over Michelle's body. Seeing that she was already transforming into Bearadon, the pilot quickly complied with her request.

When the door opened in front of Michelle, she had already reached a size at which she was barely able to squeeze through it. She pushed her body through the door and then she was in free fall as she guided herself toward GE. Michelle had completed the transformation into Bearadon just prior to landing on top of GE. When the kaiju crashed into the robot, she dug her teeth, horns, and foreclaws into the robot's shoulder. The kaiju used her momentum to slide down the robot's back, land on her feet, and then flip GE over her shoulder. GE soared through the air and came crashing down into an abandoned building. A cloud of debris and dust flew into the air from the force of the impact. Bearadon quickly turned around to see that by tossing the robot, she had created a distance of several blocks between the bulk of the fleeing mob and GE.

She turned her head back in the direction that she had tossed the robot to see it pulling itself up out of the rubble. GE's thick black armor was covered in gray dust as it walked out of the crushed building toward Bearadon. Bearadon was standing on all fours as she charged GE and drove her horns into GE's midsection. The blow caused GE to fall flat on its back. Bearadon mounted the robot and swiped her claw across its chest. While the kaiju's claw had managed to gouge the robot's chest, she did not feel it reach the rubber insulation or the CPU beneath it. Bearadon roared as she remembered that the locomotive parts used to construct GE were far stronger than the car parts used to make the robots she had faced in New York.

Bearadon felt the ground rumbling beneath her, and she looked up to see the Apetrain robot barreling toward her. As she was looking up, GE backhanded her across the jaw and then it pushed her of its chest. Bearadon rolled when she hit the ground, and then she stood up in her bipedal stance ready to take on two robots at one time. She took a quick glance to her left to see GE walking away from her and towards the fleeing people. She snapped her head forward just as Apetrain slammed into her. Bearadon wrapped arms around Apetrain and she dug her feet into the ground, but despite her best efforts, the mech's strength and momentum pushed her backward.

The kaiju felt her feet tearing through the street as the robot continued to push her backward. Apetrain had managed to push Bearadon back five city blocks before she was able to bring the robot to a stop. Bearadon tried to throw Apetrain to the ground when in a show of superior strength, Apetrain lifted Bearadon off the ground and tossed her into the remains of a nearby building. Bearadon was blinded by the dust and concrete that flew into her eyes. The kaiju was trying to regain her feet when Apetrain's huge fist struck her in the jaw and forced her back to the ground. The mechanical gorilla delivered blow after crushing blow to Bearadon's face and jaws. She was briefly able to open her eyes long enough to see Captain Okafur bring the TR-3B in behind Apetrain and open fire on the robot with his machine guns.

Bullets tore into Apetrain's back, but the robot felt no pain, and it was programed specifically to destroy kaiju. Apetrain had no concept of self-preservation. The robot's single motivation was to carry out the command of its programming.

As yet another fist slammed into Bearadon's face, she realized that she was only a few more heavy blows away from losing consciousness, and if that happened, she was fully aware that death would soon follow. When she saw the next blow coming, the kaiju quickly shifted her head to the left. When Apetrain's fist crashed into the debris next to her, she bit into the robot's left hand and then dug her claws into its arm. In a quick and fluid motion, Bearadon brought her back legs up and placed them on Apetrain's chest. The kaiju then pulled the robot's arm while using her legs to push against its chest. Bearadon felt her strength being pushed to its limits, but she was fully aware that if she was unable to tear Apetrain's arm from its body that the robot would soon beat her death. The kaiju roared as she exerted even greater pressure on the robot's arm and chest. When she heard the sound of metal tearing, Bearadon began to shake her body from side to side, twisting the damaged metal that connected Apetrain's arm to its torso. There was a loud snap as Bearadon finally tore Apetrain's arm free from its body.

As its arm tore off, Apetrain fell backward onto the ground. Bearadon quickly stood up, and before Apetrain could regain its footing, the kaiju sprang forward and attacked its right leg. The kaiju bit into the leg and tore a chunk out of it. Apetrain reached out with its right arm and backhanded Bearadon across the face, knocking her off its leg. Bearadon shook off the blow and lunged back at Apetrain's leg as the robot was trying to stand. Bearadon swiped her paw at the robot's thigh, slicing deep into it with her claw. She was still tearing into the robot's leg when she felt Apetrain's fist come crashing down onto her spine. The blow buckled the kaiju's knees and forced her to the ground. Apetrain lifted its fist to strike her again, but Bearadon rolled out of the way, causing the robot to lose its balance, forcing it to use its hand to keep itself from falling over.

With her enemy in a vulnerable position and with its damaged leg close to her, Bearadon attacked. The kaiju swung her body around and drove her spiked tail into Apetrain's leg. With the robot's leg already severely damaged, the kaiju's tail was able to tear through what was left of the damaged appendage. With its right leg and its left arm gone, Apetrain fell face first onto the ground. The disabled robot used its remaining arm and leg to spin its body around, and when it was facing Bearadon, it tried to crawl to the kaiju. Bearadon knew that she could end the robot's existence right there by jumping onto its back and tearing out its insides. While her initial instinct was to destroy her enemy, the soldier and the human inside the monster knew that she had more pressing concerns. Bearadon turned away from Apetrain, and she began running after GE who had caught up to the fleeing mass of humans and was once more crushing them beneath its feet.

Bearadon quickly looked to her left to see Captain Okafur flying around Colmar and unloading his machine guns on the robot. She could see that while the TR-3B's bullets were penetrating the mech's armor, they were not causing much significant damage to it. The sheer force of the bullet's hitting the robot was, however, delaying the mech's progress as it tried to pursue another wave of people that was trying to escape from it. Bearadon hoped that Okafur would be able to delay Colmar from reaching the fleeing people long enough for her to dispatch GE and then make her way over to finish it off.

The kaiju turned away from Colmar and focused on GE who was now reaching down and grabbing another handful of people. The robot was lifting the people off the ground when Bearadon darted forward and sank her teeth into the robot's arm. The kaiju pulled down as hard as she could, forcing the robot's hand back toward the ground. She had pulled the robot's hand to a height of roughly ten feet off the ground when GE brought its free hand around and struck Bearadon in her ribs which had not yet fully healed from her last battle. The blow rocked the kaiju, but she refused to release her grip on the robot's hand until she was able to free the twenty-some people trapped within it.

Bearadon lifted her right claw and used it to gouge out a piece of the robot's arm. GE responded by delivering another crushing blow to the kaiju's ribs. Bearadon groaned in pain as she scratched away yet another piece of the robot's arm. She saw GE pulling its hand back to punch her again. Bearadon quickly shifted her hind legs, and when her tail was positioned correctly, she swung it at the robot's head, burying her spikes in the mech's face. While the blow to GE's face didn't cause any significant damage to the mech, it caused the robot's punch to strike her flexible tail instead of her injured ribs.

GE brought its free hand to its face where it grabbed Bearadon's tail and tried to dislodge it. While the mech was removing her tail from its face, Bearadon furiously attacked the arm that she was latched onto. With three powerful swipes from her claw, the kaiju finally managed to tear the robot's hand off. Bearadon gently placed the hand with the captured people in it on the ground. GE pulled the kaiju's tail from its face and held it in its grip. Bearadon yanked her tail forward, causing her spikes to embed themselves in the robot's wrist. The kaiju then turned around and slashed at the robot's right leg, tearing out a portion of it. She then stepped forward and pulled her tail, causing the robot to fall onto its face. GE was trying to stand when Bearadon climbed onto its back and forced it back to the ground. Unlike Apetrain, she knew that she needed to completely destroy GE. The robot's primary function was to capture and kill people, and even if it had to crawl to do so, the robot would continue to carry out its programming. Bearadon slashed and bit at the locomotive parts which constituted the robot's back until she was finally able to see the rubber lining beneath it. The kaiju plunged her jaws into the robot's back, bit into a mouthful of rubber, and then tore it out. Bearadon tossed the rubber aside then she once more thrust her mouth into GE's back where she ripped out its CPU. She felt the robot cease struggling beneath her then she climbed off its back and turned in the direction of Colmar and the TR-3B.

Bearadon's entire body ached as she made her way toward Colmar. When she had crossed half the distance to her next target, she saw the still-functioning form of Apetrain crawling toward her. When she walked past the partially dismembered robot, it spun on its stomach and started pursuing her again. The kaiju made a mental note to finish off Apetrain after she had destroyed Colmar.

Each step that Bearadon took sent a shot of pain surging through her body. She had already fought six different mechs today, and she was moving toward her seventh. She knew that after this battle, she would have to take time to heal if she was going to be any help to her teammates in the next couple of days. She also knew that she would heal much faster if she stayed in her kaiju form which meant that she would be unable to board the TR-3B and meet up with the rest of her team. Despite the fact that she would be unable to join her teammates in their upcoming battle, she was still confident that she had made the correct decision. She had already saved countless lives by destroying GE, and she would add onto that number if she was able to stop Colmar. Bearadon also still had complete faith that the other members of the Kaiju Corps would be able to destroy the robots in Chicago without her help.

Several blocks ahead of her, she saw that Captain Okafur was still doing his best to battle the giant robot with his TR-3B. Bearadon watched as the machine gun that Okafur was using to attack the mech expelled the last of its bullets. Having exhausted his supply of bullets, Captain Okafur was forced to pull away from his attack.

With the TR-3B no longer impeding its progress, Colmar started moving toward the mass of fleeing people. Bearadon roared and tried to run after the robot, but with pain surging throughout her body, the best that the kaiju could manage was a quick trot. She had almost reached Colmar when, to her surprise, the robot turned around and backhander her across the face. The blow knocked the weakened Bearadon to the ground. She realized that in addition to the robots learning and taking steps such as creating robots like Apetrain to fight her that perhaps the humanoid robots were also having changes made to their programs to attack her prior to her attacking them first.

Bearadon was trying to make her way back to her feet when Colmar kicked her in her badly damaged ribs. The kaiju let out a slow and painful roar as her injured body slumped back to the ground. Colmar stomped on Bearadon's ribs several more times, causing the mammalian kaiju to start coughing up blood. The robot was lifting up its right foot to stomp on Bearadon again when she whipped her tail around and buried the spiked end in the robot's left leg. Bearadon used her tail to pull the robot's leg out from under it. When it crashed into the ground next to her, the kaiju noticed that the mech's armor cracked in the areas where it was riddled with bullet holes.

When she saw the cracks spider web between the bullet holes in Colmar's outer hull, she realized that she was not the only one who had sustained heavy damage in her previous fight. Like two weary prizefighters entering the tenth round of a match, the injured kaiju and the damaged robot staggered to their feet. Bearadon forced her body to stand on her hind legs so that she was at her full height which was at least twenty feet taller than her opponent. Colmar pulled his fist back to punch the kaiju and Bearadon responded by letting her weary body fall forward onto the mech. Despite Bearadon's massive weight leaning on it, the robot managed to maintain its footing. With her body pressed against the robot, Bearadon wrapped her powerful arms around its torso. The kaiju then began to squeeze the mech. Bearadon could both hear and feel the robot's badly damaged armor cracking and shattering beneath the intense pressure she was placing on it. The kaiju closed her eyes and roared as she squeezed and shattered Colmar's upper body to pieces.

As Colmar's body crumpled, Bearadon released her grip and returned to her quadrupedal stance. She heard a scraping sound behind her, and the kaiju turned around to see the persistent Apetrain crawling toward her. Bearadon roared and then she began limping toward the damaged mech. When she was close to Apetrain, it lifted its hand off the ground and swung at Bearadon. The kaiju easily avoided the blow, climbed on top of the mech's back, and then proceeded to tear out its CPU.

With the threat to Buffalo destroyed, Bearadon crawled down from atop of the defeated Apetrain. She wanted to roar, but she lacked the strength to do so. Bearadon quietly laid down in the middle of the street. Even though she was exhausted, she knew that she couldn't let herself fall asleep, because if she did, she would revert back to her human form, and in order to heal as quickly as possible, she needed to be a kaiju.

The TR-3B landed in the street next to Bearadon, and as the door opened, she saw Captain Okafur standing in it. He yelled as loud as he could, "We aren't going anywhere for a while, are we?"

Bearadon simply shook her head no in response.

Okafur shrugged. "Okay then. Let me get in touch with headquarters and tell them that we are not going to make it to Chicago in time to rendezvous with the rest of team. Just so you know, I think that you did the right thing by deciding to save all of these people, but I am telling the people at HQ that it's your fault we can't make it to Chicago!"

Bearadon nodded as she did her best not to let her exhausted body fall asleep.

CHAPTER 11

Catskill Mountains, Horsemen Facility

Clarissa slammed down the button that shut off the video feed from Captain Granderson's TR-3B. Her body was shaking with anger, and she needed to calm down before she reached out to Timothy and discussed how they were going to have to alter their plans. She took a look at her reflection in the computer screen and yelled, "Why can't she just follow orders! The importance of saving Buffalo doesn't even compare to the importance of reuniting Bearadon with the rest of team!"

Clarissa took several deep breaths then she turned on her computer screen to see Timothy working with several other Horsemen on still more EMP bombs. She waited a moment as Timothy finished working on the latest bomb then he turned around and walked toward the screen. When Timothy reached the screen, Clarissa informed him of their current situation. "Bearadon took it upon herself to fight the robots that were attacking Buffalo. She managed to destroy two humanoid robots and a battle robot that she designated as Apetrain. She saved close to five hundred thousand lives, but she is injured and exhausted. She needs to stay in kaiju form for several hours in order to heal. This will delay our plans to have her join the rest of the Kaiju Corps in Chicago." Her tone changed from anger to disappointment. "We can't wait for her to heal before we launch our counter-attack in Chicago. There are still over a million and a half people alive in there. Many of them are still hiding within the city or using the underground tunnel systems to try and escape from the robots. If those people have any hope of surviving, we need to launch our assault now, but without Bearadon, our chances of success decrease and the chances of losing another team member increases drastically. If we don't have all four of the Kaiju Corps alive, we won't be able to initiate the next phase of our plan at optimal efficiency." Clarissa was silent for a moment after making that comment, so that Timothy could fully process what she meant.

When she was sure that the gravity of the situation had sunk in on Timothy, she started speaking again, "We also have to face the fact that we need to follow Mr. Linke's suggestion and disconnect the TR-3Bs from outside sources to prevent them from being corrupted. With each passing second that Michelle is separated from the rest of the team, we increase the likelihood that the Signal will overtake our fastest and most powerful aircraft."

Timothy looked behind him at a woman who was working on yet another EMP bomb. He gestured her over to come over, and as the woman was walking toward the screen, he filled in Clarissa on their progress. "We have successfully dropped EMPs on twenty-eight percent of the cities in the world. The increased productivity is a testament to the workers we have here. The projections on how long our firewalls will last continues to drop drastically. Our programmers have dropped our timeline to less than thirty hours. Given that our timeline continues to be diminished at such an alarming rate, we are going to continue to cut our deadline to twenty hours. We believe that in that timeframe, we can use the EMPs on as much as forty percent of the world's cities."

The other woman who Timothy had called over had reached the screen, and she was standing next to him as he continued to fill in Clarissa of their progress. "That number should give the surviving population and the Kaiju Corps a fighting chance of surviving this invasion." He turned to the woman next to him. "Susan, Jerome, Nick, and Miki are about to engage multiple robots in Chicago. As you know, we feel that we need to disengage the TR-3Bs from external communications ASAP. We are going to recommend that the remaining TR-3Bs deliver their current payloads and then we are having them all return to this location. Once they are here, we will disconnect them from external communication, arm them with whatever weapons we have left, and then have them join the Kaiju Corps in Chicago. Having the squadron of TR-3Bs at their disposal will help the team as this war continues."

Timothy placed his hand on Susan's shoulder. "We know that you and Michelle have never had much of a personal connection, but we will not be able to communicate with the other members of the team until after their battle. We need you to explain the next phase of the long-term plan to Michelle."

Susan nodded. "I understand. Connect me with Captain Okafur."

Okafur was sitting in his pilot's chair when the screen in front of him flashed to life with Susan's face on it. She didn't waste time introducing herself, "Captain Okafur, I need you to relay my projection in front of Bearadon. I urgently need to speak to her." Okafur simply nodded and recast Susan's projection in front of Bearadon.

When Susan saw how badly bruised and bloodied Bearadon was, she gasped. While Michelle had always kept Susan at a distance, she loved the young woman as if she was her own daughter. She did her best to respect Michelle's independence in hope that one day the young woman would learn to love her as well, but now Susan realized that day would never come. She fought back tears as she addressed the resting kaiju, "Michelle, I know how badly you are hurting, but there is something that I must discuss with you. I would not ask if it was not of vital importance. I know it will be physically difficult for you, but please return to your human form, enter the ship, and ask Captain Okafur to step outside for a moment." The projection faded from in front of the Bearadon and the kaiju groaned as she began the transformation back into a human. Michelle's body was so badly beaten that she could barely stand. Her ribs were badly cracked and her face was swollen and bruised. She bit her lip to help her deal with the pain and then she started limping toward the TR-3B.

She had only taken a few steps when the door to the craft opened and the ramp extended down from it. Okafur came sprinting down the ramp and then he ran over to Michelle. He put his arm around her waist and then pulled her arm over his shoulder. "I've got you, soldier." Michelle nodded and accepted the pilot's help. As they were walking back toward the ship, he smiled at Michelle. "The world might be coming to an end, and I can't even begin to think what it must be like to be you, but I have to say that the bravery and refusal to accept defeat that you exhibited today go far beyond the call of duty." He shook his head.

"Girl, monster, soldier, however you see yourself, I want you to know that I will always see you as nothing but a hero."

Michelle smiled back at the Okafur as they walked up the ramp to the TR-3B. The pilot helped the young woman into his chair so that she was facing the projection of Susan. He quickly whispered in Michelle's ear, "I will be right outside. Just yell when you are done talking to her." Michelle nodded in reply and then Okafur exited the ship.

Tears were rolling down Susan's face as she looked at Michelle. She shook her head in acknowledgment of her own failure to connect with this remarkable woman. Susan cleared her throat and then she addressed the person who meant more to her than anything in the world, "I am truly sorry that I am not able to be there in person with you. Michelle, I have something important to tell you, but first, there is something else that I have to say because I will never have the opportunity to say it again. I want you to know that while I have always tried to respect your privacy, I have always looked at you as if you were my own daughter. I love you, Michelle, and for what it's worth, please know that no mother has ever been prouder of their child than I am of you. You are a strong and resourceful young woman who has done her species proud in its defense. I can only offer my sincerest apology for not being a better Instructor for you."

Michelle was starting to cry as she saw the face of her Instructor in front of her bearing her soul. Michelle began to vigorously shake her head. "No, you didn't fail me. You were the only person who could see that I needed space and time to confront my unique life on my own terms. Any other instructor would have tried to smother me in an attempt to clear their own conscious that they were doing what they needed to. You had the strength to allow me to be myself." Michelle wiped a tear from an eye that was half-swollen shut. "I have never been good at expressing my emotions, but please know that I love you too. I always thought that we would have more time together, and that one day we would have a talk like this face to face, but I suppose that it's now or never. I just want to thank you for letting me be me. It's all that I could ask of anyone who was assigned to me and you let me have that."

Susan wiped more tears off her face. "Thank you. That means more to me than you could ever know." Susan took a deep breath. "I am sorry to throw this additional burden on you, but I must discuss an integral part of the next phase of our plan that will put a tremendous strain on the team, but I suspect you most of all."

Michelle held up her hand to stop Susan from speaking. "I know what you are going to say. Once more, our family is going to be assigned to us, and just as you and I did, we will have to learn to love each other." A look of surprise flashed across Susan's face as she realized that Michelle had already figured out the next phase of the plan for humanity's continued existence. Michelle sighed as she revealed the truth that she had deduced earlier that day. "This is the type of war that won't be over in a few years. It will go on for generations. Once we secure a foothold for humanity, the people who live there will need the Kaiju Corps to protect them from the threat of robot abduction until every last robot on earth is destroyed. Jerome, Miki, Nick, and I will not be around to see the end of this war, but our offspring will." Michelle was silent for a moment as a tearful Susan simply nodded in reply. "There are only four people on the entire planet who can change from humans into kaiju, and with the imminent destruction of the Horsemen Facilities around the world, you won't be able to make more of us. We are humans, but we are also part of a subspecies and that subspecies can only breed within itself. You need the four of us to pair off and mate to create the next generation of Kaiju Corps members."

Susan was momentarily taken aback at Michelle's knowledge of the situation. "As always, your perceptiveness of the events around you astound me." Susan's voice took on an empathic tone. "I am so sorry, Michelle. I am sorry, because you are too young to even understand the implications of what we are asking you to do. We are asking you not only to mate with someone who you may not even feel romantic love toward, but we are asking you to raise your children to be humanity's protectors. Believe me, that is a burden no parent should have to shoulder." Susan wiped her face clean of tears. "Are the other members of the team aware of this as well?"

Michelle shrugged. "I don't believe that they are, but it's obvious that Nick and Miki are already in love, even if they don't know it yet." Michelle raised her voice, "Isn't that right, Timothy and Clarissa?"

Timothy briefly stepped in front of the screen. "Yes. We also believe that to be true."

Susan looked Michelle in the eyes. "What about Jerome? How does he feel about you?"

Michelle thought for a moment as she chose her words carefully. "I believe that he views me the same way that I do him: as a respected and valued member of the same unit. Jerome is like me though; we will do what is asked of us in order to complete our mission. "

Susan tried to smile. "I am sorry about this, Michelle. I wanted so much more for you. I wanted you to have as normal a life as possible."

Michelle shook her head. "It's all right. Things are the way they are, and there is nothing that we can do about it."

Susan nodded. "I know that we have already asked so much of you, and I know that you will heal faster in your kaiju form, but I have to ask more. We need you to meet up with the other members of the Kaiju Corps ASAP because the Signal may soon overtake the TR-3Bs. If that happens, then it will be difficult for you to reach the rest of your team and secure the designated areas, let alone carry out the next phase of the plan when the time comes. Additionally, we are going to have the remaining TR-3Bs return to base where we will disconnect them from external communications in an attempt to prevent the Signal from taking them over. We will then arm the TR-3Bs with any of the experimental weapons that we can. The pilots of the TR-3B's that are operating abroad, will be sent instructions on how to disconnect their ships from outside information as well. The TR-3Bs will then meet with you and the rest of the Kaiju Corps in Chicago. They will be part of the weapons for you to use against the robots as this war rages on."

Michelle nodded. "All right then, let me get Okafur back on board and we will start flying toward Chicago." She started to tear up again as she looked at Susan for what she knew would be the last time. "Goodbye, Susan, and thank you."

Susan did her best to control her emotions as she gave her last words of wisdom to Michelle. "You have always been so good at finding your own way in life, but let me offer one piece of advice that I hope will help you to avoid a great deal of pain. I know that you will do whatever you is needed of you to carry out your duty. If the next phase of the plan comes to fruition, you will have even a greater duty than those you currently possess. Please, for your own sake, do all that you can to win this war before you need to send your children to fight it, or even worse, inform them that they need to mate with a specific person in order to ensure the continued existence of the human race." Susan had to stop talking for a moment as her words became stuck in her throat. "I can assure you that burdening your children with responsibilities like that is an experience that no mother should ever have to endure." Susan reached out and touched the screen in front of her. "Goodbye, my daughter. I love you, and I am proud of you."

The screen went blank as Michelle broke down in tears. She was glad that she at least had that small moment to let Susan know what she truly meant to her. Michelle was never the type of person who was good at expressing her emotions verbally. She was the type of person who firmly believed that actions spoke louder than words, and as Susan went off to face the last few hours of her life, Michelle vowed that her actions would honor the Instructor. She wiped her battered face clean and then she yelled out the open to door to Okafur who was waiting outside, "Captain, we need to get to Chicago!"

Okafur hurried back into the craft. He turned his back for a second when he saw that Michelle was dressing herself. She thanked him for this discretion but assured him that he could take his seat and set course for Chicago, as she was not embarrassed by the situation. He nodded and walked over to his seat. He kept his eyes forward but he quickly asked Michelle, "Are you okay?"

She sat down in the chair next to him. "No. I am in no way okay, but I will feel much better after we meet up with the rest of the Kaiju Corps and kick some robot ass."

Okafur nodded in reply and then he lifted his TR-3B into the air and started flying toward the city of Chicago.

Back at the Horsemen facility in the Catskill Mountains, Susan quickly turned to Timothy who was still standing next to her. "What happened to the feed? I wasn't done talking with her."

Timothy shrugged. "The system is under attack from the Signal. We are losing services all over the place. It's just a matter of time before the Signal completely overrides our network. That's why we need to keep working as hard as we can until that happens."

Timothy and the other programmers were completely unaware that the reality of the situation was that the Signal had already compromised their operation. In the deepest sublevels of the Catskill Mountain Facility, was the hangar in which the TR-3Bs were constructed. The security cameras stopped recording for a nanosecond and then they started running a loop of the room on the security feed throughout the facility. Then the electronic doors in the room locked themselves shut. Finally, when the hangar was completely under the Signal's control, the robots in the room that the programmers used to construct the otherworldly crafts suddenly activated and began constructing something that was much more than a TR-3B.

CHAPTER 12

Chicago

Captain Granderson shut down his feed from headquarters. He turned around and addressed Jerome, Nick, and Miki. "I have just received word from HQ that Bearadon engaged several hostiles in Buffalo. She was able to defeat them, but she needs to rest and she will not be able to assist us in the upcoming battle. They are also reporting that in addition to a robot created to fight Bearadon that the humanoid robots she encountered were much more heavily armored and aggressive than the ones we have seen so far."

Nick laughed. "Just like Michelle to save an entire city on her own and then leave the three of us to save a city without her."

Jerome smiled for a brief moment then he refocused his team on the task at hand. "Michelle has more than done her part. Now we need to honor her by doing ours. Chicago has a large military weaponry plant located just outside of the city. We don't have any definite intel, but it is likely that we will be facing robots constructed from the same machinery that is used to make tanks and military trucks." Jerome walked up to the pilot. "Captain Granderson, drop the EMP to prevent any more robots from being created then circle the city so that we can see what we are up against here."

The pilot replied with a quick, "Yes, sir." Then he swooped down over the city and deployed the EMP weapon. The EMP washed over Chicago like a neon wave, shutting down every piece of machinery in the city including the military plant that Jerome had suspected was creating the giant robots who were attacking the city.

The TR-3B increased its altitude as Granderson brought up the visual feed from the city onto the walls of the TR-3B. Jerome stood and walked over to the feed. He closely examined the situation to see four robots each in a different section of the city. Jerome quickly developed a plan of attack, and then he turned around and gave out his assessment of the situation and his attack plan to Nick and Miki.

"There are four robots down there. Two of them maintain the humanoid form that we have seen before, but in this instance, they are heavily armed as they are constructed out of tank parts. We are designating them by their parts as PT1 and PT2. From the reports we have gotten from headquarters about Michelle's last encounter, the humanoid robots are adapting to be better equipped to protect themselves from us. We can expect a more difficult battle from these robots than what we got from the robots in Detroit." Jerome zoomed in on the images of PT1 and PT2. "As you can see, while these robots have a relatively humanoid appearance in terms of arms, legs, and torsos, it's the military-style additions that make them far more deadly than the car-based robots we faced in Detroit."

Jerome pointed to the robots' arms. "Instead of hands, these robots have cannons at the end of their arms." Jerome quickly shifted the view to show thousands of body parts and large craters scattered around the city streets. "It's easy to see that these cannons are functional and were used on the population of Chicago based on the carnage below us." He moved the projection back to the humanoid robots. One of them was crushing a building while a second one was firing his cannon directly onto the street itself, causing it collapse into the subway system. "When we were in Detroit, we were fighting to protect people who were trying to flee the city above ground. As you can see from the carnage down there, the humanoid robots' long-range weapons have taken away that option. Anyone who is trying to escape the city now is doing it underground through the subway and sewer tunnels. This is likely the reason that the robots are targeting the streets themselves. We can also assume that there may be civilians still alive and hiding in some of the buildings that the robots are attacking. Once we transform in our kaiju-selves, we should be able to use our sense of smell to determine the location of any surviving humans, be they above ground or below it. We need to use our sense of smell to make sure that we are moving the humanoid robots away from the human population as we engage them."

Jerome then shifted the view to show the two battle-ready guardian robots standing still in the center of Chicago. "Based on the way these two robots are staying still, we can assume that they are the battle bots." Jerome focused the screen on a colossal robotic rhinoceros made from tank parts. The mech's horn was in fact a tank cannon and on its back, was a gargantuan gun turret that stretched the length of the robot's shoulders. Jerome pointed directly to the gun turret. "We are designating the first battle robot as Roboceros, for obvious reasons. The gun turret on its back is an experimental weapon that is designed to attack battleships at sea. It packs a hell of a punch. So, let's try to avoid getting shot by that thing."

Jerome then shifted the view to a giant robot that was like nothing they had ever seen before. The second robot was a huge sphere with a giant blade sticking out of the top of its head like a sail, three crab-like legs on either side of its body, and two long thick arms that ended in gigantic circular saws. Jerome shrugged. "So far, the Signal has been basing its robot designs off animals found here on earth. I don't know if that second robot is a mix of earth creatures, some alien monster, or what, but it was clearly created for battle." Jerome shook his head as he looked at the monster. "I don't even know what to call it."

Nick smiled. "Phantasm. We call it Phantasm. You know, like the horror movie where the Tall Man uses spheres with blades and drills in them to kill people."

Miki gave Nick a sly smile. "You and your horror movies."

Jerome shrugged. "It's as good a name as anything. Basically, we are using the same plan as before. I will fly around the perimeter of the city and take out PT1 and PT2. Nick, you take on Roboceros. That thing looks pretty heavily armored, and as it's made out of tank parts, I am not sure that even in her Chagon form that Miki could do much damage to it anyway. Beware of that big gun turret, especially at close range."

He turned his head toward Miki. "You have Phantasm. If one of you manages to defeat your opponent before the other one does, help each other out before helping me." Jerome yelled up to Granderson, "Captain, how much more ammo do you have left?"

"A few hundred rounds but plenty of air-to-air and air-to-surface missiles. I think that I can still be of help to you guys."

Jerome nodded. "Okay, fly in a circular pattern around the city, and take shots at the robots as you can. If you see that one of us needs help, break your pattern and see what you can do."

Jerome shifted his attention to Brian Linke. "Brian, are you about ready to disconnect this craft from external sources?"

Brian shifted his head back and forth indicating his trepidation. "I think so, but I am not one hundred percent sure. I am learning all that I can, but this craft has computer programs and components that are far beyond what would be considered cutting edge in the civilian world."

Jerome nodded. "Just keep doing your best. As soon as we see Michelle's TR-3B, I want this thing offline and then as soon as possible, I want you to do the same thing to the craft that Michelle is coming in on." Brian nodded in reply.

Jerome looked around the craft. "Does everyone understand their roles?"

The other four replied in unison with, "Sir, yes, sir!"

Jerome started taking off his clothes as Miki and Nick followed his lead. When they were naked, Jerome opened the door. The craft was flying around the outskirts of the city and, approaching PT2, Jerome jumped out of the jet and started his transformation into Garudasaurus as he was in free fall.

Nick watched his friend jump and then he walked up to Miki and grabbed her hand. He looked at her and she turned to look at him. Nick's heart was racing, but it had nothing to do with the fact that he could be jumping to his death. It was because he was standing next to Miki. He wanted to tell her how he felt about her, but as they were standing there naked and waiting to transform into a kaiju, he couldn't bring himself to say anything. He was a soldier who had no qualms about fighting a giant robot rhino created by an alien signal, but he was terrified to express his feelings to the girl that he loved.

They were approaching Roboceros and Phantasm. Nick was trying to push his feelings for Miki to the back of his mind when, to his surprise, Miki grabbed him and kissed him passionately. She looked into Nick's eyes and said, "I love you, Nick." She then jumped out of the TR-3B and began changing into Chagon as she plummeted toward Phantasm.

Nick was watching Miki as she fell and his mind was almost totally blank. He heard Granderson yell to him, "Leviathan, go!" Nick's mind snapped back to reality then he jumped out of the TR-3B and began to change into the most powerful kaiju on earth.

Garudasaurus was streaking through the air toward PT1. His plan was to slam into the mech at full speed, knock it to the ground, and then to tear it apart. He was several hundred feet from making contact with the robot when, to his surprise, the mech turned around and opened fire on him with the cannons on its hands and face. Garudasaurus had never been struck by live ammo before. He could feel intense pain as each shell exploded against his thick hide. The shells were penetrating his skin, causing him to bleed, but the kaiju's thick muscles held against the explosions, resulting in the blasts as causing nothing more than painful flesh wounds. As he flew closer to the robot, the pain from each impact increased, and Garudasaurus became concerned that as he drew closer to PT1 that the robot's shells might be able to penetrate his muscles and cause serious damage.

The winged kaiju veered hard to his right and out of the direct path of the stream of cannon fire. The upper half of PT1's body began to turn at the waist as the robot attempted to adjust its aim on Garudasaurus. Garudasaurus flew in an alternating zigzagging motion to keep PT1 from being able to aim at him as he made his way toward the robot. When he was close to the robot, Garudasaurus flew to its right in an attempt to position himself behind the robot and out of its firing range. Garudasaurus screeched in frustration when he flew behind the robot and its body was still able to rotate and to continue to fire at him. Garudasaurus flew a complete circle around the robot while the upper half of PT1's body rotated a full one-hundred and sixty degrees and continued to launch rapid-fire shells at the kaiju.

With a stream of shells following him, Garudasaurus flew up and away from PT1. Once he had flown out of the range of shell fire, the kaiju turned and flew back toward the robot with a new attack plan in mind. Garudasaurus decreased his altitude as he rocketed back toward PT1. When he was in range of the robot's shells, it once more unleashed a barrage of cannon fire at the oncoming kaiju. When the first few shells hit the kaiju, he decreased his altitude even more until he was flying only a few hundred feet over the skyline of the city. Garudasaurus ignored the pain from the deadly shells, and he breathed deeply through his sensitive avian nostrils. The kaiju could detect the scent of every human that was hiding in the buildings between him and PT1. When he discovered a building that had no human scent was coming from it, Garudasaurus screeched.

Garudasaurus increased his speed as he flew toward the abandoned building. He had almost reached the building when a shell buried itself deep in his shoulder and sent a splash of blood flying into his eyes. The kaiju closed his eyes tight and reached out his hands in front of him. When he felt his fingers touch the abandoned building, he closed his claws on the upper part of it and ripped off the top twenty-five floors while he still in flight. The kaiju lifted the remains of the building he was holding in front of himself to act as a shield while he flew over the remaining few blocks between himself and PT1. The kaiju felt pieces of glass, steel, and concrete fly into his skin as the chunk of building he was holding was shot to pieces. He had nearly reached PT1 when he started to feel shells striking his skin again. The remnants of the building took the brunt of most of the shells so that when they struck the monster's body, they lacked the force to do any significant damage.

Garudasaurus's slammed into PT1 with the force of a flying aircraft carrier. The impact drove the robot through two more abandoned buildings. Garudasaurus was standing atop a pile of rubble with PT1 buried beneath it when a shell exploded up out of the debris and narrowly missed the kaiju's beak. The monster quickly reached down and grabbed PT1's face cannon. With a quick twist, the monster tore PT1's face cannon off, leaving a large hole in its place. Before PT1 could reposition his hand cannons, Garudasaurus dug his claws into the hole where the head cannon had been. The kaiju quickly stood up, and with both of his claws, he pulled up and back, tearing the steel off the robot's torso from its shoulders its waist. Garudasaurus was staring at the insides of the mech when he saw the hand cannons aiming at his chest. The kaiju quickly leaned back just as the robot fired, causing the shells to graze his skin instead of piercing his heart. Garudasaurus then reached down into the exposed interior of PT1 and removed the computer system that controlled the robot.

The kaiju stood, and as soon as he spread his wings to fly, he felt a sharp pain in the back of his left shoulder then saw pieces of blood, muscle, and bone exploded out of the front of the shoulder. Garudasaurus fell on top PT1 face first, clutching his badly wounded shoulder. He rolled over onto his back to see PT2 aiming all three of his canons at him at nearly point-blank range.

Miki had completed her transition to Chagon as she landed on the ground near the spherical Phantasm. As Chagon slithered toward Phantasm, she tried to clear her mind of the thought that she had just kissed Nick. She didn't know if kissing him and expressing her feelings toward him would change things between them. She didn't know how the other members of the Kaiju Corps or the Instructors would react to the revelation that she had romantic feelings for Nick. All that she knew was that kissing him felt right. She was on the front lines of the war that would end the world, as it was currently understood. She had decided that with the reality of her situation, she could no longer keep her feelings toward Nick to herself. If she was going to die, she wanted Nick to know that she loved him.

Chagon hissed in an attempt to focus her mind on the task at hand. With the understanding that Phantasm had two buzz saws in front of its body and a large blade on top of its back, Chagon quickly decided that the most effective way to attack the robot was from behind. Chagon moved with incredible speed as she slithered through debris and half-destroyed buildings. Within a few seconds, Chagon had managed to make her way behind Phantasm. The serpentine kaiju darted out of the debris when, to her surprise, Phantasm's buzz saw arms rotated a complete one hundred and eighty degrees so that they were facing her.

With its arms repositioned, Phantasm charged the oncoming kaiju. Phantasm swung its right buzz saw at Chagon, causing the kaiju to halt its forward momentum and swerve to the right in order to avoid being sliced in half. The buzz saw cut deep into the ground as the kaiju coiled her body away from it. Chagon was coiling her body and lifting her head to strike at the robot when it swung its left buzz saw at her. The kaiju quickly dropped her head to the ground, causing the buzz saw to miss decapitating her by only a few feet. The moment that Chagon's head touched the street, she saw Phantasm's right buzz saw sliding along the ground toward her. The monster pulled her head back once again, narrowly avoiding the robot's attack. Chagon managed to dodge one more strike from the robot's left buzz saw attack then she quickly withdrew from the exchange and headed for a nearby abandoned building. Phantasm lifted its buzz saws into the air then it scrambled after the fleeing kaiju.

When Chagon reached the building, she plowed into its base and coiled her thin body up inside of its interior. The kaiju's sensitive body could feel the vibrations created by the robot's legs as it scurried toward her. When the robot had almost reached the building, Chagon began uncoiling her body and slithering up to the top of the abandoned structure. The kaiju's head smashed through the roof just as Phantasm had reached the building and began ravaging the structure with its buzz saws.

Chagon pulled her entire body out onto the top of the building then she looked down to see Phantasm still slicing into it in an attempt to reach her. With the robot's buzz saws engaged in trying to cut an entrance into the building, Chagon attacked. She slithered down the building and wrapped her body around the mech, being careful not to press herself around the large blade on Phantasm's back. In a matter of less than three seconds, Chagon had completely enveloped the mech within her grip. The kaiju constricted her body, hoping to crush Phantasm in the same manner that she had crushed the robots in Detroit. She quickly realized that crushing the mech's body was nearly impossible. She was applying pressure to Phantasm's entire body, but the robot's spherical shape was equalizing that pressure across its hull. Chagon's own strength was canceling itself out and preventing her from crushing the mech.

She was starting to release her grip on the mech when the large blade on Phantasm's back began to close creating something like a giant paper slicer with Chagon's body wedged in its fulcrum. Chagon could feel the giant blade descending and cutting deep into her body. The kaiju pulled her body out from the under the giant blade and off the mech's outer hull, as quickly as she could.

Chagon's body slumped to the ground next to Phantasm's legs. The kaiju had a deep cut in the middle of her slender body and she was bleeding badly. She did her best to ignore the injury and keep her focus on her opponent. Phantasm turned and swung its buzz saws toward Chagon. The kaiju managed to avoid the weapons by slithering underneath the mech's body. Chagon found herself beneath Phantasm's round body and in between the mech's crab-like legs.

Seeing her chance to damage the mech, Chagon shot her head out from underneath the mech's midsection, and she quickly constricted herself around the base of Phantasm's left arm, crushing it flat and causing it break off from mech's body. Phantasm tried to reposition itself in order to attack Chagon, but the kaiju slithered back under the mech's body and out of the range of its remaining buzz saw. Once she was under the robot's body, she wrapped herself around its left arm at the base and crushed it as well. With both of its arms destroyed, Phantasm attempted to move away from Chagon, but the kaiju refused to let the mech escape from her. Chagon darted forward and once more slid her body beneath the mech's body. Once she was beneath Phantasm, Chagon intertwined her body throughout Phantasm's legs making it impossible for the robot to move. Chagon then placed her head against the bottom of the robot's body and began pushing up on it. Even to the kaiju, the weight of the robot was immense. Chagon felt her muscles and tendons being taxed to the limit, and she could feel the cut in her midsection tearing even further apart from the strain she was placing on her body.

Chagon could feel the robot's legs starting to lift up off the ground, but she was beginning to doubt that she had the strength to completely flip Phantasm onto its back. For a brief moment, she thought of Nick and she wished that she had his strength. The thought of Nick had no sooner entered her mind that she remembered kissing him and the feelings of fear, elation, and relief that went along with it. She didn't give Nick a chance to react to the kiss, but she knew that she desperately wanted to see him again and to discover what his feelings were toward her. The thought of seeing Nick again gave Chagon a renewed determination. The kaiju forced every last bit of energy out her muscles that she could. With the extra effort, she could slowly feel Phantasm's body beginning to lift off the ground. When Chagon had forced the mech's body into a vertical position, she felt gravity take over and pull the mech onto its back. The giant blade on Phantasm's back was driven into the ground by the weight of its body. Chagon saw the robot's legs flailing helpless in front of her. She hissed at them and then slithered on top of the robot and in between its legs.

Chagon wrapped her body around the mech's thin legs and then she crushed them as well, leaving the mech crippled and stuck to the ground. Chagon slid off the defeated mech and then she started slithering toward the battle that was raging between Leviathan and Roboceros.

Leviathan crashed into the ground almost directly in front of Roboceros. Leviathan's mind was racing with a flood of emotions. Aside from the stress placed on his mind by the transformation from human to kaiju, Leviathan had also just been enlightened to the fact that the woman he loved also loved him. The thought that Miki loved him had energized the saurian monster.

The kaiju roared at Roboceros, and in doing so, the monster condensed the whirlwind of emotions that he was experiencing into the single emotion of rage. Leviathan needed an outlet for that the rage, and he was determined to vent his anger on the robotic pachyderm. The kaiju leapt forward and placed one arm under the robot's right leg and the other around its neck. Leviathan then lifted Roboceros off its front legs and tossed it into a row of buildings which collapsed on top of the mech.

Roboceros was working its way out of the rubble when Leviathan ran over to the mech and began stomping on it. Leviathan delivered blow after blow to the heavily armored robot's frame, but even he was finding it difficult to penetrate Roboceros's outer hull. Leviathan lifted his foot into the air to deliver another blow when Roboceros lifted its head off the ground and drove its horn cannon through the kaiju's left foot.

Leviathan roared in pain as he looked down to see the horn cannon sticking out of the top of his foot. The kaiju has started to pull his foot off the horn cannon when a shell fired out of it and struck him in the head. The shell deflected off Leviathan's thick skull, but the force of the impact was still enough to stagger the monster. Leviathan fell flat on his back with his foot still impaled on Roboceros's horn cannon. Roboceros stood and shook his head to free it from Leviathan's body. Leviathan saw the robot lower its head in preparation to gore him, and he instinctively unleashed a blast of flames from his mouth at the robot. The flames washed over the robot's armor but did nothing to prevent it from thrusting forward and driving its horn cannon into Leviathan's left hamstring.

The pain was on a scale that Leviathan had never experienced before. He could feel the muscles in his legs being torn apart. The pain increased exponentially when Roboceros shook its head from side to side as it pulled its horn cannon from the monster's leg.

When the mech had freed itself from his leg, Leviathan quickly rolled to his side so that he was no longer directly in front of Roboceros. The robot was turning his body to once again gore Leviathan when the monster reached out and wrapped his left claw around the robot's horn. Leviathan then quickly sat up and delivered three punches to the robot's face. He then pulled the robot closer to him and used his free arm to place Roboceros in a headlock. The kaiju pushed down on the robot's horn while pulling up its neck, and in doing so, Leviathan was able to tear the horn cannon off the robot's face.

Leviathan used the horn cannon like a giant knife, and he drove it into the robot's side. He then pulled Roboceros even closer to him so that he was able to place his shoulders beneath the robot's stomach while wrapping his left arm under the robot's neck and around its shoulder and his right arm under its back leg and around its thigh. With Roboceros in his grasp, Leviathan roared and then, placing his uninjured foot and leg firmly on the ground, the monster executed a fireman's carry by lifting the mech off the ground, leaning to his right, and then slamming the mech back first into the street. Roboceros hit the street with such force that it collapsed and dropped the robot several feet lower into the subway system.

Leviathan looked down to see Roboceros rolling around and tearing up the street and the subway below as it tried to right itself so that it could climb back to street level. The kaiju let out a small sigh of relief when he realized that there were no civilians in the tunnel he had thrown the robot into.

Leviathan grabbed onto the side of a nearby building, and he used it to help pull himself back to his feet. Despite the damage to his foot and leg, the monster was managing to stand. He had started to walk back toward Roboceros when he saw the robot step out of the crevice it had fallen into and back into the street. The robot's head was down, and the huge gun turret on its back was aimed directly at Leviathan. The kaiju immediately threw his body down and to the right when he saw the cannon move. The maneuver shifted Leviathan's body enough so that the shell grazed his hip instead of tearing through his stomach. Even with the shell just grazing him, it had managed to tear flesh off the left side of Leviathan's hip. With even more damage to the left side of his body, Leviathan was nearly immobile. He looked up to see Roboceros aiming its gun turret at him.

Leviathan roared at the mech in defiance of his imminent death. When he finished his roar, he saw Chagon slither up behind Roboceros. She coiled her body around the robot's rear legs and then she constricted, crushing the mech's legs as if they were made of cardboard. Roboceros lower body dropped to the ground, causing his shell blast to fire harmlessly into the sky. Leviathan limped over to the crippled mech as Chagon slithered out from under its metal body. Leviathan roared his thanks at the woman he loved then he grabbed the gun turret and ripped it off Roboceros's back. The kaiju leaned his head over the hole in the robot's back where he had just ripped off the gun turret. Leviathan took a deep breath, and then he unleashed a sustained blast of flames into the interior of the mech. The acrid smell of burning rubber filled the air, and the exterior of Roboceros's armor began to glow a bright red. The mech fought to break free of the kaiju's grip until the flames churning inside it finally liquefied its CPU.

Leviathan dropped the deactivated robot to the ground and then he turned to his left to see that Chagon had crawled up next to him. Leviathan looked into Chagon's eyes and then both kaiju roared as they professed their victory. The two badly injured kaiju then turned and began heading toward the outskirts of the city to assist Garudasaurus.

Captain Granderson saw PT2 shoot Garudasaurus in the shoulder and then he saw the kaiju fall to the ground. Granderson immediately armed his TR-3B, locked two missiles onto PT2, and then fired them. The missiles exploded against the cannon on the robot's head, destroying it and knocking the robot off balance. The cannons on PT2's hands were still operational, and they fired on Garudasaurus, but because the robot had been knocked off balance, the shells it fired buried themselves in Garudasaurus's arms and wings instead of his chest, creating painful but not fatal wounds.

Captain Granderson circled back around and emptied what was left of his high-powered machine guns on PT2. He cursed loudly when he finished his attack and saw that PT2 was still standing over Garudasaurus and threatening to kill the leader of the Kaiju Corps.

Garudasaurus's body was racked with pain, but the kaiju knew that he had to act quickly if he was going to save his own life and destroy this mech. Garudasaurus thrust his leg out and swept PT2 at its legs, knocking the robot down. Garudasaurus stood, and as he did so, he realized that his wings were too damaged to fly and his arms were too damaged to fight with. He looked down to see PT2 starting to stand up. The kaiju also saw the mountain of rubble that was between him and the robot. Garudasaurus's wings were too damaged to fly with, but they were still far from useless. The kaiju screeched then he started to flap his wings. The wind gusts generated by Garudasaurus's wings started with the force of a large storm and quickly accelerated to the force of a level five hurricane. The concrete, steel, and cars that littered the ground were caught up in the strong winds and were hurled at PT2 at speeds over one hundred and fifty miles per hour. The shrapnel that was being tossed at the robot was slowly shredding it ribbons.

The winds were so strong the Granderson had to fly his TR-3B away from the battle to avoid being caught in a wind shear. He looked down to see that the constant stream of shrapnel had all but torn the outer layer of armor off PT2. Granderson was shocked to see that despite the damage to it, the mech was still operational. Granderson was considering trying to arm two of his remaining missiles and fire them at the mech in an attempt to finish it off, but he was concerned that the high winds would push them off target.

He decided that he was going to attempt it when he heard his radio come to life, "Granderson, this is Okafur. Pull away from the target, I have something that will finish it off."

Granderson replied, "Copy that." Then he flew his TR-3B away from the battle.

Okafur flew his craft in low and from behind Garudasaurus. When they were almost directly over the kaiju, Michelle opened the door to the TR-3B, jumped out of it, and transformed into Bearadon. She was still falling when she dropped directly in front of Garudasaurus and into the wind gusts that he was creating, adding the force of the wind to the speed of her free fall. Bearadon was fully formed when she slammed into the mech with the force of her jump and Garudasaurus's wings propelling her massive weight. Bearadon's body smashed through what was left of PT2's body, ending the robot's existence.

As soon as Garudasaurus saw Bearadon plow through the mech, he stopped flapping his wings and slumped to the ground. The still badly injured Bearadon walked over next to Garudasaurus and laid down next to him. Granderson and Okafur both landed their TR-3Bs and exited from them. The two pilots shook hands as Brian ran from one ship to next as he continued his efforts to prevent the Signal from gaining control of the TR-3Bs.

Okafur pointed to the computer programmer. "Who is that guy, and what's he doing running onto my ship?"

Granderson shrugged. "His name is Brian Linke and he is a civilian programmer. He has been more or less drafted by the Horsemen. Right now, he is cutting the ships off from external communications based on the Horsemen's orders." Granderson looked at the two giant kaiju that were lying on the ground near them. "Why haven't they turned back into humans yet?"

"They heal faster in the kaiju forms. From the looks of them, they may have to stay in those forms for a little while."

Leviathan and Chagon moved their injured bodies as best they could toward Garudasaurus's position. When they saw that he was not only alive but that he had Bearadon with him, they both roared and hissed respectively to inform Garudasaurus that they were alive and that they had won their battles as well. Garudasaurus screeched in reply.

Satisfied that the battle was over, Leviathan sat his exhausted body down on the street. Chagon then gently wrapped her body around that of Leviathan and she looked up into his eyes. Leviathan stared back into her eyes and then he ran his claw slowly over her head. They were in their kaiju forms, badly injured, and surrounded by death, but they were together, and for the first time in their lives, they both felt complete.

CHAPTER 13

Catskill Mountains, Horsemen Facility

Clarissa turned off her tablet, cursed loudly, and then she exited her office. She took the long walk down three floors to the hangar five. When she entered the hangar, she saw Timothy and Susan working on several of what appeared to be a series of pencil detonators. Jerome's Instructor Thomas was with them as well. He had just overseen the deployment of four of the TR-3Bs who had come back to base, been fitted with updated weaponry, and then sent to Chicago. Aside from the four Instructors, there were other Horsemen scientists in the hangar who were working on a variety of other weapons and projects as quickly as they could.

Clarissa tried to calm herself down as she walked toward the other three Instructors. When she reached Timothy and Susan, she simply said, "We are just about out of time. Our network is falling apart. I could barely keep an incoming transmission from falling apart while I was conferring with Granderson and Okafor. Bearadon is now with the rest of the team in Chicago. They were able to defeat the robots that were attacking the city. During the battle, however, all four members of the Kaiju Corps were badly injured. They may need to stay in their Kaiju forms for a day or two in order to heal." She looked toward Thomas. "What is the status of our TR-3B squadron?

Thomas pulled out a notepad that he had been using to keep track of information in place of his tablet. "We just armed and deployed four of the TR-3Bs that had returned to base with our newest sonic cannons and magnetic compression missiles. The sonic cannons can punch a hole through a mountain. They can be utilized as either a single burst or as a continuous blast. The magnetic compression missiles attach to a metal object and then create a powerful but concentrated magnetic field that will cause the structure to condense upon itself into the smallest unit possible.

We also restocked their typical ammunition and disconnected them from external input to help protect them from the Signal. Those four ships are also transporting sonic cannons and magnetic compression missiles to be attached to Granderson's and Okafor's crafts. In addition to new weapons, they will also carry supplies, including ammunition and missiles, to restock Granderson and Okafor's crafts as well as food and water supplies to last the team several weeks if needed. The four TR-3Bs should reach Chicago within the next few minutes." He flipped to the next page of notes. "We have ten more TR-3Bs here that are currently being fitted with new weaponry and are being disconnected from external communications. Once the necessary weaponry installations are complete, we will send them to Chicago as well. Our reaming eight TR-3Bs are scattered around the world, delivering the last of EMP bombs. The last instructions that they were given were to deliver their payloads and then to fly to Spain where they will follow instructions sent to them by Mr. Linke on how to disconnect their craft from external communications. Once they have completed that task, they are to fly to the Great Lakes area of the United States and Canada. They are to search that area and the US East Coast for the Kaiju Corps and other survivors so that they can become a part of the resistance."

Clarissa nodded and then turned toward Timothy. "What is the status our bombing raids."

"Our targets have attacked fifty-three percent of the major cities in the world. It's a remarkable pace, but with still nearly half of the planet's manufacturing plants creating robots at a pace of every half an hour, the effectiveness of phase one of our plan has been greatly diminished. Had our original two-week projection held out, we may have been able to completely stop the production of the robots across the globe, but with our time frame being cut to twenty-four hours, we will never reach that goal. With the craft that we still have in the air, our best estimate is that we will be able to the stop production giant robots in about fifty-five percent of cities using the EMP bombs. The good news is that we were successfully able to stop production of new robots in the targeted cities along the Great Lakes and along the US East Coast from New York City to Atlanta. The Kaiju Corps will have to contend with the robots that already inhabit those cities, but no new ones will be created in them."

Clarissa nodded. "What about the other robots across the planet? After they capture all of the remaining humans in their cities of origin, will they move into other areas?"

Timothy shrugged. "We have not seen any of the robots leave their city of origin yet, but given how efficiently the Signal has approached the invasion so far, we believe that robots moving from their cities of origin to be a logical next step."

Clarissa threw her hands into the air "Then our plan is a failure. The Signal will just continue to create new robots until they overwhelm the Kaiju Corps and the remaining humans with sheer numbers!"

Susan walked over and placed her hand on Clarissa's shoulder. "That's not necessarily how things will play out. While the Signal has managed to take over our technology, it's still limited to the finite resources of our planet. Currently, the robots it has created have all been made from vehicles and other forms of transportation. The main reason for this approach is because that when the Signal entered the internet, it was able to determine that we had the technology to shut down their robots with EMPs. In order to prevent this from occurring, the Signal has thus far created all of its robots in plants where there is an ample supply of rubber, usually tires, to insulate the mechs against an EMP attack. As long as EMPs continue to be a threat, the Signal will be limited to the number of robots it can create by the amount of available rubber. Granted, there is a lot of excess rubber out there, but we can least be sure that the number of possible robots created is limited by something."

Timothy spoke up, "Our surgical EMP strikes may have been too high tech an approach to dealing with this problem, and we are currently considering other options. Specifically, we are looking at using a low-tech variation on Program 437."

Clarissa shrugged. "The program that focused on detonating nuclear bombs in the upper atmosphere in order to create wide-spread EMP dispersion? That program was put on ice in the 1960s."

Timothy nodded. "Yes, it was put on hold because it was difficult to predict exactly how the EMP would disperse. The US and the Soviets were unable to ensure that they could launch the attack without affecting their own satellites. That is no longer a concern for us. In fact, we want as wide-spread a dispersion as we can get."

"Even if we could gain access to our nuclear weapons, how do we get them into the upper atmosphere without having launch capability? The TR-3Bs are not capable of flying that high."

Thomas walked over to the group. "That's where our low-tech approach comes into play. The Signal has taken over most our technology, but apparatuses without CPUs will be totally free of the Signal's influence. Our delivery method will be weather balloons. We can attach our nukes to them and let them loose into the atmosphere. We can detonate the bombs with the delay switch pencil timer that we are currently constructing. These timers would be unaffected by Signal's ability to override computer systems."

Thomas then led the group over to a world map. The map had several red dots with large areas of blue emanating out from them. The blue areas of the map overlapped in numerous places, and together, they covered nearly the entire planet. Thomas waved his hand over the blue areas of the map. "We would only need to release roughly ten nuclear balloons to cover the parts of the world that we have yet to address with EMP bombs."

A small glimmer of hope was starting to work its way into Clarissa's mind. "Where are we going to get access to nuclear weapons? All of our military bases have been totally compromised."

Thomas motioned for Clarissa to follow him over to one of the other several large maps that were hung along the walls of the hangar. "With our network failing, we have had to dust off some of these old maps to help us locate targets." He pointed to an area of the map that showed a wooded area in New Jersey. "The forest known as the Pine Barrens, which is located in New Jersey between The Delaware River and The Atlantic Ocean, houses underground nuclear missile silos. It is in a rural area with a small and dispersed population. Not only are the Pine Barrens within our targeted area along the US East Coast, but because it is so sparsely populated, the last data that we have suggests that there is no robot presence in the area."

Clarissa pointed over in the direction of the detonators that had already been created. "We are almost at zero hour. How many of those detonators have already been created?"

Thomas shook his head. "Only two so far, but we can make more from scavenging materials from old clocks and other similar machines if we had to leave the base. Creating the detonators is not the problem. The issue would be our balloon-based attack would have to occur simultaneously from various sites around the world. If we were to release one balloon at a time, the robots would quickly figure out our plan and then they would be on the lookout for our balloons. We also have the benefit of knowing the TR-3Bs circuits are shielded from EMPs. They will still be functional after the warheads are detonated."

Clarissa's eyes lit up as the full meaning of what Thomas was saying occurred to her. "You have found a method that doesn't require us to stay until the last minute creating EMP bombs and deploying them before blowing up the facility! We can live on and continue to fight against the robots!" She sprang forward and hugged Thomas.

As she was hugging Thomas, there was crashing sound that shook the entire facility. Clarissa's eyes went wide as she yelled across the hangar to anyone who could answer, "Are we under attack?"

A voice yelled back, "No, ma'am. There is no sign of any attack coming from outside the structure."

The facility shook again and the floor split beneath their feet. Timothy looked down at a newly formed crack in the floor. "That was an impact tremor that came from below us." His face took on a crimson hue, as his mind ran through the schematics of the building they were standing in. He began to scream out orders in a panicked fashion, "Open the bay doors! Load the detonators onto one of the TR-3Bs!" He grabbed Clarissa and Thomas then he began pushing them toward one of the TR-3Bs. "I want Clarissa and Thomas in the TR-3B closest to the bay door! Get them in the air as soon as they are on the craft! Then we need the TR-3B with the detonators to follow in the air right after that! Once those two craft have taken off, evacuate the building!"

Thomas picked up Clarissa and ran onto the TR-3B closest to the bay door. The craft's pilot ran in behind him, jumped in the pilot seat, and took off out into the sky.

Thomas could see that Clarissa was still trying to process what had occurred. "The tremors were coming from below Hangar 5! Hangar 6 houses most of our computer banks and Hangar 7 is where we construct the TR-3Bs. We were worried that we were running out of time and that the Signal would soon infiltrate our network. It seems that the Signal had infiltrated our system some time ago. The Signal has also taken over the hangar where we construct our TR-3Bs and has likely created a giant robot using TR-3B parts."

Clarissa gasped. "My God! The TR-3Bs are the fastest and most advanced aircraft on the planet. They are dangerous enough on their own, but in Hangar 5, we also had the sonic cannons and magnetic compression missiles with recent modifications made to allow them to be attached to a TR-3B! If the robot is able to incorporate that technology into itself, we may have just given the Signal the tools to create a robot that is powerful enough to wipeout our TR-3Bs and the Kaiju Corps!"

Thomas nodded. "I know. That is why Timothy sent us out first. You know what areas of the world have been bombed, and you have the most current information about what area we are going to attack next. I know how to create detonators from scavenged clock pieces, and where we need to launch the balloons from for maximum effectiveness." He reached out and grabbed her hand. "It's up to us to make sure that we get those EMPs into the air and give the Kaiju Corps and the resistance a fighting chance."

Back in the Catskill Facility, Timothy watched as the TR-3B that he had just run a detonator onto took off out the bay doors and into the sky. He saw Susan running another detonator onto a TR-3B and he yelled at the craft, "Take off! Go! Go!" The craft was moving through the hangar, and it had just reached the bay door when the ground behind it exploded. Susan yelled at the TR-3B, "Show me rear visual, now!" Susan screamed when she looked at the hangar and saw a colossal black robot climbing out of the floor. The mech was clearly created out of TR-3B parts. It had a roughly humanoid appearance with notable differences on its extremities. The robot's triceps, thighs, and the back of its head all had triangular-shaped protrusions sticking out of them. Its shoulders were also large and rounded. They also had the appearance of a human who was wearing football pads.

The most terrifying aspect of the robot was that Susan could clearly see the rockets which propelled the TR-3Bs attached to its back. The TR-3B that Susan was on increased its speed as it gained altitude, and she quickly lost sight of the robot and the hangar. She whispered, "Goodbye, Timothy. You were the best of us, and if there is heaven above us, I hope to see you there one day."

Pieces of the concrete floor that had been thrown into the air as the robot tunneled its way into Hangar 5 rained down on the Horsemen who had not managed to escape. The robot quickly scanned the room, and the first thing that it did was to destroy the remaining TR-3Bs. Timothy was in awe of the robot's speed and power. It took the robot less than ten seconds to smash eight TR-3Bs to pieces using nothing but its hands.

What happened next terrified Timothy even more as the robot picked up one of the sonic cannons that was going to be attached to a TR-3B and effortlessly connected the weapon to its right arm. Timothy grabbed his tablet and entered in the code to cause the building to self-destruct. To his horror, nothing happened. He quickly looked toward the bay door operators who were staring at the robot. Timothy screamed, "Shut the bay doors! We need to keep that thing in here! We are going to have to initiate the self-destruct manually!"

One of the men near the bay door hit the button to close it causing the doors to slowly slide shut. The closing of the bay door made no difference to the robot. The bay doors were far too small for the robot to exit through. The robot aimed its sonic cannon at the exterior wall of the hangar, set it continuous fire, and then blasted an opening large enough for it to walk out of right through the side of the mountain. The robot stepped away from the facility and then it ignited its thrusters and leapt into the sky. The robot altered its course to head east then it rocketed over the horizon.

A second TR-3B robot's head appeared out of the hole in the middle of the floor created by its predecessor. Timothy screamed, "Attack that thing with whatever we have! We need to keep it in the building!" Timothy motioned for one of the security guards to follow him. Timothy and the guard ran over to one of the magnetic missiles. They picked up the rocket and then Timothy motioned for two other guards to follow him. The four men then ran out of the hangar as guns opened fire on the robot. Timothy, the guard who was helping him carry the magnetic weapon, and the other two guards turned the corner and ran down the stairs leading to the basement and the explosives that constituted the facility's self-destruct apparatus.

In Hangar 5, rifles blazed as security forces fired their bullets in vain at the kaiju-sized robot that was tearing through Hangar Five. To their credit, each person in the hangar knew that they were going to die, and despite that fact, they fought with the courage of a pride of lions. Even the research team members grabbed emergency flares, fire hoses, and whatever else they could find to try and use to try and keep the robot from exiting the building.

Timothy and the guards that had accompanied him ran to the doors that housed the explosives for the self-destruct system. Timothy pulled the magnetic missile over toward the door and quickly attached it. He activated the weapon and then he stepped back as the weapon created a small but powerful magnetic field that pulled the six-foot-high and two-foot-thick steel door into a sphere that was no larger than a bowling ball. Timothy could see the explosives that lined the bottom and the sides of the facility staring at him. He could hear the security forces above as they continued to fire at the TR-3B robot. Timothy looked at the guards who were standing next to him with their rifles in hand. He yelled at them, "Shoot it! Shoot it now!"

The two guards unleashed the fury of their rifles on the explosives. Several floors above Timothy and the guards, the second TR-3B robots was making its way toward the opening created by its predecessor when the entire facility blew up in an explosion with a payload equal to a small nuclear bomb.

CHAPTER 14

Chicago

Thomas and Clarissa arrived in Chicago roughly thirty minutes after the destruction of the Catskill Mountain facility. As their craft flew over the city, they were able to see the utter devastation that had occurred to it. They Instructors knew that death and destruction were occurring on a scale that was unprecedented but to actually behold what had occurred with their own eyes forced them to confront the horror that the Signal had brought to their planet on a personal level. The hundreds of thousands of dead bodies that lined the streets were difficult enough for them to look at, but when they saw the saw bloodied bodies of Garudasaurus, Bearadon, Chagon, and Leviathan resting in the middle of the city, it brought them to tears.

They had helped in creating the Kaiju Corps for the very purpose of standing on the front lines of a battle to prevent the extinction of humankind. They had instructed and trained the members of the team to be soldiers, and like all soldiers, to be willing to give their very lives in order to complete their mission.

While Thomas and Clarissa had worked with the Kaiju Corps toward this end for over two decades, they had also helped to raise to them. The Instructors had no other family save for the Horsemen themselves. The Kaiju Corps were their children. The scientist and trainers within the Instructors looked down on the soldiers they had generated to see that they had performed their duties to the utmost and it filled them with a sense of pride. Simultaneously, they looked down at the children they had raised to see them bloody and injured at the hands of the robots they had fought off, and the parents within the Instructors were overwhelmed with sorrow at seeing their children in such pain.

Clarissa was starting to tear up when Thomas looked at her and put her feelings into perspective. "As I look down at them, I am filled with a sense of accomplishment and empathy. They are exactly what we had hoped they would be when we created them and prepared them for this moment. As scientists and teachers, we successfully prepared them to defend the planet. This is something I was prepared for. It's the other feelings that I am experiencing that no one can prepare themselves for." He shifted his gaze so that he was looking down at Garudasaurus. "Every parent eventually reaches that point of their children's life when the child they raised has become an adult. The parent must face the realization that their capacity to protect and shield their children from the world is now limited to a role of merely supporting them as they can. I suppose that this must be particularly difficult for the parents of soldiers who watch their children place their lives on the line in order to protect others." He looked back toward Clarissa. "Jerome is his own man now. He is a soldier, and I could not be prouder of him for what he has accomplished so far. I may not be able to protect him from what lies ahead, but I can support him in his cause."

He shifted gaze back to Clarissa. "They are going to need at least twenty-four hours to heal before we can talk to them anyway. Even after they return to their human forms, they are going to need time to eat and sleep before they can battle in another city." He pointed to the six TR-3Bs that were lining the streets roughly ten blocks from where the Kaiju Corps were resting. "Let's use our timely wisely and support them as best we can. We are going to fly those TR-3Bs over the city, and we are going to broadcast a message that the robots are defeated, the monsters are here to protect us, and that we need all remaining citizens to report to designated areas where they can best be utilized to help us enact the next part of our plan. We will need physicists, chemists, mechanics, meteorologists, and even people like jewelers and watchmakers who can help us with the collection, assembly, and deployment of the nuclear bombs that we are going to use to disperse our EMPs across the world." He looked back toward the ruined city. "Then we are going to find police officers, firefighters, and teachers. People who are skilled at organizing others and conveying information to them to help us move the remaining population to an area where they can rebuild. Then we will need doctors and nurses to help address medical needs as well."

Thomas looked back to Clarissa. "If we can support the Kaiju Corps in this way… If we can organize the beginnings of the next stage of human civilization as well as orchestrate the attacks that will cease the creation of more robots across the globe, we can make a difference in this war. We can give our children the opportunity they need to recover and continue to fight."

He reached out and grabbed Clarissa's hand. "Most importantly, we will be able to increase the chances that our children will survive this war."

Clarissa nodded. "We have a lot of work to do." She yelled up to the pilot, "Bring us down near those other TR-3Bs."

The craft quickly landed next to the other TR-3Bs, and as soon as Thomas and Clarissa stepped out of their craft, they saw the TR-3B that was carrying Susan flying toward their location.

Clarissa jumped off the TR-3B, and she as did so, Brian Linke came running over toward her. She smiled at him. "Mr. Linke, my name is Clarissa. I am one of the people who was communicating to you through your tablet. I understand that you think you have made progress on disconnecting the TR-3Bs from outside communications?"

Brian nodded. "Yes, ma'am, and please, call me Brian. As far as I can tell from the TR-3B's schematics and its internal programming, all of the ships that I have addressed so far should be safe from being compromised by the Signal. The downside is that for now that TR-3Bs are also unable to communicate with each other when they are in the air."

Clarissa nodded. "Brian, you have been tremendously helpful. In the face of the greatest crisis humankind has ever faced, you have stepped up and done everything you can to fight against the threat. I want to thank you on behalf of everyone. Without you, the TR-3Bs may have fallen under the control of the Signal, and if that were to happen, this war would already be over." She placed her hand on his shoulder. "I know that you are exhausted, but if you could disconnect this TR-3B and the other that has just landed, we will see that you can get some food and some much-needed rest."

Brian smiled. "Thanks that would be much appreciated. Let me get these two crafts disconnected before they start turning into giant robots."

Clarissa smiled at the young man's attempt at humor, but in the back of her mind, she was thinking about the TR-3B robot that emerged from the Catskill Mountain Facility and disappeared.

As Brian was disconnecting the TR-3Bs that had escaped from the Catskill Facility, Clarissa called over the pilots of the crafts. She immediately began outlining the next steps of her plan to the pilots, and in doing so, she was forced to rely on tools and methods that she had not used since her days in grade school. Clarissa quickly jotted down an announcement that she wanted the pilots to read over their loud speakers as they flew over the city.

Citizens of Chicago, we represent the Horsemen. We are an organization that is dedicated to protecting the Earth from potential extinction-level threats. The giant robots that had attacked the city were created by a Signal that has taken over the planet's technology. For the foreseeable future, we will not have power or electricity available to us. We are working to rectify this issue and to fight the threat presented by the Signal and the robots it is creating. We will require your help in continuing to fight this war. Please listen carefully to the following orders and enact them as quickly as possible. We understand that following these orders will require many of you to leave your families during a time of crisis. We will reunite you with your families at a later date, but for now, their safety and the safety of our entire species depends on you doing what you can to assist in this crisis. We need all physicists, chemists, mechanics, and watchmakers to report to Wrigley Field. All doctors, nurses, and EMTs, please report to the nearest hospital. For the rest of you, if you are near one of the many people who are badly wounded, please take them to the nearest hospital. Everyone else, please report to the waterfront where further instructions will be given.

Clarissa had recopied the announcement for each of the pilots, and then within an hour, the TR-3Bs were slowly floating over Chicago as the pilots read the instructions over their loudspeakers to the people who were hiding throughout the city. Clarissa moved between hospitals, and she did the best that she could to coordinate the efforts of the medical staff there.

Susan was stationed at the waterfront where she worked with the civic leaders that Thomas had mentioned on preparing the survivors for the lives that they would now have to lead. She instructed them on how they would need to work in cooperation as best as they could to scavenge food, use what they could to heat water so that it was potable, and to fish the lake for food. Some of the more forward-thinking survivors voiced their concerns about the lack of power and the harsh winter that was headed their way to Susan. She recognized their fears, but she also dissuaded them from discussing this issue with the other survivors for as long as possible in order to prevent a panic. Susan knew that more than half of the survivors within the city would die in the next year from cold, starvation, and disease, but she also explained to the people that approached her with these concerns that there was nothing they could do about it. She suggested that what they could do right now was to help the survivors deal with the challenges they currently faced in hopes that it helped them to find an inner strength that would allow them to face the greater challenges that awaited them down the road.

Their current challenge was to remove the corpses and body parts that littered the streets before disease spread across the city. The people of Chicago were forced to gather up the remains of nearly half of the city's population, including their friends and loved ones, and carry them to mass funeral pyres. The bodies of the dead were piled up in the streets, doused in accelerants, and then burned. The smell of the burning dead blanketed the entire city by nightfall.

Thomas worked with the scientists and craftsmen. He gave them very specific details on the materials that they would need to construct the detonators needed to arm the nuclear bombs located in New Jersey.

To the credit of both the Instructors and the people of Chicago, everyone was where they were supposed to be, working on the tasks given to them within twenty-four hours. During that time period, that Kaiju Corps remained in their monster forms and healed. When they had finished healing, they returned to their human forms. They ate a quick meal and then occupied one of the many hotel rooms where they were given twelve hours to sleep before they discussed their next mission with the Instructors.

CHAPTER 15

Once the Kaiju Corps had returned to their human forms, the pilots and the Instructors had to help them walk to the hotel, force them to eat a least an energy bar, and then help them into their rooms. Nick and Miki didn't even have the chance to talk to each other about what had happened. He had no doubt that the time they spent embracing each other in their kaiju forms had conveyed to Miki that he shared her feelings, but he desperately wanted to talk to her in their human forms. He could see though as Susan had half-carried Miki to her room that she was in no condition to talk about anything until she had some rest.

As Michelle and Jerome were being helped to their rooms, Michelle briefly asked Jerome if after a few hours of sleep that he would come to her room to discuss their plans regarding the continued war against the Signal and its robots.

Jerome managed five hours of sleep before he woke up. He knew that his body needed more rest, but he pushed that thought aside, forced himself to get dressed, and walk down to Michelle's room. Jerome had always taken his role of team leader very seriously. He had always tried to be available to his team members when they needed him. He also knew that if Michelle wanted to talk to him that meant she had something very serious to discuss.

He walked down to her door and he knocked gently on it so as not awaken Miki who was sleeping in the room next door.

Michelle was completely naked when she opened the door. Jerome didn't think much of this, as all of the members of the Kaiju Corps had regularly seen each other without clothes as a result of their transformation process. Michelle would often forgo clothes if they were in the middle of a training session in order to transform into a kaiju as quickly as possible. Given the threat they were facing, he didn't blame her for wanting to be ready to fight as quickly as possible. He was even a little ashamed that he did not think of it himself. Still, even though he knew that she was simply keeping herself in a state of being ready for battle, he kept his eyes fixed on her face. Michelle was a beautiful woman, but she was also a fierce warrior both as a human and a kaiju, and Jerome had no intention of aggravating her in any of her forms.

To Jerome's surprise, she smiled as she opened the door. Jerome only took note of this fact because Michelle hardly ever smiled. She was the type of woman who kept her feelings to herself. Even when she was in her Bearadon form and engaged in battle, she never seemed angry. Michelle was always in control of her emotions, and she was always surveying the situation around her with a keen eye.

She motioned for Jerome to come into her room. "Thank you for coming, Jerome. As I said, there is something of the utmost importance that I need to discuss with you."

Jerome walked over to a chair in the room and sat down. "As always, I value your perspective on missions, and given what we currently face, I can use your input now more than ever."

Michelle smiled at him and Jerome did his best to smile back. He could tell that something was bothering Michelle because her usual sense of self-confidence was gone. She seemed unsure of herself and how she should proceed. Jerome tried his best to probe her feelings without hurting her pride. "Michelle, I can see that something is bothering you. Whatever it is, if there is anything that I can do to help you with it, please just let me know. I know I don't often discuss personal matters with you, but that doesn't mean that I don't care about your feelings. What we are currently facing is beyond what any of us were ever prepared for. If you feel the need to share what you are feeling with someone, you can feel free to do so with me. Nothing that you can say would ever change the respect that I have for you as a person or as a soldier."

Michelle did the one thing that Jerome would not have expected from her when she burst out laughing. She was laughing so hard that her eyes were tearing up. She looked at the confused Jerome, and she did her best to apologize to him in between laughing. "I am sorry, Jerome. It's not you or what you said. It's just that with what you and I are facing, I don't know how to handle it, and for some reason, it just came out as laughter."

Jerome smiled at her. "Hey, it's all good. We are fighting a war where the best outcome we can hope for is to save less than twenty percent of the world population. The stress is getting to all of us in different ways."

Michelle took several deep breaths to stop herself from laughing. "It's not the war, Jerome. It's the other thing we have to do." She walked closer to Jerome, knelt down in front of him, and grabbed his hands. "I talked to Susan after my battle in Buffalo and before coming out here. Do you know what the rest of the plan for our counter-attack is from here?"

Jerome nodded. "We are going to secure several other cities along the Great Lakes and then the East Coast. The Instructors also have some type of plan to use nuclear bombs to create EMPs in the upper atmosphere that will stop the production of the robots."

She stopped him from talking. "Think about right now and tomorrow, Jerome. At best, we can secure two cities, and even if the Instructors are able to successfully enact their plan tomorrow, we are still facing insurmountable numbers. Think about how many giant robots have already been created. Then think about how many more robots will be created by the end of tomorrow in cities that have yet to be exposed to an EMP. We have seen factors generate a robot every half an hour in some cases. Even after we secure the Lakes and the East Coast, there will still be hundreds if not thousands of robots across the planet. After those robots clear out the human population around the area they were created in, they are going to look for more people. Their programming will not be complete until they have set up their fully functioning farm here on Earth." She looked away from Jerome. "We are going to spend the rest of our lives fighting to protect what's left of the human population, and even then, it won't be enough."

Jerome shook his head and he placed his hand on her shoulder. "Michelle, we can't look at this war like that. We can only address each battle as it happens and all that we can give is ourselves and everything that we have. We have to believe that we can win this war. We have to believe that one day we will once again live on a relatively peaceful planet."

Michelle stood up and walked away from Jerome. She was silent for a moment as she collected her thoughts. She shook her head and turned around to face her team leader. "Jerome, I have never been good with approaching issues in a delicate fashion." She sighed. "The truth is, I thought that I could accept what we have to do without issue, but now seeing you here, this is more difficult than I ever would have imagined." She took a step back in Jerome's direction. "I have talked to the Instructors about the next phase of their plan going forward. The truth of the matter is they firmly believe that this war will rage on long after we are gone. With the destruction of the Horsemen facilities around the world, they lack the means to create more soldiers like us." Michelle moved slightly closer to Jerome so that she was standing directly in front of him. "Jerome, we need to ensure the continuation of our species so that humanity will still have a Kaiju Corps to protect them after we are gone."

Jerome's jaw dropped and his eyes widened as the realization of what Michelle was saying dawned on him. "Wait, what? Do you know what you are saying? Do you know what you are asking of me?"

Michelle nodded. "I know what I am asking of you. I am also fully aware that neither of us fully understand what the full implications of what I am asking means to either of us."

Jerome stood up. "Michelle, only yesterday we first entered into a war. Since then, we have lost millions of people, we have lost our home, and we still have countless battles ahead of us. We could die in any one of those encounters." He began to pace around the room. "Then they want me to be a father in all of this? Not only to be a father who could die at any second, but a father who is raising a child specifically to be a weapon!" He looked toward Michelle. "How are we supposed to be parents when we never really had parents ourselves? Then why are you and I just supposed to breed? Don't we get any say in who we love and who we want to be with?" Jerome realized what he had said and he looked at his teammate. "Michelle, I am sorry that wasn't meant as a slight against you. I do love you as a friend and a teammate. You are a stunningly beautiful woman. It's just that the thought of being with someone and of having a family… These are things that I thought I would never have. I have always focused on the mission. On what I had to do to win a battle. This is just something that's out of my depth, something that I am not prepared for."

Michelle walked to Jerome and she wrapped her arms around his neck. "I know how you feel, Jerome. Believe me, I know exactly how you feel. You know that I more than anyone have been a person who was focused on my mission and on doing what I had to do. I had thought that this might come up when the war first started. I was preparing myself for it, and I was preparing for you. It looks like Nick and Miki have finally admitted their feelings for each other. It won't be long until those feelings lead them to having a child on their own." She placed her forehead against Jerome's. "This may be something that we have to do as part of our mission, but it can also be more than that. This war has caused all of us to reevaluate our lives. I had never thought about having a child, let alone who I would have it with, but you are correct when you said that we could die tomorrow. There is a good chance that we won't make it to the end of this war. I don't want this war to be my life. I want someone to fight for other than just the faceless numbers that are the human race. Whatever life we have ahead of us, I want it to have as much meaning for us as possible. I know that we don't have feelings for each other the way that Nick and Miki do, but I do know what feelings I have for you. I feel that you are the bravest, most selfless person that I know. I know that you are a born leader and that your sense of determination is second to none. I am proud to call my friend and my commander. If there was anyone whose traits I would want to be a part of my child, it would be you. If there was anyone who I thought would be the best possible father to a child, it would be you. Do you find any of those traits in me?"

Jerome nodded slightly. "You are the bravest person I know. You would fight until every last ounce of energy left your body to protect someone that you love. When everything crumbles around me, you are the rock that I look to for stability. I have no doubt that you would be a loving and devoted mother."

Michelle kissed him. "We can work out how we feel about each other later. Right now, let's focus on ensuring that we have more to life than just endless war. You and I are always focused on other people around us and what they need. For now, why don't we focus on each other and take our next step from there." She kissed Jerome again, and as she did so, she pulled him over toward her bed.

Nick had slept for six hours when there was a knock on his door. He eagerly sprang out of bed, hoping that he would open his door to find Miki standing there. Nick was surprised to see Thomas standing in his doorway. It had been over an hour since he had spoken to Thomas, but every word of their conversation still resonated within his mind. He found himself running one sentence through his mind over and over again.

"I am sorry, Nick, to have to be the one who tells you this, but Timothy is gone. He died a hero. He and many other people sacrificed themselves to prevent an army of TR-3B based robots from being constructed. You should be proud of him just as I know that he is proud of you."

Thomas would go on to tell Nick that if he needed him that he would be there for him. That Nick could always come and talk to him especially now in light of what had occurred. Nick's already overwhelmed emotions caused him to shut down. He thanked Thomas for the information and then asked for so time to himself.

Nick couldn't fathom the fact that Timothy was gone. Everything in his life that he trained for and longed for was occurring and the one constant in his life, the one person he could truly confide in, was gone forever. Nick wanted to cry, but he couldn't. His mind was beginning to fill with anger. He could feel his muscles and bones shifting beneath his skin and he knew that if he didn't do something soon that he would change into Leviathan in the middle of the hotel. He ran out into the hallway and toward Jerome's room. Nick pounded on the door and called for his friend, but there was no answer. His spine cracked as it was in the process of realigning itself. Nick strained his back as he tried to fight the transformation. He then ran to the stairs and sprinted down to the floor that Miki and Michelle were staying on.

He ran into the hallway to see that his foot had already turned green. He rushed toward Miki's door and he went to knock on it, but instead of a hand wrapping on the door, a clawed fist burst through it.

Miki was immediately awoken from her sleep when she heard Nick yell, "Miki, I need you!"

She ran to her partially destroyed door to see Nick's changing face through the hole he had punched in it. She flung open the door, grabbed the man she loved, and pulled him into her room. She cradled him just as he had cradled her the day before when her emotions had overwhelmed her. She whispered to him, "Nick, calm down. You have to calm down."

Nick screamed, "I can't! Timothy is dead."

Miki gasped. "Oh my God, Nick." She could feel him changing in her hands. She knew that he was only moments away from reaching a height and weight that would destroy the floor they were on and then the entire hotel. She whispered in his ear, "Nick, the anger is causing you to change, but that's not what you really feel. The anger is just what's easiest for you to express, but it's the pain and sadness at your loss that you need to let out. Look at how far you have come in being able to control both your emotions and your kaiju-self in the past few days. You have shifted in and out of your kaiju form with ease because you were in control of your emotions and you expressed them. You expressed your love for me, you directed your anger at the robots, and now you have to let yourself feel the sorrow that is within you from losing Timothy. Please, Nick, let the pain come out."

Nick wailed loudly as tears burst out of his eyes, "Timothy is gone! I need him now more than ever and he is gone!"

As he cried, Miki could feel his body shifting back into place in her arms. She whispered to him, "I have got you, Nick. I will be here for you from now on."

When Nick's body had fully settled back into his human form, he hugged her. The two of them cried for several minutes as Nick let loose his pain. Miki held him the entire time, and when it was over, he looked into her eyes. He smiled at her. "Miki, I love you too. I have loved for years, I just didn't know how that applied to us. I didn't know how the Horsemen or Jerome and Michelle would react to my feelings, but I have learned over the past two days that none of that matters. The world that we knew is gone and the only way that I can face this new world is with you. I love you,

Miki, and whatever lies ahead of me for the rest of my time on this planet, I want to experience it with you."

Miki kissed him back and said, "We will be there for each other, Nick. I have loved you for as long as I can remember. No matter what this world has in store for us, not matter what battles we have to fight, I will love you."

The two of them hugged then Miki pulled Nick over toward her bed. She gently laid down on the bed and then she pulled him close to her. The two of them embraced each other as they slowly drifted back to sleep.

CHAPTER 16

The Atlantic Ocean

Captain Erik Creany was piloting his TR-3B over the ocean with the other remaining seven TR-3Bs flying in a V pattern behind him. The last communication that any of the TR-3B pilots who were operating outside of the US had received was from their squadron leader Captain Richards. Richards had ordered them to deliver their last EMPs then to meet at Horsemen facility in Spain. When the pilots met outside of the facility, they were instructed to follow the directions of a civilian programmer who had sent them instructions on how to disconnect their craft from external communications. The programmer's instructions were easy to follow, and it took the pilots less than an hour to protect their craft from possible take-over by the Signal. With the TR-3Bs secure against the Signal's influence, the pilots' final order was to fly to the Great Lakes area and to search for the Kaiju Corps, the remaining Horsemen, and other TR-3Bs. There they would join the insurgency and aid in the war against the machines.

Captain Creany was doing his best to keep the fleet in a tight formation, as visual confirmation was the only way that the TR-3B pilots could keep track of each other. Beyond their line of sight, the pilots had no idea what was in the sky with them. As their lead pilot in the formation, Creany took it as his personal responsibility to lookout for any potential threats. There was a good deal of cloud cover in the skies below them, but the air in front of them was clear.

The middle-aged pilot was staring intensely at the sky in front of him when he thought he saw some sort of oddly shaped dark black object flying toward them from the east. He tried to focus his vision to get a better look at the object when it dove down and flew into the clouds. Creany cursed because he had no idea if any of the other pilots had seen the object, and he had no way to contact them to warn them of the potential threat. Creany said a quick prayer that either his eyes were playing tricks on him or that he had seen something as mundane as a flock of geese. Creany decided that in the current environment that it was better to proceed with caution. The pilot banked his craft to the left and away from the cloud bank he had seen the object fly into. Once he was sure that the other TR-3Bs had followed his lead, he increased the speed of his craft beyond the capabilities of any other craft on the planet. Creany shifted his chair around and was glad to see that the other crafts in the squadron had also increased their speed. Creany wasn't sure what he had seen, but now he was not overly concerned about it. Whatever he had seen was now behind the squadron, and there was no way possible that the object would be able to catch up to them let alone engage them.

The pilots continued to make their way toward the United States for another five minutes when Creany looked down to see the black object flying roughly a thousand feet below them. He shook his head in disbelief as he realized that he was looking at a giant robot that was constructed from the parts of TR-3Bs. The ace pilot felt a cold chill run through his body when the robot's pitch black and pointed head turned toward him and stared back at him.

Creany cursed, "Damn it! The Signal must have compromised the TR-3B plant in the Catskills!" Creany pulled his ship hard and to the left as he engaged in evasive maneuvers. While his craft was shifting its position in mid-air, he saw the robot point its arm at the squadron. Creany screamed when he saw what looked like circles of pure force pulsating out of the robot's arm and streaking toward the TR-3Bs. The two TR-3Bs that were directly behind Creany were ripped to pieces when the robot's sonic blast came into contact with them.

The remaining five TR-3Bs followed Creany's lead, and they engaged in evasive maneuvers. Creany circled his craft around; he didn't need to have radio contact with the other craft to know that they were following his lead. Despite the fact that no one could hear him, Creany talked to the robot, "All right, you metallic bastard. You now have the attention of the top pilots in the world behind our most advanced weapons. Kiss your alien-controlled ass goodbye!"

Creany armed his rockets and machine guns then he opened fire on the oncoming robot. He saw the missiles and bullets of the other TR-3Bs streak past his ship on their way toward the robot as well. Creany cursed when he saw the robot make a ninety-degree turn straight down to avoid the bombardment. Creany and the rest of the TR-3Bs also performed the ninety-degree dive as the pilot yelled, "You're not the only one with TR-3B technology. We can follow you wherever you go!"

Creany unleashed another torrent of bullets at the robot. His first few bullets hit the robot, and as soon as they did, the robot began spinning and then it veered to the left. The robot turned around and fired another of its sonic blasts. Creany veered to the right and the other TR-3Bs behind him also veered off course to avoid the blast. Creany laughed. "Fool me once..." Before he could finish his sentence, the robot streaked past Creany and grabbed one of the TR-3Bs behind him. The robot pulled the TR-3B off its flight path and then it tore the craft in half. Creany could see the face of his fellow pilot as he fell past him and the G-force from the speed he was traveling at shredded him to pieces.

Creany flew his TR-3B in a circle then he flew straight up toward the robot who was positioned above him. Creany launched two more missiles at the mech while a second TR-3B that had positioned itself above the robot opened fire with its machine guns. Creany couldn't believe his eyes as the robot curved up and out of the path of the duel attack. The robot flew directly at the TR-3B that was firing its machine guns on it and then with a single blow, it sent the craft tumbling to the ocean below. The robot then turned its sonic cannon at another of the advanced craft that was pursuing it, and when the blast struck the craft's propulsion system, it exploded.

Creany was moving his craft into position to try and attack the robot again when he saw it dive toward one of the other three craft with a speed and precision that he had never seen exhibited by a TR-3B. When the pilot noticed the robot coming toward him, he veered his craft to the left and accelerated to top speed. Despite the fact that the TR-3B was moving at top speed, the robot was able to catch up to it in a matter of seconds. The robot flew over top of the fleeing TR-3B then it pulled its fist back and drove it through the hull of the craft, causing it to explode.

Creany shook his head in disbelief as he realized that he was engaging an enemy that was beyond his capabilities to defeat. The robot had the combined speed and power of multiple TR-3Bs, and in addition to that, it obviously had some additional weapons that most TR-3Bs didn't possess. While the robot's superior weaponry and speed made it formidable enough, the mech was made all the more dangerous by the fact that it possessed more processing power within its CPU then the combined minds of every human brain on the planet combined.

Creany turned his craft around and tried to flee from the battle. He was no coward, but he knew what the TR-3Bs meant to the survival of humanity going forward. If Creany's craft and the other three remaining craft were lost here, the chances of humanity winning this war would decrease dramatically. As he flew away, Creany shifted his TR-3B from side to side which was the signal to scatter that he and the other pilots had worked out before heading out over the Atlantic.

As Creany flew east, the other remaining TR-3Bs flew toward the south. The robot took off after the ship that was flying south. Creany could no longer see the robot or the other TR-3Bs. All that he could do was continue to push his craft as hard as he could in an attempt to reach the Great Lakes where he could find the remaining TR-3Bs, and more importantly, the Kaiju Corps. His craft had been moving at top speed for nearly three minutes when he looked to his left to see the robot streaking toward him. He guessed that the robot had destroyed the TR-3Bs that had flown south and now it was coming for him. Creany shook his head in disbelief at the speed the robot was capable of attaining. He quickly looked through the transparent bottom of the craft to see that there was only ocean below him. He had yet to even reach the East Coast and he was still hundreds of miles from any possible help.

Creany gritted his teeth then he veered directly at the oncoming mech. Creany screamed as he unleashed every weapon that he had at the stark black robot. Creany watched as the robot shifted its body around every bullet and missile that he had fired at it. The last thing the Creany saw was the robot's fist as it pierced the hull of his craft and drove through his body. Creany's TR-3B exploded as the robot passed through the flames unscathed. The robot flew in a tight circle and then it flew away in a southwest direction.

CHAPTER 17

The next morning, the remaining Instructors, the Kaiju Corps, Brian Linke, and The pilots of the TR-3Bs were all meeting within the conference room of the Hyatt. Thomas sat at the head of the large conference table in the middle of the room with Clarissa and Susan on either side of him. Jerome and Michelle sat on opposite sides of the table. The two of them were strangely quiet, and they were doing their best to avoid making eye contact with each other. Nick and Miki sat next to each and they were holding hands. After the events of the previous two days, they no longer cared how anyone else felt about their relationship.

Brian Linke and the TR-3B captains filled out the table. Thomas stood up and he looked around the table with his eyes setting directly on Nick. "I would like to suggest a brief moment of silence for all those that we have lost in the past few days." He then bowed his head, as did everyone else. When the moment had passed, Thomas resumed his briefing. "Thank you. I have asked you all here so that we can discuss the next steps in our war against the robots. To this point, we have cleared four cities of giant robots completely, and we have stopped the production of giant robots on roughly fifty percent of the world. Bringing the construction of new giant robots to a complete halt would truly enable us to turn this war into a war of attrition, and more specifically, a war that we can win. To that end, we have developed a plan in which we will shall use weather balloons to carry ten nuclear warheads into the upper atmosphere where they will be detonated and create an EMP that will cover the entire planet. This planet-wide EMP will completely stop the production of any new robots. In order to prevent the Signal from overriding the warheads, we will use a delay-switch pencil timer constructed from clocks and other mechanical devices that we have scavenged from the city. Mr. Linke and I have been working in conjunction with several of the physicists and mechanics in the area. We have been able to cobble together six of the necessary ten detonators required for this mission. We were fortunate in that the Emergency Weather Service located in Chicago had more than enough of the weather balloons that we require to complete this task."

He looked toward Clarissa. "I will now turn this briefing over to Clarissa who will hand out mission parameters and discuss the logistics of our current operations."

Clarissa stood up. "From this point on, our attack will be two-fold, with our initial plan to secure the Great Lakes area and US East Coast still intact but with the additional objective of using our nuclear warheads to create a global EMP. We are giving the nuclear warhead plan the codename Program 437. We currently have eight TR-3Bs at our disposal. There are eight additional TR-3Bs that are still MIA. Without communication from them, we are not sure where they are or what has happened to them. We do have a new factor to concern ourselves with in that prior to the destruction of our main facility in the Catskill Mountains. The Signal managed to compromise our network and create a TR-3B giant robot. The TR-3B robot or Blackbolt, as we have designated it, is the first mech that is capable of flight. Blackbolt has also managed to arm itself with the latest in Horsemen-developed weaponry. The construction of this robot is the culmination of our fears. It is entirely possible that Blackbolt engaged and destroyed the missing TR-3Bs. With the threat of Blackbolt in mind, we shall split our forces to best accommodate possible attacks from the super robot. All of the cities in our target areas have already had EMP bombs dropped on them, so we know that no new robots will be created in these cities, and we know the number of robots that were present in the city at the time of the bombings."

Clarissa rolled a map of the Mid-Atlantic states across the table. "The primary objective is to secure Philadelphia and the surrounding area. The old naval shipyard in Philadelphia will have the remaining delay-switch pencil timers that we require to enact our plan. The Pine Barrens across the river from the city house the nuclear warheads that we require to generate our EMPs. Captains Okafor and Granderson will take the Kaiju Corps to Philadelphia as well as Thomas, Mr. Linke, and several other engineers that we have found in Chicago who can be of assistance in this mission. The two TR-3Bs that brought me, Susan, and Thomas to Chicago will fly a holding pattern around the area as lookouts for Blackbolt."

She quickly consulted her notepad. "The same naval shipyard that is holding the detonators that we require was coopted by the Signal to create the giant robots in Philadelphia. When the EMP was dropped on Philadelphia twenty-seven hours ago, three giant robots were spotted within the city. Two of the robots seem to be the standard collect-and-destroy robots that are actively attacking the city. In Philadelphia, these robots are constructed from parts of two different naval ships, and we are designating them based on those parts. The first robot is known as Battleship and the second robot has been given the codename Cutter. Each of these two robots stands at slightly over two hundred feet tall and has more firepower than any of the previous collection robots that you have faced thus far. The third robot appears to be one of their battle bots. This robot had been given the call sign Carrier. As I am sure that you surmised, this robot is built from parts of aircraft carriers. It has a height of over three hundred feet, making it a hundred feet taller than even Leviathan. Carrier will be the largest and likely the physically strongest robot that you have encountered thus far. The city was first attacked over thirty hours ago, and most of the buildings in Philadelphia are destroyed. The death toll in Philadelphia is easily over five hundred thousand. Based on the robot's movements, we can assume that any people who are still alive within the city are hiding underground or within the remains of a partially destroyed building. In your previous battles, you have used the tactic of having Leviathan engage the battle robot while the rest of you take on the collection robots. Given the size and strength of Carrier, I recommend that Bearadon, Leviathan, and Chagon engage Carrier directly as soon as you enter the city."

She turned her head toward Jerome. "While three of the kaiju are battling Carrier, Thomas's team will recover the required detonators from the naval shipyard and then load them onto Captain Okafor's TR-3B. As they complete this operation, Garudasaurus will stand guard over them in the likely event that one of the other two robots detects their presence and attacks. Once Thomas's team has successfully located the detonators and loaded them onto the TR-3B, Captain Okafur will then fly them to the nearby Pine Barrens with the two lookout TR-3Bs accompanying him as protection from Blackbolt. This team will modify the warheads to fit our new detonators and then load them onto Captain Okafor's TR-3B. He will then pilot his craft to the various locations around the world that we need to launch the weather balloons from to carry our nuclear warheads into the upper atmosphere. It should take Captain Okafor roughly seventeen hours to reach every destination on his mission. At each stop, he will leave one person from his team to arm and launch our attacks. These launching points will include Brazil, Argentina, Algeria, South Africa, Finland, India, China, Russia, Australia, and the US West Coast, likely California. Eighteen hours after leaving from the Pine Barrens facility, we launch our balloons and create a World-Wide EMP. As Captain Okafor and his escorts are transporting the EMP team around the world, the Kaiju Corps will continue to make their way down the East Coast, clearing out cities from giant robots and saving as many people as possible in the process."

Clarissa quickly unrolled a map of the Great Lakes on top of the map of the Mid-Atlantic states. "We still feel strongly that securing the area around the Great Lakes is vital to the survival of the resistance of the human race. The four TR-3Bs that were armed with sonic cannons and magnetic missiles will engage the robots in Cleveland and Toronto. We feel confident that with the upgraded weapons at their disposal that they can defeat the robots who are still stalking those two cities. This attack will be led by Captain Larry Richards, as he is our longest-tenured and most experienced pilot."

Clarissa turned to the veteran TR-3B captain. "Captain Richards, is your team prepared for this mission?"

Richards looked directly into Clarissa's eyes. "Cleveland and Toronto will be robot free by the end of the day."

Clarissa nodded. "Very good." She then looked around the room. "Are there any questions?"

Miki immediately raised her hand. "Clarissa, what about the suspected launch site in Cape Canaveral? When are we going to move on it to prevent the robots from sending their cryogenically frozen captives into space?"

Clarissa looked at the young woman who she had mentored as a girl. Inwardly, her heart felt for Miki and her concern for the people who were destined to end up as food for some alien race in the distant future, but she needed to focus on people who could still be saved. She glared at Miki. "As we discussed previously, we need to focus on saving the lives of people who can help us rebuild humanity. While most of the people in Philadelphia, Baltimore, Washington, and Atlanta are dead or have escaped the cities, there are still thousands of people trapped there. People who are not frozen and who we can save." She softened her voice somewhat. "I appreciate your concern, Miki, but we need to help those we can and accept the fact that in war there are going to be casualties."

Miki's eyes were burning with anger as she screamed, "Anyone who is still alive within the cities at least has a chance of survival! If they can hold out until after we save the people who are going to be sent into space, we can save double the lives! If we don't move on the Cape Canaveral location, all of those people won't have a chance at all and they will be facing a fate worse than death. We need to save them!"

Clarissa's voice changed from the soft voice of a caregiver to the authoritative voice of a commanding officer. "You are a soldier. Your job is to worry about following orders and winning a war. The difficult burden of deciding whose lives need to be saved first falls on me. We will focus on saving the people along the East Coast. Once we secure Atlanta, we can move onto Cape Canaveral but not before that."

Miki stood glaring at Clarissa when Jerome spoke up, "I would suggest that the success of our mission may lie entirely with the Cape Canaveral site."

Susan was intrigued by the young commander's suggestion, and she also saw it as an opportunity to end the debate between Clarissa and Miki. "Elaborate on your thoughts, Jerome."

Jerome stood up. "Everything that we have seen the robots do so far is based on securing resources to send back to their home plant. They are reducing the human population to a number that won't put a strain on the planet. They are freezing some people to send back to their home planet and presumably they are starting to take some live prisoners to the farms that we suspect they are creating. The robots have taken steps to ensure that this plan is successful. When we attacked the robots, they responded by creating battle robots to oppose us. They also made a slight change in the programming of the typical robots to attack us first if we were to approach them, when at the first, they didn't even bother with us until we had attacked them."

He looked toward Clarissa. "You have also suggested that this new super robot Blackbolt has taken down a large portion of our TR-3B fleet. The robots have clearly deduced that the TR-3Bs are transporting us from location to location and decided that the best way to prevent us from further disrupting their plans was to take away our transportation. If Blackbolt is targeting TR-3Bs, it is likely that it will target Captain Okafor's craft and the other craft that are accompanying him. You suspect that Blackbolt was able to take out eight TR-3Bs. If it was able to do that, the robot will easily be able to destroy three of them. If we are unable to launch those balloons and deploy the EMPs, then we are all in agreement that this war is a lost cause."

Jerome started to walk around the room. "Every move that the robots have made was to ensure the success of their prime objective which is to send resources back to their home planet. Their supply resource chain ends with their ability to send those resources back to their home planet. We have been raised to be soldiers. We have spent countless hours learning military history, and one of the key factors in operating a successful military campaign is protecting your supply chain. Given that the Signal has created battle robots to protect the multiple robots that are at the start of that supply chain in the cities, it would stand to reason that their most powerful robot would be stationed at the bottleneck at the end of their supply chain."

Clarissa realized the point that Jerome was getting at. "You are suggesting that Blackbolt is stationed at Cape Canaveral and that it is conducting hit-and-run operations from there?"

Thomas nodded. "Jerome has a point. We don't know anything for sure, but given the methods in which the robots have operated so far, we can make the assumption that their primary shipping point is Cape Canaveral. His suggestion that Blackbolt is likely acting as a protector of the robots' operation would also seem to hold true with how they have operated so far."

Jerome nodded. "I figure that if Blackbolt was designed specifically to attack the kaiju Corps, then it would have already headed to Chicago. I mean, it's not like it doesn't know that we are here. It also knew that there was no chance we were on the TR-3Bs that were on their way to Chicago. As long as Blackbolt is operational then our plan for deploying the nuclear warheads around the world and stopping the production of new robots is in jeopardy. I would like to respectfully propose some small changes to our current course of action."

He walked over toward the maps on the table and separated them. "The first few steps of the plan will remain the same with Captain Richards and his TR-3Bs attacking the robots in both Cleveland and Toronto, as well as the Kaiju Corps securing Philadelphia and Thomas's team acquiring the warheads in the Pine Barrens. I would suggest, however, that Captain Okafor and Thomas's team holds their positions there while Captain Granderson transports the Kaiju Corps to Cape Canaveral. Once we can fully determine that Blackbolt is there and that the robots are using that location as their launching point, we can attack Blackbolt, which will ensure that it is occupied and cannot attack Captain Okafor and Thomas's team."

Jerome pointed to the cities of Baltimore, Washington DC, and Atlanta. "With us engaging Blackbolt, it will free up not only Captain Granderson's TR-3B but also the crafts that were going escort Captain Okafor. I would suggest that Captain Granderson and one of the TR-3Bs that was going escort Captain Okafor should meet above Atlanta and try to clear that city of robots. The second TR-3B that was going to escort Captain Okafor should take half of the warheads and fly west while Captain Okafor flies east. It will cut the time to execute the launch of the balloons in half from seventeen hours to eight hours."

Jerome looked toward Brian. "Mr. Linke, have you learned enough about the materials needed for this operation to help the people who are heading east to arm the warheads and set the detonators?"

Brian thought for a minute and then shook his head. "I think if the process was reviewed with me one time that I could set the bombs for the people who are going to be launching the balloons."

Jerome nodded. "Good. Lastly, any of the TR-3Bs which survive the battles in Cleveland and Toronto can attack Baltimore. Assuming that both groups of TR-3Bs are successful, they then converge on Washington DC."

Thomas smiled at the young man whom he had raised. "Jerome, you have proven to be a greater soldier and commander than we could have ever imagined. I find your suggested course of action to be prudent." He looked to Clarissa and Susan who both nodded their heads in approval.

Clarissa turned her attention to rest of the table. "Very well then; we shall proceed with Jerome's plan. Captain Williams will take his TR-3B and fly west from New Jersey with half of the nuclear warheads while Captain Okafor flies east. We will take one hour to make preparations for the adjusted plan and then we shall commence our operation."

The group disbanded and went their separate ways. Nick and Miki walked outside of the hotel, and they sat on what was once the front porch of the Hyatt. They looked over the devastation that was Chicago. Miki placed her head on Nick's shoulder. "Look at the city. This is a city that we fought to save. What are the cities that we are headed to next going to look like? The cities where the robots have had days to destroy them and slaughter the people there?"

Nick placed his arm around Miki's waist and hugged her. "We have to keep our focus on the future. We know that it's going to be bad as we move from city to city, but we need to think about what life can be like on this planet later. When we jump out of the TR-3B later on today, we won't be fighting for the cities of today. We will be fighting for whoever is still alive and the cities that they can build tomorrow." He turned Miki's head toward him. "For me, it's even more personal than that. I am going to be fighting for you. I am going to be fighting for our future together. I finally have a relationship with the woman I love. For the first time in my life, I also feel like I have a place in this world. I always saw myself as a freak, a monster, who would forever be known as the kaiju that killed thousands of people when I first changed into Leviathan. Now I see myself as not only having a chance at redemption by saving as many people as possible, but also as someone who can be an integral part of society. It almost seems horrible to say as we stare at all of this death and devastation, but I am right on the precipice of finally having everything that I want in life and no dammed robots are going to keep me from that."

Miki leaned in and kissed him. "I know exactly what you mean. I finally feel as though I am washing the blood off my hands from those people I killed at the lake when I first became Chagon. I never even dreamed of a future outside of continually training with the Horsemen. As horrible as this war is, it has brought me both a purpose in life and it has brought me you. I have gotten a taste of what I want in life, and we both know that in order to hold onto it, we have to win this war. Like you, I had always felt disconnected from humanity so fighting to save it always seemed like a well-intentioned but hollow concept to me. The short time that I have spent with you since revealing my feelings has not only brought me joy but it has shown me what all of the other people in the world have. Being loved and loving someone else is the greatest experience I can ever imagine. There is no way that I am allowing these robots to take that feeling away from everyone on this planet. We are going to win this war, Nick, we are going to love each other, and we are going to see what remains of the human race rise from the ashes of this war and build a new society based on the love they have for each other. In the next few hours, we will have a chance to earn our place in that society, and I can't think of a greater cause to fight for." She gently kissed Nick once more and then the two of them spent the last of their time together holding onto each other as a reminder of what they for fighting for.

CHAPTER 18

Cleveland

It was just after 10am when the four TR-3Bs with the updated weaponry of sonic cannons and magnetic missiles were flying over the decimated city of Cleveland. The squadron was led by Captain Larry Richards. As the pilots flew over the city, they were unable to see a single standing building. The entire city of Cleveland had been reduced to rubble.

Cleveland had been one of the first cities to have an EMP dropped on it which kept the number of robots made in the city to a minimum. There were only two robots rummaging through the debris of the city. The two robots were constructed from plane parts. One of them was given the designation Airbus and the second robot was given the designation Boeing. Both of the robots had an overall humanoid appearance with some enhancements due to their construction from airliners. The robots had wings on their arms and legs as well as propulsion systems attached to their backs. Aside from their airliner-like appendages, both of the mechs appeared to be the typical kill-and-collect robots. The early bombing of the city had prevented the Signal from constructing any of the so-called battle robots in Cleveland.

As the pilot who was designated the leader of the squadron, it was up to Richards to initiate the attack. Richards gritted his teeth and then flew by Airbus, designating the robot as the first target for the squadron. The pilots had discussed their strategy prior to leaving from Chicago, and as soon at the lead TR-3B flew past Airbus, the two craft that were trailing Richards fired magnetic missiles at the robot, hitting it in the chest and left leg. Airbus's chest and left leg immediately condensed into themselves, crushing the robot's upper body and leg. Airbus fell to the ground, and as soon as it hit the street, the fourth TR-3B in the squad flew in low and blasted what remained of Airbus with its sonic cannon, reducing the robot to a twisted pile of scrap metal.

Captain Richards circled around and flew toward Boeing. As Richards flew past Boeing, the propulsion system on the robot's back ignited. The mech leapt into the air and took off after the lead TR-3B. Richards had not expected the mech to be capable of flight, and as a result, the mech was nearly able to reach the TR-3B before the pilot realized that he was being pursued. Richards quickly increased his speed and put some distance between himself and the mech. While Boeing was capable of flight, the mech's commercial airline parts were no match for the speed and maneuverability of a TR-3B. Richards made a wide circle and the mech mirrored the maneuver in pursuit of him. As Boeing was halfway through completing its circle, it flew directly into the flight path of two of the other TR-3Bs who utilized their machine guns to destroy the mech's propulsion system. With its ability to fly taken from it, Boeing fell to the ground. It slid along the blood-soaked streets of Cleveland until it crashed into the remains of a destroyed building. As soon as the robot stopped sliding, it grabbed two handfuls of concrete in its hands, stood up, and threw them at the TR-3Bs flying above it. The TR-3Bs were easily able to avoid the debris. The crafts circled around the robot, shooting it with machine guns which caused damage the robot's outer hull and decreased its stability. After the TR-3Bs had riddled Boeing with bullets, the lead craft dove toward the robot and hit it with a sonic blast that shattered the damaged mech.

With the mechs destroyed, and the city now free of giant robots, the TR-3Bs slowly drifted over Cleveland, playing a recording that instructed anyone who was still alive in the city to come out of hiding and to organize themselves in a similar fashion to the way that the people of Chicago had on the previous day. The message ended by saying that the members of the benevolent group known as the Horsemen were making their way to the city from Chicago and that they would help anyone who was alive to acclimate to the new world in which they would live in. The TR-3Bs circled the city a few times, replaying the message until they saw people climbing out of subway tunnels and other shelters.

Once the pilots were satisfied that the citizens of Cleveland were following their directions, they set course for Toronto.

In the state-of-the-art TR-3Bs, the flight from Cleveland to Toronto only took a few minutes. As the squadron approached Toronto, Richards could see the utter devastation that the robots had wrought upon the city. Not a single building was left standing in Toronto. Every single structure within what had once been one of Canada's greatest cities had been reduced to rubble. Even with the city destroyed, the three robots who had attacked it were still rummaging through its remains, looking for survivors. Two of the robots in the Toronto had a humanoid shape and were constructed from car parts. The first robot was a huge black robot with red stripes on its sides. These robots were made out of parts from the experimental Ford GT, and in his mind, Richards labeled them as GT1 and GT2.

The third robot was the battle robot. It was obvious to Richards that the battle robot was constructed from some manner of farming machinery. The battle robot had a thick rectangular body with three legs on either side of it and a series of large spinning blades attached to both its front and rear flanks. Richards had designated the robot as Reaper. Richards planned to use the same attack pattern against these robots as he had used on the mechs in Cleveland. He turned toward Reaper to fly by the robot and designate it as the first target. Richards went into a dive when something suddenly caught his eye to his left. He turned his head to see a dozen battle drones flying toward him. Richards cursed. "Damn it! They must have found some drones that were clear of the EMP drop zones!"

Richards quickly swerved toward the drones to engage them while the craft directly behind Richards maintained his attack path toward the battle robot. The second that Richards had altered his flight path, Reaper and the drones initiated their coordinated attack.

Reaper fired two of his spinning blades at the oncoming TR-3B. The pilot who was diving toward Reaper at full speed did not have time to alter his course. The huge spinning blades embed themselves into the TR-3B, destroying several of its vital systems, including navigation. The pilot could do little else but scream as his TR-3B continued its dive and crashed into the ground behind Reaper.

Captain Richards cursed when he saw the TR-3B explode in a ball of flames when it hit the ground. He knew from the briefing in Chicago that the robots were in contact with each other across the world. He concluded that the machines must have relayed the information on his attack in Cleveland to the robots in Toronto. When the robots saw him engage in the same attack pattern that he had used only moments ago in a different city, they immediately employed a counterattack that it had taken them only microseconds to develop. The drones were merely a distraction. As deadly as the drones were, they were no match for the maneuverability and weaponry of the TR-3Bs, but the drones had served their purpose. They had allowed Reaper to destroy one of the TR-3Bs. Richards was well aware that this was a war of attrition, and his failure to anticipate the robots adapting to his attack plan had just cost the human race one of their most powerful weapons and one of their few remaining pilots.

Richards quickly pushed his thoughts of self-doubt aside and refocused on the task at hand. He flew his TR-3B into attack formation to lead the squadron against the drones. As the other TR-3Bs fell into position behind Richards, the drones unleashed a barrage of missiles. Richards responded by firing his sonic cannon which destroyed not only the missiles that were heading toward him but also two of the attacking drones. The other TR-3Bs followed Richards' lead and used their sonic cannons to destroy the oncoming missiles as well several of the drones who had fired them. With the use of their sonic cannons, the TR-3Bs had managed to destroy eight of the twelve original drones within seconds of engaging them.

The reaming four drones converged into a diamond formation, descended in altitude, and flew over the city. Richards saw one of his three remaining TR-3Bs go into a sharp dive to pursue the drones. The moment that he saw the TR-3B go after the drones, he screamed, "No!" but with his communication system disconnected, his warning went unheeded by the other pilot. The TR-3B chased the drones low above the city where he used his sonic cannon to destroy them. The TR-3B had no sooner destroyed the drones then it was struck and destroyed by a large chunk of debris tossed by GT2.

Captain Richards cursed; he had now lost half of the TR-3Bs that were under his command in the battle for Toronto. He flew his craft near the last TR-3B that remained under his command. Richards dipped his wings from side to side, indicating that he was ready to reinitiate an attack on the robots. The other craft responded in kind indicating that he understood Richards' communication. Richards flew in a tight circle then he headed directly for Reaper. The battle robot lifted the front of its body into the air and then fired another set of spinning blades at Richards which both he and his wingman were easily able to avoid. Richards responded by hitting the robot with one of his magnetic missiles. The missile caused the front half of Reaper to implode. Rather than finishing off Reaper, Richards pulled up, causing his craft to rapidly increase in altitude. Richard's wingman followed his lead, causing a chunk of debris thrown by GT1 to narrowly miss his TR-3B.

Richards looked down in disdain GT1. "You are not the only one who can change tactics in the middle of a battle." Richards turned to the left and dove toward GT2. As Richards suspected, GT2 was attempting to attack him while he was seemingly distracted by GT1. There was a piece of a building flying directly at Richards, but this time, he was ready for it. Richards turned on his sonic cannon which reduced the concrete projectile to dust. Richards flew through the cloud of dust and then fired his sonic cannon at GT2, hitting the robot in its torso. The blast tore a hole right through the center of the robot, destroying its CPU and ending its existence.

Richards looked to his right to see his wingman blasting out GT1's torso with his own sonic cannon. With GT1's defeat ensured, Richards turned his attention toward the still-functioning Reaper. With the front half of its body crushed, the mech's maneuverability was greatly reduced, but it was still far from helpless. Reaper was turning his back toward Richards' wingman in preparation to fire another series of blades at him. Richards quickly switched his sonic cannon's controls to continuous fire. The pilot screamed as he sent a steady barrage of sonic blasts towards Reaper, reducing the mech to little more than shards of metal.

After they had defeated the robots, Richards and the other remaining TR-3B began flying over the city and broadcasting directions for any survivors to head toward the lake where representatives from the Horsemen would meet them shortly. Given that every building in the city was destroyed, Richards didn't see any reason to ask medical professionals to report to the nearest hospital.

As Richards looked down at the acres of rubble that had once been Toronto, he doubted that there would be many survivors to hear his directions. Richards completed four sweeps over the city, and he was able to count little more than two hundred people who crawled out of ruins to start heading to the shoreline.

Several thoughts crossed Richards' mind as he looked down at the minute amount of survivors walking through the rubble. The first thought that popped into his head was if two hundred people were worth the cost of two TR-3Bs. His second thought contradicted his first as he reminded himself, that given the current state of the human race, that every life he could save made a difference. The last thought that Richards had shook him to the very core of his being. Richards was a lifelong military man. He had gone from high school to the Airforce, and after distinguishing himself there, the Horsemen recruited him. He had flown countless missions which brought small victories to whatever cause he was fighting for, and no matter how small the victory, he always felt that his efforts were worthwhile. With only two hundred some people left alive in Toronto, and the majority of the East Coast still under siege by robots, he wondered how many survivors were still out there for him to fight for.

Richards did his best to push any doubts out of his mind. He flew by the last remaining TR-3B and tipped his wings, indicating that it was time to move on to the next city. The pilot positioned his craft next to Richards' TR-3B and then they flew toward Baltimore as Richards prayed that there were still people alive there for them to rescue.

CHAPTER 20

Philadelphia

The flight to Philadelphia was a quick one in the TR-3B, giving the Kaiju Corps only a short time to discuss their strategy for attacking the robots there. Jerome did his best to come up with a strategy that would best utilize the team member's individual skills. "Leviathan will attack Carrier head on while Bearadon and Chagon wait for hit-and-run opportunities to strike. I want the two of you to try and take out a leg and ground that big mech. Once it is on the ground, its size and weight will work against it." He turned to Nick. "I know that I am asking a lot of you. Leviathan is the strongest and heaviest kaiju that we have. I have faith that you will be able to hold your own against that giant until the girls can find an opportunity to strike."

Nick nodded. "I am ready. I can keep Carrier busy for as long as we need." He reached over to Miki who was sitting next to him and grabbed her hand for support.

Michelle said, "I am going to help Nick engage Carrier directly. In my Bearadon form, I have the strength and mass to fight that thing with Leviathan's help. Chagon should wait in the rubble and look for a chance to wrap herself around a leg and crush it."

Jerome shook his head. "I don't think that's our best option. I think you should hit and run with Chagon. It's the best way to ensure that we ground Carrier as quickly as possible."

Michelle's voice became defiant. "Chagon has a slender body that is designed for quick strikes, so it makes sense for her to operate in an ambush fashion. I am a big heavy monster who is not overly quick. I am more likely to accidently step in Chagon's way while she is trying to attack then I am to be a help to her. Clarissa said that three of us need to attack this robot head on. While I agree with your idea of Chagon using stealth to attack, I need to be engaged in a frontal assault with Leviathan." She glared at Jerome. "I am still the second physically strongest kaiju on this team. A few days ago, you would have had me attacking head on with Leviathan. Don't let what happened last night change your approach to how to best utilize Bearadon in the field."

Nick and Miki both had quizzical looks on their faces. "What do you mean about last night? Was there some kind of meeting that we missed?"

Jerome was trying to think of what to say when Michelle stood. "Jerome and I had sex last night." She could immediately see the stunned looks on the faces of the newly involved couple. She shrugged. "There is no reason to hide this from you anymore. The Instructors have known from the start of this war that it was going to last longer than our lifetime. This is a war that will take generations to win. Even if we are successful at stopping the production of giant robots across the world, the humans of the future are going to need a Kaiju Corps to protect them from the thousands of robots that are currently on the planet. With the Horsemen facilities around the world destroyed, they can't genetically engineer new Kaiju Corps members like they did with us. Which means the only way that there can be a new generation of Kaiju Corps members in the future is for us to give birth to them."

Nick and Miki stared at Michelle in wide-eyed disbelief. She shrugged at them. "Look, I know that this is a lot for you guys to take in since you finally just admitted your feelings for each other. If I know you two, you have been cuddling and haven't even had sex yet. Jerome and I are not in love like you two and we don't have the luxury of dating. We could all die on our next mission, and before that happens, we needed to take steps to ensure our chances of success in this war." She turned toward Jerome. "The fact that we are having sex and trying to conceive doesn't mean that you should` treat me any differently than you did before. I am not your girlfriend, and I don't need you to put me in positions to try and protect me. Especially when doing so decreases our chances of success and increases the likelihood of another team member being seriously injured or killed."

Jerome looked at Michelle in stunned silence at the revelation that she had just given to Nick and Miki.

Miki shook her head. "You are saying that the two of you are having sex because it's part of a battle plan for us to have kids? Do the Instructors expect Nick and I to do the same thing?"

Jerome quickly responded, "It's not as cold and direct as Michelle made it sound." He quickly looked at the outside feed on the wall of the TR-3B. "We are above Philadelphia." He took a deep breath and he turned first to Michelle. "Look, maybe I was trying to treat you differently based on last night; honestly, I am not sure. I have not had the chance to process how I feel about what happened between us. You are right. Your skills would be better utilized, and it would be better for Nick if the two of you attacked head on." He quickly looked at Nick and Miki. "What Michelle said shouldn't change what is happening between the two of you. I am sorry that you found out about this right now, but as long as you two love each other, like I know that you do, then it doesn't matter what the Instructors want to become of your relationship. Whatever the future holds for you two will come, and you will deal with it as best as you can when it happens." He pointed to the colossus that was Carrier standing in the remains of the fallen city as if it were Atlas holding up the very heavens themselves. "We have a mission to complete and right now that is what we need to focus on. You three get ready to jump. Leviathan and Bearadon will attack Carrier head on. Chagon, you look for a chance to disable the robot. Do you understand?"

Michelle continued to stare at Jerome while Nick and Miki just nodded. Jerome could see that all three of them were still thinking about their relationships with each other. He could also see that Nick and Miki were looking at him as a friend and Michelle was looking at him like a whatever their relationship defined them as now. Jerome realized that for their sake, he needed to change that mindset. He hardened his voice and shouted, "Soldiers, do you understand your orders?"

Nick and Miki replied with a quick, "Yes, sir!" while Michelle nodded. Nick and Miki walked over to the hatch and opened it. They quickly kissed each other then they jumped out of the craft toward the imposing form of Carrier.

Michelle took one last look at Jerome. "I may not love you, Jerome, but it's leadership qualities like the ones you just displayed that are the reason I admire you." The young woman then unzipped her flight suit, threw it to the back of the TR-3B, and then jumped out of the craft.

Leviathan crashed to the ground in front of the gigantic Carrier. As soon as he looked at Carrier, Leviathan knew that the report of the mech being roughly a hundred feet taller than him was grossly underestimated. Carrier was twice the size of Leviathan and weighed more than four times what he did. The robot's size and bulk did nothing to deter to Leviathan from his mission. As Bearadon landed on the ground beside him, the reptilian monsters roared and charged at Carrier. Leviathan ran up to the mech and began pounding on its right hip. While Leviathan's punches were denting the huge robot's leg, his blows were unable to penetrate its outer hull. Carrier threw a sweeping backhand that struck Leviathan in the chest and sent the kaiju flying over the rubble of what had once been Philadelphia. The blow carried Leviathan for three blocks before he came crashing back down into the remains of the destroyed building.

The moment that Carrier struck Leviathan, Bearadon rushed in to attack. The kaiju spun around in front of the mech and used her spiked tail to tear a piece out of the mech's right leg. Carrier ignored the damage to its leg and brought its fist crashing into Bearadon's back. The blow forced the kaiju to her knees. With the kaiju stunned at its feet, Carrier reached down and grabbed Bearadon by her neck and the base of her tail. The mech then lifted Bearadon over its heads and slammed her into the ground with enough force to toss dust and rubble into the air over an eight-block radius.

Carrier was reaching down to pick up Bearadon and repeat the move when Chagon wrapped her long body around the mech's left leg. The serpentine kaiju was starting to constrict her body when the mech reached down and grabbed her by the throat, stifling her ability to breathe. Chagon was awed by the strength of the robot when it started to unwrap her body from around its leg. Chagon shifted her head as far to the side as she could then she bit down on the base of the robot's thumb. Chagon attacked the robot's thumb with every ounce of her waning strength. She knew that no amount of pain would cause the robot to release its grip. The serpentine kaiju's only hope was to completely tear off Carrier's thumb so that it was physically unable to maintain its grip.

Swirling colors of blue, purple, and finally black flashed in front of Chagon's eyes as she started to lose consciousness. She tried to keep her mind focused on simply continuing to bite the mech's thumb, knowing that eventually she would inflict enough damage to cause the thumb to release her. Chagon had almost completely passed out when she finally managed to sever Carrier's thumb from its hand. The serpentine kaiju slid out of the robot's grip and fell hard on the ground. She was taking quick gasping breaths as her body tried to resupply itself with oxygen. Chagon looked up to see Carrier reaching down for her. She tried to slither away, but her body had not yet recovered enough oxygen to move itself. Chagon braced herself for the robot's grip when she saw Leviathan slam into the mech with the force of a living earthquake.

Leviathan had been dazed by the blow Carrier had struck him with to the point that when he first tried to stand up, he fell back down. When he lifted his head, he saw Carrier holding Chagon in its grip and choking her. Seeing Chagon in distress angered Leviathan and once again gave him a new sense of strength. He stood and charged the mech, determined to stop the mech from hurting the love of his life. Seconds before Leviathan was able to reach Carrier, he saw Chagon free herself from the mech's grip. He then saw the mech turn and reach out to grab the dragon-like monster again. Leviathan roared at the robot then launched his body into the air. The saurian monster's body slammed into the mech's torso, sending both of them crashing to the ground.

Leviathan found himself laying on top of the gigantic mech and immediately pressed his advantage. The kaiju delivered a series of hammer fists to the mech's torso in hopes of crushing the CPU located within its chest. Leviathan was still pounding on Carrier when the mech reached up with its right hand, placed it on Leviathan's ribcage, and then pushed the monster off itself.

Carrier sat up and turned around to see Bearadon rear up on her hind legs. With carrier sitting down and Bearadon standing on her hind legs, the robot and the kaiju were roughly the same height. Bearadon wrapped her thick arms around the robot's torso and then forced it onto its back. Bearadon roared, lifted her claw into the air, and then brought it down across Carrier's chest, leaving three deep gouge marks in her wake. Bearadon was preparing to strike again when Carrier's good hand reached up and grabbed the mammalian beast by the throat. Carrier maintained its grip as it pushed the kaiju off its chest. Carrier then stood up, lifted Bearadon off the ground by her throat, and then choke slammed her into the street.

The mech was preparing to continue his attack on Bearadon when it was suddenly engulfed in flames. The mech looked to the right just as Leviathan dove at its knees and tackled it to the ground. Leviathan grabbed the robot's huge head, and with one twist, he yanked it off the mech's torso. He then threw his weight onto Carrier's right arm and pinned it to the ground. The reptilian monster turned his head briefly to see Bearadon standing up behind him. He roared and then motioned his head in the direction of Carrier's left arm. Bearadon understood her teammate's suggestion and crawled up on top of the robot's body.

Carrier was lifting its left arm to strike Leviathan when Bearadon wrapped her arms around it and then pinned it to the ground. Both Leviathan and Bearadon looked up to see Chagon crawling through the rubble toward the exposed cavity where Carrier's head had once been. As strong and as heavy as both Leviathan and Bearadon were, they were having difficulty holding the powerful Carrier to the ground. Bearadon looked at Chagon and she roared, pleading with her friend to move as quickly as possible. Chagon doubled her speed, and when she reached the downed mech, she crawled into its body.

The moment that Chagon entered Carrier's body, the mech sat up and thrust its arms forward, sending both Leviathan and Bearadon tumbling down the street. The two kaiju rolled with the force of the attack and quickly regained their feet. Leviathan looked over at Bearadon who nodded. Then the two monsters sprang onto the robot. Bearadon attacked the robot's left leg and Leviathan its right while Chagon continued to tear the robot apart from inside. Carrier backhanded Bearadon, knocking her over then it reached down and grabbed Leviathan by the throat. The mech had lifted the kaiju off his feet and then suddenly stopped moving. Leviathan pulled the mech's fingers off his throat, and as he dropped to the ground, he saw Chagon crawling back out of the hole atop the robot's body. She slithered down the side of the defeated robot just as Bearadon had finished standing up. The three kaiju looked to the waterfront and the naval base to see Garudasaurus engaged in battle with both Battleship and Cutter. Bearadon roared and then led the charge as the three kaiju raced to assist their leader.

Jerome took an extra second to look at Michelle as she jumped out of the TR-3B. He had not consciously meant to try and put her out of harm's way, but when she pointed out to him that he had done just that, he tried to own up to his decision. Jerome strove to be the type of leader who listened to those under his command and who could admit when he was wrong. The issue he was facing now was that his relationship with Michelle had literally evolved overnight from one of commander and trusted lieutenant to something that he couldn't define. He also admitted to himself that a small part of him was concerned that he may just have sent Michelle off to fight the largest battle robot ever constructed with the possibility that she was carrying his child.

Jerome had never considered having a relationship with anyone, let alone being a father and having a child with another member of his team. Granderson yelled that they were hovering over the naval yard and that he was bringing them in for a landing. Jerome made a note that in order to continue being as effective a leader as possible that he would need to better comprehend his own feelings about his relationship with Michelle and then to discuss it with her and what it meant for them. He also realized that part of that conversation would have to occur with Nick and Miki as their already new relationship was now affected by the revelation that the world was depending on them to reproduce as well. Jerome shook his head and convinced himself that for now all that he could do was to acknowledge that his inner turmoil was affecting his ability to lead and to make sure that he would address the situation as soon as he could.

Jerome saw the hatch to the TR-3B open and knew that Thomas, Brian, and the rest of the people they had recruited in

Chicago needed him to be totally focused on protecting them. Jerome reminded himself that none of the issues between himself and Michelle would matter if they failed in their mission to create the World Wide EMP and put a stop to the ever-increasing number of giant robots around the world.

Captain Granderson landed his TR-3B next to the naval base and the other three TR-3Bs landed next to them. When the hatch opened, Jerome was pleased to see that while the rest of the city was utterly destroyed that the naval base was relatively undamaged. Thomas and Brian Linke were both relatively sure that this would be the case as the Signal was using the base to create its giant robots. Based on the destruction he had witnessed in other cities, Jerome had a hard time believing that the robots would leave anything intact but he was glad to see that the majority of the base and hopefully the detonators were relatively undamaged.

Jerome jumped out of his TR-3B just as Thomas and his team were exiting Captain Okafor's craft. The young soldier yelled to his mentor, "Run for the naval base. I will stay out here! We don't want to alert the robots to the fact that we are here! I won't transform unless if I see Cutter or Battleship heading over this way! Get in and out of there as quickly as you can. The world is counting on you!"

Jerome watched as Thomas led the group of volunteers into the abandoned naval base. He then quickly looked to the center of the city to see his teammates engaged in a battle with the Gargantuan Carrier. He wished that he was able to help his friends in their struggle against the titanic robot, but he knew that his role in this mission was of vital importance. He turned his attention to the north end and west ends of the former city where Battleship and Cutter were rummaging through the remains of buildings. Both of the robots had numerous cannons and turret guns positioned on various parts of their bodies. It was obvious to Jerome that the robots were searching for any surviving humans that might still be hiding in the remains of the city. Every fiber of Jerome's being screamed for him to transform into Garudasaurus and to destroy the robots before they found another human, but he knew that he needed to hold his position. As much as it pained him that the robots might be killing or capturing people that he could save, he knew that the fate of the entire species was resting on the success of his current mission, and his current mission called for him to ensure that Thomas and his science team were able to retrieve the detonators they need.

Jerome's fears came true when he saw Battleship move a pile of rubble to find a group of roughly five survivors. Jerome could see a man, a woman, and three young children. He watched as the robot pointed its gun at the family who had resorted to falling on their knees in prayer. Jerome wanted desperately to change into Garudasaurus and fly to the praying family like a guardian angel, but he knew that even if he was already in his kaiju form that he would not reach them in time. Jerome felt the urge to look away from the horror that was about to occur but he forced himself to watch it so that he remembered who and what he was fighting for. As he watched the family blown to pieces before his eyes, the image of he and Michelle holding a young child in their arms as a robot stood above them with its guns ready to fire flashed through his mind.

Jerome gritted his teeth and made a small promise to the family that had just been slain by Battleship. "I may not have been your guardian angel, but I will be your avenging angel."

Thomas and his team were moving through the naval base as quickly as possible. While they knew that the detonators were within the facility, they were not sure exactly where they were located. Their first step was to locate the records department. The naval base and the detonators were both relics of a bygone era. The base had volumes of paper records that would tell them exactly where all of the resources and materials within the base were located. Thomas had guessed that the records room would be in the basement and he quickly lead the team there.

The Instructor was pleased when he found a door marked *Records Room and Archives*. Thomas grabbed the door handle, but he was surprised when he found that the door was locked. He checked the handle to see that the thick metal door had an electronic lock that had been magnetically sealed. He turned around to the rest of his group. "The door lock must have been engaged when the EMP was dropped on the city. It appears to be sealed shut."

One of the volunteers shouted, "There must be something on the TR-3B that we can use to blow the door open!"

Thomas shook his head. "Undoubtedly there is, but we cannot guarantee that when we blow the door that we won't also inadvertently destroy the records that we need as well."

Brian Linke walked to the front of the group and he examined the locking mechanism. After taking a close look at the lock, he turned to Thomas. "This door is under tons of concrete. The lock itself doesn't seem to have been damaged by the EMP. I think that it's just stuck in the locked position because the network it is connected to was destroyed." Brian reached into his backpack and pulled out his laptop. "I think that I can connect this laptop directly to the door and override the locking system, but if the lock is still intact, it will likely reconnect to whatever is left of the internet. There is a good chance that as soon as I plug this into the lock that the robots will know that we are here."

Thomas nodded. "Do it. We need those blueprints. Garudasaurus can protect us from the robots."

Brian took out several cords from his backpack. He attached them to his laptop then he pulled a panel off the wall that housed part of the locking mechanisms interior wiring. Brian used a knife to peel the covering off the wires in the panel and the wires he had connected to his laptop. He quickly spliced the wires together then he turned on his laptop. The expert programmer began feverishly typing on his computer, and in under three minutes, he had managed to get the door to unlock. The door slid open, and when it did, the entire building shook and the loud-pitched screech of Garudasaurus could be heard echoing through the empty base.

Thomas helped Brian up to his feet. "We have to hurry!"

Jerome was keeping a close eye on the robots, and he was surprised to see that both of them were looking directly at him. Cutter had started walking toward him while Battleship was raising its arm and aiming one of its many cannons at the naval base. Jerome cursed out loud. "Damn it, they know that we are here." He started to change into Garudasaurus when he saw Battleship fire two shells toward him. Jerome was in mid-transformation as he leapt into the air to avoid the blast. The shells exploded beneath him and tossed him even higher than his half-transformed legs had been able to carry him. Jerome had reached the apex of his ascent and was starting to fall when he completed his transformation into Garudasaurus. The kaiju screeched and then he flew toward Battleship.

Garudasaurus was flying toward the heavily armored robot as it continued to fire shells and bombs at him. The air around the flying kaiju was full of explosions and shrapnel, but Garudasaurus was managing to avoid direct hits from the mech's attack. The kaiju circled around the robot as it continued to fire at him. When the monster had completed two circles around the robot, he had managed to gauge the robot's timing. The kaiju waited for the robot to fire another shell, and the moment that it did, the monster dropped in altitude and then flew directly at Battleship.

Garudasaurus slammed into Battleship's torso and he knocked the robot to the ground. Rather than trying to outright destroy the robot, the kaiju used his claws, talons, and beak to damage or break the numerous cannons on the robot. He had just managed to tear off the last of the mech's long-range weapons when he looked back toward the naval base to see Cutter attacking what remained of the building that Thomas's team was in. Garudasaurus was suddenly knocked off Battleship when the robot struck him in the face. The kaiju tumbled off the mech, but rather than re-engaging the robot, Garudasaurus took to the sky and flew in the direction of Cutter and the naval base. Battleship stood and then it began walking in the direction of Garudasaurus and the base.

Deep within the bowels of the naval base, Thomas's team was sifting through rows and rows of file cabinets and their contents in search of the location of the detonators. What seemed like an eternity had in reality only been a few minutes when one of the volunteers screamed, "I have it! The detonators are in Building 3, 2nd floor, Room 215!"

Thomas yelled to his team, "All right, let's move!" Thomas led the group outside and he cursed when he saw the massive form of Cutter waiting for them. The robot reached down to grab them, but the group scattered, causing the robot to grab nothing but a handful of pavement. Thomas, Brian, and several others were running toward building three when Cutter turned in their direction and started chasing them. The mech had almost reached the humans when Garudasaurus landed in front of them. The kaiju screeched at the robot, and as Thomas and his team ran between the kaiju's legs, Garudasaurus reached out and grabbed Cutter.

The monster and the robot grappled for several seconds before Garudasaurus was able to overpower the mech and toss it into the parking lot. Cutter was picking itself up off the ground when Garudasaurus threw a shoulder block into the mech that caused it to tumble farther away from building three. The kaiju delivered two quick roundhouse punches to the mech when he was suddenly struck from behind and sent falling face first to the ground.

Garudasaurus rolled over to see Battleship standing above him. The mech had lifted up its foot to stomp on Garudasaurus, but the kaiju quickly reached out and grabbed the mech's foot before it could bring it down. Garudasaurus twisted and pulled the mech's foot, causing it to fall to the ground. Garudasaurus stood just in time to find himself face to face with Cutter.

Cutter punched Garudasaurus in the ribs and the were-monster responded by throwing a jab into the mech's face. The monster and the robot exchanged several blows as Battleship was making its way back to its feet. When Garudasaurus noticed that Battleship was standing, he quickly pushed Cutter away from him. The kaiju then spun around and hit Battleship with a hammer strike to its right shoulder. The kaiju followed up the hammer strike with a kick to the mech's midsection that created some space between himself and Battleship. Garudasaurus tried to take to the sky so that he was no longer trapped between the robots, but he had no sooner left his feet than Cutter grabbed his wings and slammed him back into the parking lot.

Garudasaurus was lying flat on his back as both Cutter and Battleship stood next to him and reigned down blows on his body. The kaiju did his best to protect his face and torso, but the robots' attack was relentless. Garudasaurus tried to grab Cutter's foot in order to trip the mech when he saw Bearadon rear up behind the robot and then wrap her powerful arms around it. Bearadon sank her fangs into the robot's shoulder then spun it around and tossed it to the ground. Bearadon climbed on top of the downed robot and began to tear it to pieces.

Battleship was still kicking Garudasaurus in the ribs when Leviathan stepped over his fallen friend and pushed the mech, causing it to stumble backward and fall into a sitting position. The second the mech hit the ground, Chagon wrapped her body around it. With the robot trapped in her grasp, Chagon swung her face in front of the mech. She hissed at the robot and constricted her body. The sound of metal bending and breaking could be heard throughout the naval base as Chagon crushed Battleship.

Chagon slithered off the defeated mech and crawled back over to the other members of her team. Garudasaurus stood and then he heard a shouting sound coming from Building 3. The kaiju turned around to see Thomas's team loading the detonators onto Captain Okafor's TR-3B and informing them that their mission was a success. Thomas waved briefly to the kaiju as he climbed onto the TR-3B and shut the hatch. The craft then slowly lifted into the air and flew toward the Pine Barrens to retrieve the nuclear warheads located there.

Garudasaurus started to change back into his human form, and the other members of the Kaiju Corps followed his lead. When all four members of the team had reverted back to their human forms, Miki looked at Jerome and simply said, "Cape Canaveral?"

Jerome nodded. "Cape Canaveral." With that, they ran toward Captain Granderson's TR-3B.

CHAPTER 21

California

Captain Williams made his first drop in the woods of northern California. The drop was quick and easy. Brian Linke and the first volunteer ran out of the TR-3B. Brian quickly reviewed with the man how to arm the warhead and set off the balloon, then he reviewed the contingency plans with the man should he be attacked by a giant robot. The entire process took less than three minutes. Brian quickly reentered the TR-3B and then Williams pushed his TR-3B as hard as he could in an effort to reach Australia and set the next warhead.

Baltimore

Captain Richards and his wingman flew several large circles around Baltimore prior to attempting to engage the robots in the city. After losing nearly half of his force in the battle for Toronto, Richards was determined to not be caught by surprise again. Once he was convinced that there were no drones waiting to distract them in the middle of the battle, he motioned for his wingman to follow him into the city. With Baltimore being so close to Annapolis, Richards was concerned that they would run into more robots constructed from military parts and machinery.

Richards and the last remaining TR-3B under his command flew high above the remains of yet another ruined city. Richards was trying to see what type of robots they would be engaging when they dropped down and started their attack. Richards looked down to see three robots that were clearly constructed from Cyclone-class patrol ships. Richards nodded, thinking to himself that with the naval academy using large numbers of Cyclones in training exercises that they most likely had a plant nearby that manufactured the boats. The pilot quickly designated the robots as

Cyclone 1, Cyclone 2, and Cyclone 3. The good news was that while the robots did possess high-powered machine guns, they were not nearly as heavily armored as they could have been had they been constructed from the parts of other warships. One thing that puzzled Richards from his sweep over Baltimore was the apparent lack of any of the battle robots that they encountered in every other city.

Richards circled around back toward the city in preparation to attack the Cyclone robots and the other TR-3B followed him. As they were diving toward the city, a large shape emerged from the sky above the TR-3Bs. The robot had the appearance of hundred-foot-tall metallic pterosaur. The robot had been the partially completed project of one of the students in the military research and development program. It was an advanced drone based on the pterosaur because of the ancient reptile's proficiency at high speeds for long distances and because of the student's love of dinosaurs and other ancient creatures.

When the Signal took over the computer systems at Annapolis, it found the half-completed project. When the Signal started to receive information that the TR-3Bs were destroying its robots, it modified the robotic pterosaur to serve as one of its battle robots and increase its presence in the air. The pterosaur, named Pterodrone by its creator, initially possessed stealth technology and was equipped with rockets that could help the robot attain supersonic speeds. The Pterodrone was designed predominantly as a spy and scouting drone, but the additions made the by the Signal had turned the robot into a killing machine. The Pterodrone was equipped with surface-to-air missiles and machine guns for long-range attacks and its beak, teeth, and talons were constructed from titanium and powered by hydraulic presses that were capable of crushing a tank.

The Pterodrone flew in behind the TR-3Bs as they were preparing to attack the Cyclone robots. Even if the TR-3Bs had their radar capabilities they would not have been able to detect the oncoming robotic pterosaur.

Captain Richards quickly looked to his right to see Pterodrone swooping down on his wingman. He screamed in vain as the flying robot latched its claws onto the TR-3B. Richards watched helplessly as the pilot did his best to shake the robot off its hull, but Pterodrone's titanium claws held fast to the craft. Richards watched in horror as Pterodrone bent its head down and tore off the roof of the TR-3B. The robotic terror then reached into the cabin of the TR-3B and pulled the entire cockpit out of the craft including the pilot. Pterodrone bit down into the cockpit, crushing and killing the pilot in a single move. The now pilotless TR-3B fell to the earth as Pterodrone disengaged from the craft and turned its attention toward Richards' TR-3B.

Richards swerved to his right and away from the robot. He felt that he had to engage this robot at a high altitude because he was sure that if he flew too low above the city that the Cyclone robots would open fire on him. Richards had no idea of the exact capabilities of the robotic creature, but he doubted that it was a match for a TR-3B piloted by a man with his skills.

Pterodrone was closing on Richards when the pilot quickly increased his altitude at a nearly impossible forty-five-degree angle. The Pterodrone followed Richards into the ascent and then it fired two sidewinder missiles at the TR-3B. Without radar or any of his other external computer systems, Richards had nothing other than his experience in combat to warn him that he was being fired upon. The moment that Richards started his ascent, he thought that if he was pursuing a craft that had made such a move, he would have fired on it. Figuring that the robot might make the same decision, he quickly dropped several hundred feet in altitude and banked hard to the left. He then looked overhead to see Pterodrone's missiles streaking past his craft.

Richards briefly saw the back of Pterodrone as it followed him in his dive. He was starting to wonder if the robot was able to match the maneuverability of the TR-3B. Richards leveled out his craft, and he was immediately bombarded by a machine gun fire. He heard the bullets bury themselves inside of the hull of TR-3B and quickly veered to his left, increasing his altitude in order to move out of Pterodrone's line of fire. Richards then cut hard to the right and increased his altitude even more. The robotic monster again followed Richards, firing bullets at him. Richards swerved to left then dropped his altitude as Pterodrone was still trying to follow him in his previous ascent.

Richards had finally managed to maneuver himself into a position where he could attack the robotic creature, and he didn't hesitate to open up on the mech with his own machine guns. He hit the creature several times, but his bullets didn't cause much damage to the mech. He had considered using his sonic cannon, but the weapon was much more difficult to operate than his guns were. He decided that it would be best to damage the mech with some of his other weapons in order to slow it down to a speed where he could successfully use the sonic weapon.

Pterodrone shifted its flight pattern down and to the left in an attempt to move out of the TR-3B's range, but the pilot was able to match the robot's maneuvers. As Richards watched the robot move through the air, he developed a plan to defeat it. First, Richards lifted his craft slightly above Pterodrone and then fired a volley of bullets at its left side which forced the robot to pull to its right. As soon as the robot started to pull to the right, Richards fired two of his incendiary missiles followed by one of his magnetic missiles at it. As Richards suspected, Pterodrone detected the missiles coming toward it and it shifted its body down and to the left. When the robot started to shift, the magnetic missile activated and pulled the incendiary missiles toward it, causing them to explode near the robot. Pterodrone avoided the worst of the blast, but the shockwave from the explosion caused the robot to lose control of its flight pattern.

With Pterodrone tumbling out of control in the sky before him, Richards armed his sonic cannon and fired it at the mechanical beast, cutting it in half. With Pterodrone destroyed, Richards turned back toward the city below. When the Cyclone robots came into view, it was clear that they were aware he had destroyed Pterodrone because they were all looking up at him with their guns at the ready. When he was within range of the robots, they opened fire on him. Richards easily avoided the robots' bullets and fired a magnetic missile that struck Cyclone 2 in the chest, crushing the robot's torso and CPU.

Richards flew over the other robots, and when he cleared the city, he circled around to renew his attack. Once more, the robots were waiting for him and firing at him. Richards set his sonic cannon on continuous fire then he aimed it first at Cyclone 3.

When the sonic blast hit the robot, it utterly destroyed the mech within seconds. Cyclone 1 had managed to hit the TR-3B with a few bullets, but the damage to Richards's craft was minimal. Richards aimed his cannon at the last robot, and then he destroyed Cyclone 1 as well.

With the last of the robots vanquished, Richards brought his TR-3B into a slow hover over the city. He played the message for people to report to the Inner Harbor where members from Horsemen would meet them to help them establish a settlement. The loss of the last of the TR-3Bs under his command was slightly offset when he saw what he guessed to be over one thousand people heading toward the Inner Harbor.

After he had finished playing his recording, Richards set a course for Washington DC, and he silently uttered a prayer that Granderson and the other TR-3Bs were successful in their missions and that they would meet him over DC because he doubted that he would survive another battle with the robots without additional support.

Argentina

Captain Okafur landed his TR-3B at the base of Mount Aracar in Argentina where Thomas quickly helped a civilian volunteer unload his warhead, detonator, and weather balloon from the craft. Just as he had for the man at the drop point in Brazil, Thomas quickly reviewed with the man how to arm the weapon and send up the balloon. His last command to the man was that if he saw a giant robot coming toward him before the designated release time was that he was to release the balloon and then to do his best to make his way north where the TR-3B would return to look for him. The man didn't reply verbally, but instead simply nodded. Thomas quickly shook the man's hand then he ran back to the TR-3B to continue their mad dash around the world.

CHAPTER 22

Atlanta

Captain Granderson had two TR-B3s with him as they flew over the border between Florida and Georgia. He had just dropped off the Kaiju Corps a few miles outside of Cape Canaveral. Jerome thought that it was best if the TR-3B not risk being attacked by Blackbolt, and he felt that the time it would take his team to walk to Cape Canaveral would also give them time to discuss strategy. Given the brief conversation that Granderson had heard between the team members, he thought that they might have a little more to discuss than simply how to the best attack the super robot who they expected was waiting there for them.

The other two TR-3Bs had briefly escorted Captain Okafur to the underground nuclear silos in the forests of New Jersey. After helping Thomas and his team to load the warheads onto Okafor's TR-3B, they flew south where they rendezvoused with Granderson over the Atlantic Ocean. With the speed of the TR-3Bs, Granderson only had to circle over the Atlantic for a few minutes before the other craft found him. Once the three craft were united, Granderson took point as he led the other craft toward Atlanta where they would attempt to clear what remained of the city from the giant robots who had attacked it.

As Granderson expected, Atlanta was a wasteland much like the other cities that had endured several days' worth of siege by giant robots. Not a single building was left standing, and Granderson guessed that if anyone was still alive within the city that they were likely still hiding in the subways or sewers.

Granderson and his wingman circled the city to see what they were up against. Atlanta seemed to be following the blueprint that the Signal had utilized in the other East Coast cities with two humanoid kill-and-collect robots and one less-conventional battle robot. The two humanoid robots were made from many of the tool-

and-steel manufacturing companies found in the city. Both of the robots were long and thin. Their arms and legs were constructed from steel girders that were typically utilized to create the frameworks of buildings. Their torsos were constructed of several layers of steel girders that formed a make-shift ribcage for the robots that held their CPUs and the rubber that insulated them. The robots had no heads which gave them the appearance of decapitated skeletons. Granderson estimated their height to be roughly one hundred and seventy feet tall. The robots' offensive capabilities stemmed from the rows of wielding torches that were attached to their arms. Granderson figured that the torches didn't have much range, but he was concerned that they could damage the hulls of the TR-3Bs if they flew too close the mechs. He named these two mechs Blowtorch and Acetylene respectively.

The battle mech was an all-together different entity. The mech was clearly constructed from the parts of two different machines. The bottom of the machine looked like two colossal forklifts that had been connected back to back. Each of the forklifts used in the construction of the robot was almost twenty feet across and twenty-five feet long. The top of the mech was made from the parts of at least four Apache Helicopters with the cannons and missiles that would accompany the military helicopters they were made from. Granderson identified the forklift/helicopter hybrid as Whirlybird.

Granderson was confident that the TR-3B's could fly circles around Whirlybird, but he was fully aware that the seemingly awkwardly constructed mech had more than enough firepower to destroy multiple TR-3Bs. From the areas where the robot's armaments were positioned, he also guessed that the mech would be able to fire at an opponent in a full three-hundred-sixty-degree range.

Granderson and the other TR-3B had just about completed their flight around the city when Whirlybird rose off the ground and took to the sky. Granderson turned his craft toward the ascending robot and tipped his wings from side to side, indicating to the other pilot that he wanted them to engage Whirlybird before attacking the humanoid robots on the ground. The second TR-3B fell into an attack pattern behind Granderson and they flew toward Whirlybird.

The moment that the two craft fell into an attack pattern, Whirlybird began firing on them with a blitzkrieg of shells and missiles. Granderson pulled his craft to the left out of the firing range of the robot, while the other TR-3B pulled to the right. Without craft-to-craft communications, Granderson wasn't sure who the other pilot was and he was not able to communicate changes in attack plans directly with him. When Granderson pulled left and the other pilot pulled right, Granderson was pleased to see that the other pilot seemed to know enough about air-to-air combat to coordinate movements based on what Granderson was doing.

Granderson had hoped that by circling around the robot, they would be able to clear its line of fire, but as they circled the mech, Granderson quickly realized that his fear of the mech being able to fire in a full three-hundred-sixty-degree arc around itself was confirmed. Granderson had flown halfway around the robot and it was still firing upon him as well as the other TR-3B.

Neither of the TR-3Bs was able to get close enough to Whirlybird to use either their sonic cannons or their magnetic missiles, and engaging the mech in a traditional firefight was only going to result in both of the TR-3Bs being shot down. Granderson decided that he needed to alter his plan of attack, so he increased his altitude and pulled away from Whirlybird and the other TR-3B followed his lead. Once he was well out of the range of the robot's weapons, he slowed his craft to a hover in order to let the other TR-3B catch up to him. When the other craft caught up to him, it slowed to a hover as well. Granderson bobbed his TR-3B up and down several times in an attempt to communicate a new attack plan to the other TR-3B. When the other TR-3B reversed the maneuver by having his craft dip down and then come up several times Granderson was satisfied that the other pilot understood his plan. The two pilots then turned their craft around and flew back towards Whirlybird.

As they were approaching the flying mech, Granderson increased his altitude while the other craft descended. As before, when they were in range of Whirlybird's weapons, the mech fired on them. Granderson angled his TR-3B so that it went into a nosedive, while the other TR-3B ascended. The two TR-3B's then shifted their craft towards Whirlybird with Granderson flying straight at the mech from above while the second pilot flew his craft straight at the mech from below. Granderson had thought that by flying directly at the mech from above and below that they would not only be out of its range of fire, but that they would also have it trapped in a crossfire.

Granderson's new plan was quickly put to an end when Whirlybird repositioned its cannons and began firing directly above and below itself at the two TR-3Bs. A shell struck Granderson's craft, and while it caused some damage, he was still able to keep the craft in the air, but as he and the other pilot continued to struggle to get close enough to Whirlybird to use their modified weapons, he wondered if he should keep the craft in the air.

Granderson quickly decided on a desperate course of action that he prayed the other pilot would pick up on and assist him in pulling off. Granderson sent his TR-3B careening toward the ground and he only pulled up on it slightly. Just prior to hitting the ground, Granderson pulled up on his controls so that his TR-3B skid along the ground instead of smashing into it. Sparks flew as Granderson's TR-3B skidded across the debris and human bodies that lined the streets of Atlanta. When Granderson saw a piece of rubble large enough to severely damage his TR-3B, he turned on his propulsion system so that he slowed his descent somewhat while still bumping into the rubble. Granderson's entire craft shook, throwing him from side to side and creating a large dent in the rear of his craft as he slammed into the rubble. He breathed a sigh of relief when he realized that he had managed to prevent his TR-3B from being damaged to the point of no longer being functional while still making it look as if he had died while trying to save himself.

Granderson turned on the outside cameras to his craft so that when he looked in any direction it was as if he was looking through a glass ceiling. Granderson first looked at Blowtorch and Acetylene. He smiled when he saw that both robots were continuing to sift through rubble rather than trying to attack him.

He smiled. "Good then, I guess that they think I am dead." He then looked to see Whirlybird still flying above him. Granderson aimed his sonic cannon at the mech and he set it for continuous fire. Then he looked at the other TR-3B and said, "Come on, bring it down a little, bring it down a little."

The other TR-3B was circling Whirlybird and firing his machine gun at the mech while the robot continued to attack him with shells and missiles. Each time the TR-3B completed a circle around the mech, it slightly decreased its altitude. Granderson smiled. "That's a good boy, just a little bit lower. Hang in there for a few more seconds."

Whirlybird had just about descended to the point where Granderson could hit it with his sonic cannon when the mech struck the other TR-3B with a missile. Granderson screamed when the saw his fellow pilot perish in a ball of flames. He stared at Whirlybird as the mech continued its descent toward the ground, and when it came with range of his weapon, Granderson unleashed the fury of his sonic cannon on the mech while screaming, "It's called playing possum!"

The sonic cannon cut Whirlybird in half, causing the two pieces of the robot to fall from the sky like shooting stars. As Whirlybird crashed to the ground, both Blowtorch and Acetylene looked in his direction. Acetylene was standing almost directly in front of Granderson, and before the mech could move, the pilot repositioned his cannon toward the mech and fired it cutting the robot's leg off. The top half of Acetylene fell to the ground with a loud clang. The mech was using its arms to push itself up when Granderson fired another blast of his sonic cannon that shot clear through the mech's chest, destroying its CPU.

It felt as if an earthquake was emerging from beneath Atlanta as Blowtorch was running toward the TR-3B. Granderson quickly looked behind him to see the giant robot coming for him, and he immediately performed a vertical take-off. He had managed to lift his TR-3B a little over on hundred feet off the ground when Blowtorch punched it, causing the craft to spin as it pulled away from the mech. Grandson's TR-3B spun completely around several times before he was able to regain control of it. He turned his craft toward Blowtorch to see the mech running directly at him. The pilot quickly fired a magnetic missile into the robot's chest that caused it to implode upon itself mere seconds before the mech would have destroyed his craft and killed him.

Granderson shook his head. "Damn, it's just me and a damaged TR-3B heading to Washington." He then set his craft to slowly float over Atlanta while he played a prerecorded message for any survivors to head for Turner Field where they would soon receive instructions from members of the group known as the Horsemen. The pilot only saw a few dozen people crawl out of sewer grates, and he quickly prayed that there were more survivors who would follow them before he turned his craft north toward Washington and his probable death.

CHAPTER 23

Africa

Okafur had pushed his craft to its limits and beyond, and in doing so, he crossed the Atlantic Ocean in just over two hours. Once they had reached South Africa, the volunteer and the warhead were quickly set into place. As soon as everything was prepared, Okafur had his TR-3B back in the air and rocketing toward Algeria. He and the team he was transporting were ahead of schedule for setting up the World Wide EMP. Okafur just hoped that Williams, Richards, Granderson, and the Kaiju Corps were having as much success as he was.

Two miles outside of Cape Canaveral

The members of the kaiju had been walking in silence for a good hour since they had been dropped off by Captain Granderson. Nick and Miki were holding hands but looking at the ground instead of at each other. Michelle kept her head up straight, but she was walking well ahead of the rest of the group. Jerome could see that the revelation that the Instructors expected them to reproduce was weighing heavily on them. Jerome felt that they would need to address this issues before going into battle with Blackbolt, because if they faced the super robot with their minds not fully focused on it, he feared they would perish.

He took a deep breath and said loud enough for all three of his friends to hear him, "Okay, we are going to discuss all of the unsaid things between us right now so that we have clear minds when we confront Blackbolt." First, he looked toward Nick and Michelle. "I can see that something is still bothering you two. Like I told you before, I don't think that it matters what the Instructors want to be the result of your relationship. All that matters, is that you two love each other. So, what's still bothering you?"

To Jerome's surprise, it was the usually reserved Miki who spoke up first. "We agree with what you said about it not mattering what the Instructors want from us." She looked at Michelle. "What matters is that Michelle knew this information for a while and she never disclosed it to us. To me!"

Michelle gave Miki an unsympathetic look. "What did you want me say to you and when did you want me to say it? When you and Nick were pining over each other but neither of you wanted to make the first move? Was that when I was supposed to tell you that if an apocalyptic war broke out that would take generations to win that you and Nick would have been expected to give birth to the next generation of monster soldiers? Or would you have preferred the real truth? That the Instructors didn't really care who mated with who? That their plan would have called for either one of us to mate with Nick and the other with Jerome?"

Miki began to tear up as she yelled, "You still should have told me, Michelle! You are my friend; more than that, you are my sister. You are the only person in the world who I felt I could trust unconditionally! Now that trust has been shaken."

Nick nodded in agreement. "Jerome, I feel the same way. How could you have kept something like this from me?"

Michelle's voice softened. "I am sorry, Miki. I have never been the best at gauging how to deal with other people. I have often looked to you for a model about how to handle social situations. My mind is always focused on how to be a better soldier, on how I can best complete a mission. When I was considering some of the scenarios that we were created for, I came to the realization that we may one day face a threat that would go beyond the scope of our lifespan. It was then that I realized we may have to mate in order to create the next generation of the Kaiju Corps." She looked toward Nick. "Jerome only learned about this yesterday. In his defense, he truly did not have time to discuss the issue with you."

Nick nodded and Miki walked over to Michelle. "You still could have told me when you figured this out, Michelle. If for no other reason than you would not have to carry the burden yourself." She placed her hand on Michelle's shoulder. "I want to be there for you just as much as I want you to be there for me. I can see how it would have been a difficult discussion for us to have, but it could have been a difficult discussion that we had with each other. We could have worked out our feelings about this together instead of you just moving forward with the knowledge that the people who created us, that our parents for all intents and purposes, had scenarios of what at best can be looked at as a prearranged marriages." Miki hugged her friend. "More than anything, Michelle, we could have discussed the anguish about giving birth to children specifically to be used as soldiers! If there is anyone who understands that pain, it's us! You said that I am your sounding board for how to deal with other people emotionally. If that is true, why didn't you talk to me about this before trying to mate with Jerome? Did you even consider what it must be like for him to send you into battle knowing that you might be pregnant with his child?"

Miki's words hit Michelle harder than any giant mech she had faced. She walked over to Jerome. "You didn't want to put me on the backlines because you felt differently about me after we had sex. You were concerned that putting me on the frontlines could have put our potential child in danger."

Jerome nodded. "I didn't even realize it at first, but when I tried to look at my decision introspectively, I came to the same conclusion." He looked at Michelle. "I don't know that I can serve as your commander and use you effectively in the field if you are carrying my child." He looked at Nick and Miki. "If they were in the same position, I don't know that Nick could effectively work with Miki in combat situation either? Could you?"

Nick was wide eyed with an overwhelmed look on his face. "I don't know. Miki and I just admitted our feelings to each other on the same day that we entered a war. These are deep questions. Will we have kids? Will we raise them to be soldiers? Will we be able to fight with the girls if we know they are pregnant with our kids?" Nick threw his hands in the air. "I don't know the answer to any of these questions! Right now, I want to focus on winning a war. We will have to face these questions later just as a result of the world that we now live in, but we don't need it to bog us down now. As long as I know that Jerome wasn't purposely hiding something from me then I can move forward with this mission and we can cross those other bridges when we come to them."

Jerome nodded. "I would never hide anything from you. Personally, you are my friend, and when we are in the field, you are my responsibility. I am obligated to give you whatever information that I can to help you succeed."

Michelle walked over to Jerome. "Jerome, I am sorry. I should have thought things out more before I approached you." She shook her head as she started to tear up. "I only ever look at things concerning how to complete a mission. When I realized that this war was going to go on for a long time, I just started taking the next steps needed to win it. I never considered how the possibility of being a father would affect you."

Jerome walked over and hugged her. "It's okay. I..." Jerome's sentence was cut short by the sound of a rocket's ignition starting. All four of them looked toward Cape Canaveral to see a huge rocket lifting off the ground.

Miki shouted, "That must be the first shipment of people being sent back to the Signal's home planet! We are too late!"

Jerome threw his clothes off. "No we are not!" He quickly changed into the awesome form of Garudasaurus and took to the sky. The rocket was carrying several tons of fuel that it would need to burn to reach escape velocity. The weight of the fuel made the initial part of the rocket's ascent relatively slow when compared to the speeds that it would reach in the stratosphere. Garudasaurus knew that if he hurried, he could catch the rocket before it left the atmosphere. The avian kaiju flapped his wings as hard as he could, and he slowly gained on the rocket.

As Garudasaurus was streaking toward the rocket, his keen raptor-like vison saw a pitch-black shape with triangular appendages flying toward him. Garudasaurus knew that the shape had to be Blackbolt, but the kaiju was determined that nothing was going to prevent him from stopping the rocket from leaving the planet. Garudasaurus had almost reached the rocket when the powerful slipstream generated by its thrusters pushed him away from it. The kaiju screeched as he looked up to see the rocket pulling away from him. Garudasaurus flapped his wings as hard and as fast as he could, and in a matter of few seconds, he caught up to rocket and positioned his body to compensate for the slipstream.

The kaiju dug his clawed talons into the side of the rocket and began tearing into it with his claws and beak. Garudasaurus had managed to punch a hole into the hull of the rocket when Blackbolt slammed into his side. The robot tried to pull Garudasaurus off the rocket, but the kaiju refused to release his grip. In his mind, he thought, *I'll show these robots what it truly means to be committed to succeeding in a mission!*

Blackbolt delivered blow after blow to the kaiju, but Garudasaurus ignored the pain and continued to cause damage to the ever-ascending rocket. Garudasaurus threw his elbow back, striking Blackbolt in the face, but the kaiju was unable to generate enough force to pry the robot off him. Garudasaurus could feel the air growing thin as the altitude continued to increase. The kaiju tore another section of the exterior off the rocket then he reached into it and grabbed as many wires and control panels as he could. The kaiju was in the process of pulling the wires out of the rocket when he felt Blackbolt place its sonic cannon against his ribcage. Garudasaurus pulled out the handful of wires at the same moment that Blackbolt set its sonic cannon to continuous pulse and fired through the kaiju's ribs and lungs.

Garudasaurus screeched in pain as he grabbed the robot's hand with the active sonic cannon on it and pointed it at the rocket. The sonic blast cut through the rocket and caused it to explode in midair. Both Garudasaurus and Blackbolt were sent tumbling away from the blast. Garudasaurus took small pleasure knowing that he had prevented the rocket from leaving the planet, but he also knew that he was mortally wounded. It was difficult to breathe and he could feel his lungs filling up with blood. Garudasaurus knew that he was going to die, but he was determined to inflict as much damage on Blackbolt as he could before that happened.

Garudasaurus's entire torso was in excoriating pain as he flapped his wings and flew toward the free-falling Blackbolt. The robot turned toward Garudasaurus, ignited its propulsion system to halt its freefall, and quickly delivered two strikes to the kaiju's face. Garudasaurus shook off the blow and hit the robot twice in its chest, hoping to damage its CPU. With each blow that

Garudasaurus delivered to the robot, the pain in his lungs increased and his vision grew dimmer. The leader of the Kaiju Corps took two more strikes to the face, and he was only able to respond by landing three weak punches to the robot's midsection.

Blackbolt delivered a crushing blow that splintered Garudasaurus's already-broken ribs. Garudasaurus's vision went dark, and he used the last of his strength to punch the robot in the chest with enough force to crack its outer hull. With the last of his energy spent, Garudasaurus, the leader of the Kaiju Corps, died.

Nick, Miki, and Michelle were still in their human forms, and they watched helplessly as the lifeless body of the man/monster who was their brother, leader, and lover respectively crashed into the ground. The impact created a deep crater and sent a plume of dust flying up into the air. The dark form of Blackbolt briefly flew over Garudasaurus's body then it returned to the launch site.

The other three members of the Kaiju Corps continued to stare at the body of Garudasaurus for several long seconds before Nick finally whispered, "Jerome. No."

CHAPTER 24

Australia

Captain Williams landed his TR-3B in the middle of the Great Victoria Desert. He had succeeded in his latest goal of flying across the Pacific Ocean in record time. Once more, the team was quick to run off the craft, set up the warhead, and then review the instructions with the volunteer about when to deploy the warhead. The team was then quickly back on the craft and Williams set a flight plan for China.

Finland

Captain Okafor's TR-3B landed next to a lake in northern Finland. By now, the team had the running out and deployment of the warheads, detonators, and balloons down to a science. The team members quickly set up the latest volunteer and then they were back in the TR-3B, heading toward Russia.

Washington DC

Captain Richards was circling the city, and he sighed in disappointment when he noticed that there were four giant robots roaming through the city as opposed to the three he had encountered during his previous battles. The robots were clearly constructed from car parts found at the GM plant in DC. Richards was easily able to name of the robots from the car parts that they were constructed from. The first of the humanoid capture and kill robots that he saw he gave the name of Yukon. The second robot was rooting through the remains of the capital building, and he gave that robot the code name Acadia. The third robot was standing on top of a mountain of destroyed treasures in the location where the Smithsonian was located, and Richards gave it the name Sierra.

The fourth robot was a battle robot that was constructed from the parts of the SUV known as the Terrain, and it was standing directly over what had once been the White House. Due to the robot's arachnid appearance, he referred to the mech as Terrainantula. Richards decided that he would best be suited to destroy Terrainantula before engaging the other robots.

The veteran pilot was sure that when he attacked Terrainantula that the other mechs would try to attack his blindside, but he had no other option. Richards circled around the city then aimed his TR-3B directly at Terrainantula. As he rocketed his TR-3B toward the battle robot, he pictured himself as a fly charging at a giant spider. Richards locked one of his two remaining magnetic missiles on Terrainantula and then pulled the trigger. He watched in disbelief as Terrainantula lifted one of its long front legs and used it to block the missile from striking its body. The magnetic field given off by the missile crushed Terrainantula's foremost right leg, but the damage that it caused to the giant mechanical spider was negligible. The mech stepped forward, showing that it still possessed all of its speed and maneuverability.

Richards looked to his left to see an eighteen-wheel truck flying towards him that been hurled by Acadia. Richards pulled up hard on his controls in an attempt to dodge the projectile, but he knew that he would be unable to avoid the flying vehicle. To his surprise, the truck was torn to pieces in mid-air. In the spot where the flying truck had previously been, a TR-3B flew through the air.

Richards cheered loudly when he saw the face of his friend and protégé Todd Granderson piloting the second TR-3B. Richards flew over the head of Terrainantula as the robot reached out with its foremost left leg at his craft. Richards was flying past the mechanical spider when it spun around and sprayed a mist of liquid nitrogen at his TR-3B out of its mouth. The outer hull of Richards' craft became coated in frost, but he managed to fly out of the mist before the freezing chemical caused any significant damage to his TR-3B. He took a quick glance over at Granderson to see him flying in a tight circle around Acadia and Yukon, who had positioned themselves next to each other, indicating that he would handle the humanoid robots, leaving Terrainantula for Richards. Richards tipped his wings in response to his friend, indicating that he understood Granderson's intentions.

Once Granderson was sure that Richards understood what he wanted to do, he dove and flew toward Yukon. The robot picked up a large handful of debris and threw it at the right side of his TR-3B. Granderson swerved to his left then immediately dropped in altitude, allowing the chunk of concrete that he knew Acadia was going to hurl at him soar over his craft. He laughed. "We are getting used to you guys and your tricks."

Once Granderson had dodged the second projectile, he fired his last magnetic missile at Yukon. To his surprise, the robot picked up a delivery truck and threw it directly at the missile. The missile activated when it hit the truck, compressing it into a sphere the size of a basketball. Granderson looked down at Yukon. "I guess that you are learning our tricks as well."

Granderson circled back around and found himself faced with an onslaught of small baseball-sized pieces of concrete being hurled at him by both Acadia and Yukon. With all of the concrete in the air, it was impossible for him to successfully target the robots with his sonic cannon. The pilot's frustration was further exasperated by the fact that the small pieces of concrete were starting to damage his TR-3B. Granderson set his sonic cannon to continuous fire then he used to it clear the debris that was flying toward him. While the sonic cannon was managing to clear him a path toward Yukon and Acadia, and the beam was still being fired in their general direction, the process of the sonic blast moving between solid and gaseous matter was greatly weakening its effectiveness by the time it reached the robots. Granderson tried to increase his altitude and switch the direction and angle of his attack, but the moment that he flew back toward the robots, they repeated the process of throwing a debris field in his way.

Granderson pulled up again from his attack. He looked over at Richards to see him flying high above Terrainantula and firing his machine guns at the mech which it was easily avoiding. Sierra was looming near Terrainantula and most likely waiting for Richards to fly low enough for it to attack him. It was obvious that the robots had figured out how to effectively create a stalemate between themselves and the TR-3Bs. The robots had observed the TR-3B's previous battles, and they had devised a plan that would require the pilots to put themselves into a vulnerable situation in order to attack them. The robots had surrounded themselves with debris that they could use to intercept any missile and would reduce the effectiveness of the sonic cannon unless the TR-3B was at near point-blank range.

Granderson quickly looked over at Sierra and shouted, "Fine, then that's how we will do it!" He armed one of his incendiary missiles and fired it at Sierra. He knew that the robot would throw something at the missile that would stop the projectile before it reached the mech, but Granderson hoped that his missile would give Richards an opportunity to attack Terrainantula.

After firing his missile at Sierra, Granderson once more set his sonic cannon to continuous fire then he dove straight at Yukon and Acadia. The moment that he started his dive, the robots began tossing a maelstrom of small debris at him. Granderson screamed as he used his sonic cannon to plow through the flying debris field and make his way toward the robots. He had to fly to point-blank range before his sonic cannon was able to punch its way through the makeshift shield and hit the robots. Granderson's TR-3B was floating directly in front of Yukon as his sonic cannon tore into the robot's chest. Yukon's torso was falling to pieces, but before the robot was rendered inert, it reached out with its right hand and crushed Granderson's sonic cannon. Yukon's deactivated husk was still standing when Acadia smashed through it and grabbed Granderson's TR-3B.

Every time that Richards decreased in altitude to attack Terrainantula, he saw Sierra reach down and pick up something to throw at him. He also glanced over to see the other two robots throwing enough pieces of steel and concrete into the air to prevent Granderson from attacking them, let alone attacking Sierra. Richards was too far away to use his sonic cannon on Terrainantula, and he was reduced to using his machine guns to try and damage the robotic spider from a distance, but the agile mech was easily avoiding his bullets.

Richards was sending another barrage of bullets toward Terrainantula when he saw Granderson fire a missile at Sierra.

Richards knew that Granderson was opening a window for him to attack and the veteran pilot jumped on it. Richards waited for Sierra to counter the missile then he set his sonic cannon to continuous fire, and dove at the oversized mechanical spider.

Richards' sonic cannon dug into the ground in front of Terrainantula, causing the mech to turn away from it and scurry away. The mech was movingly quickly and in a sporadic pattern which made it difficult for Richards to score a direct hit on it. Richards gritted his teeth, decreased his altitude, and then flew directly over the battle robot. The second that Richards was hovering only a few feet above Terrainantula and hitting it with his sonic cannon, the mech spun around and sprayed Richards' TR-3B with a cloud of liquid nitrogen. Richards' sonic cannon destroyed Terrainantula, but the exterior of his TR-3B was frozen solid. Richards' frozen craft fell out of the air and crashed on top of the remains of the battle robot. Richards still had power in his TR-3B, but he was totally grounded and immobile. With the exterior of his TR-3B covered in a thick sheet of ice, all that his exterior cameras were able to show him was a wall of white.

The pilot tried to open the hatch to the TR-3B, but the frozen door simply groaned in response to his attempt to open it. Richards felt an impact tremor shake the ground beneath his feet. He immediately knew that the two-hundred-foot-tall Sierra was moving toward him and would reach him with only a few quick steps. Richards tried to manually position his remaining incendiary missiles in the direction that he had last seen the mech, but his efforts were met with the same groaning sound that he heard when he tried to open the hatch. Richards wrapped his hand around his weapons controls as he felt another footfall shake his frozen craft. Richards then started counting. He got to ten before he felt the next footfall. The pilot quickly calculated the distance between where he had last seen Sierra and the robot's stride length. He sighed when he completed the math and realized that his only hope of surviving was that Granderson was able to destroy Sierra within the next thirty seconds.

Granderson heard Acadia's fingers crushing the back half of his TR-3B, causing the pilot to instinctively grab the trigger to his machine guns and squeeze them. Granderson's guns were positioned at point-blank range on Acadia's chest, and even as his craft was being crushed around him, the pilot continued to fire into the robot's chest, hoping to penetrate its armor and the tires beneath it to reach its CPU. The back half of Granderson's TR-3B snapped off and fell to the ground, leaving the pilot with nothing but open air behind him. He closed his eyes and continued to squeeze his trigger as he expected the robot's huge hands to slide forward and crush him at any second. After a few seconds had passed, Granderson opened his eyes to find not only that he was still alive but that he was pulling a trigger for a machine gun that had spent all of its rounds. The pilot looked forward, but all that he saw was a wall of black. He smiled. "The cameras must have gone out when the back of the ship broke off, but I am guessing that the machine gun finally hit something vital within the robot."

Granderson climbed out the back of his shattered TR-3B and he peeked around it to see Acadia with a massive smoking hole in its chest still holding the remains of his craft in its hands. Granderson looked down to see over one hundred and fifty feet between himself and the ground. The pilot was sure that either the robot or the remains of the TR-3B would collapse at any second, so he quickly jumped out of the craft and pulled his parachute. As he was drifting to the ground, Granderson looked over at Sierra to see the robot moving toward the frozen white form of Richards' TR-3B laying helplessly on the ground.

Richards' entire TR-3B shook, and frozen pieces of it rained down on his head. The pilot knew that the next footfall would be the one that crushed him. Richards counted to eight, then, knowing that his missiles would explode exactly where they were, he fired every last one that he had.

Granderson touched down then he felt a blast of heat and saw a massive explosion beneath Sierra's foot. The explosion destroyed the entire left side of the robot's body, and as he fell to the ground, Granderson saluted his fallen mentor who he knew had given his life to defeat the robot. Granderson said a small prayer for Richards and all of the brave TR-3B pilots who had died fighting the robots. Then, with nothing but his own voice to convey the message, Granderson began walking around the remains of Washington DC and calling for any survivors to come out from hiding to join him.

CHAPTER 25

Nick followed up his whisper with a shout, "Jerome!" The lifeless body of Garudasaurus did not move inside of the huge crater that it was positioned in.

Tears were streaming down Miki's face. "He is not going to change back into his human form, is he? We are going to have to bury him like that, aren't we?"

Michelle stared at the space center were Blackbolt stood guard while a flurry of activity was taking place behind it. She growled, "Right now, I am more concerned about making sure that there is nothing left of that robot to bury when I am done with it."

Nick and Jerome had been more than best friends growing up. They had been brothers both in blood and in arms. Nick had listened to Jerome on many a night talk about the team's strengths and weaknesses. He could still hear Jerome talking to him about his anger and how while it powered Leviathan, that it also cost him from seeing how to best attack an opponent. How Miki's feelings towards others helped to drive her and support others but how it could inhibit her from unleashing her inner beast when she needed to. How Michelle's brashness and willingness to work on her own was a credit to her bravery but how it also took away from her ability to maximize her skills within the context of a team.

Jerome had once said to Nick, "Pay attention, Nick. There may come a day when there is a mission that I am not around for, and I will need to know that I can count on you to act as team leader in my place."

Nick wiped the tears away from his eyes and he said to himself, "I won't let you down, Jerome." He then looked at Michelle and Miki. "We need to pull ourselves together. There will be time to mourn Jerome later. He would want us to put our feelings aside and focus on completing the mission."

Miki wiped her eyes and she stopped crying as she stood. "You are right; he would want us to act like the soldiers that we are. Completing this mission, his mission, is the best thing that we can do to honor him.''

Michelle nodded. "Enough talk! Let's wreck that robot and everything else on that base!"

Nick reached out and grabbed her. "Wait! Jerome wouldn't want us to just rush in there. You saw how easily Blackbolt killed Garudasaurus. We need a plan to attack that thing or it will cut us to pieces." Nick thought back about the encounter between Garudasaurus and Blackbolt. As he was reviewing the battle in his mind, his eyes went wide. "The robot's main advantages over us are its ability to fly, its speed, and its sonic cannon. If we can ground Blackbolt and destroy its sonic cannon, we can fight it on equal terms. Then we can destroy the launch site and significantly impede the Signal's ability to send resources back to its home planet."

Miki shook her head. "How do we get close enough to attack Blackbolt without having it take to the air and slicing us apart with the sonic cannon?"

Michelle shrugged. "I think that the sonic cannon was only able to kill Jerome because it hit at him point-blank range. Like any soundwave, it will lose potency as it travels through the air. I think that a blast from a farther distance will hurt us, but I don't believe that a single blast from a distance will be lethal."

Nick was still staring at the launch site as the women were talking. Miki walked over next to him. "It's not a city, it's a space center. Blackbolt is the only robot there. There are no collect-and-kill robots walking around killing people."

He turned back toward Miki and Michelle. "Have we ever seen the battle robots moving through the cities searching for survivors?"

Michelle shook her head. "No. They seem to just wait for a threat to show up and then they spring into action."

Nick pointed to the robot. "I think that in our human forms, we can just walk up to Blackbolt. It is programmed to protect this site, so as soon as we change into our kaiju forms, it will attack us, but it isn't programmed to do anything with humans. We will walk up to it just as we are now. When we reach Blackbolt, I will position myself next to its arm with the sonic cannon. Michelle, you stand next to its other arm. Miki, you position yourself behind it. When we are in position, we will change into our kaiju forms. Bearadon and I will restrain Blackbolt, and I will knock the sonic cannon off its hand." He placed his hand on Miki's shoulder. "The mech's primary propulsion system is on its back with its secondary navigation systems on its triceps and quadriceps. As soon as we have the robot restrained, you will change into Chagon, slither up Blackbolt's body, and destroy the main propulsion system on his back. With that gone, it won't be able to fly. Once you destroy that, start working on the back-up systems in its arms and legs that propel it forward and backward and help it to steer."

Michelle looked directly into Nick's eyes. "We are taking a big risk by not approaching that thing in our kaiju forms. With the speed it can move at, if it decides to attack us in our human forms, it could kill us before we even have a chance to change."

Nick shrugged. "If we change into kaiju this far away from Blackbolt, it will take to the sky and cut us down before we can lay a hand on it. I think that approaching it as humans is our only chance."

Michelle nodded. "All right then. We approach it as humans." She then turned and started walking toward Blackbolt with Nick and Miki trailing her.

When they had covered about half the distance between Garudasaurus's body and Blackbolt, Miki slipped her hand into Nick's and she kissed him on the cheek. "He would have been proud of you. The way that you stayed calm, assessed the situation, and determined how we can best operate as a team. Those are exactly the things that Jerome would have done."

Nick looked at Miki and smiled. "I know he would be proud of me. Now let's make him proud of all of us by destroying Blackbolt."

Nick's heart was pounding in his chest as they walked toward the monolithic robot. He had already lost Jerome, and if he was wrong about Blackbolt not be programmed to attack humans, he would watch Michelle and Miki die, and then he would perish himself. With each step that he took, he became less afraid of that occurring as the robot simply continued to stand still and stare at the horizon.

When they reached the robot itself, Nick breathed a small sigh of relief. The robot had not killed them on their approach, which meant that they would have at least have an opportunity to battle the mech. He walked underneath Blackbolt's sonic cannon and stared up in disdain at the weapon which had killed his brother. He then looked at Michelle and nodded. When she nodded in reply they both changed into their kaiju forms.

Leviathan wrapped his arms around Blackbolt's right arm and Bearadon did the same to its left. Before Blackbolt had a chance to react, Leviathan swatted the sonic cannon off the robot's arm. Blackbolt ignited the boosters on its back, and Leviathan and Bearadon could feel themselves being pulled off the ground with the robot. Leviathan looked down at Chagon and roared, urging her to hurry up and destroy the rockets on Blackbolt's back.

Chagon slithered up Blackbolt's body then carefully wrapped herself around the robot's propulsion system, positioning her body away from its exhaust port. She was starting to constrict around the boosters when Blackbolt activated the propulsion ports on its arm. The extra force provided by the boosters allowed the robot to break free of Leviathan's and Bearadon's grip. The robot then took off into the sky with Chagon still wrapped around its primary booster.

Blackbolt flew to an altitude of over two thousand feet then it turned on its boosters and shattered the sound barrier. Chagon could feel the skin being flayed off her body by the tremendous winds that were whipping around her. The heat given off by Blackbolt's thrusters was enough to burn and blister Chagon's body. Despite the pain that she was experiencing, the serpentine kaiju continued to apply pressure to the robot's propulsion system. The robot cleared the twenty-five-thousand-foot mark and it was approaching Mach 2 when Chagon felt the thrusters crack. A second later, Chagon felt the jet pack attached to Blackbolt's back crumble beneath the pressure she was applying it.

The robot immediately angled its arms so that its directional thrusters were slowing down its descent. As they were in freefall, Chagon wrapped her body as tightly as she could around the robot's midsection without applying enough pressure to crush it. As much as it would have pleased her to end Blackbolt's existence, she needed the robot to cushion her descent as well because even in her kaiju form, she would not have been able to survive a fall from their current height.

The robot's directional thrusters were keeping it from falling straight to the ground, but even with them operating at maximum capacity, they were still falling at a speed of several thousand feet per second. When the entwined monster and robot finally hit the ground, they did so with such force that it threw a cloud of dust into the air and shook Chagon loose from Blackbolt's body. The robot quickly stepped away from Chagon then it reignited its directional boosters. While the boosters were not powerful enough to let the robot fly, they did allow it to skim across the ground at blazing speeds.

Leviathan and Bearadon were still staring at the unsettled cloud of dust when a black blur shot out of it and struck Leviathan in the face with enough force to knock the huge monster to the ground. Bearadon was able to roar in the direction of the blur, but before she was able to do anything else, Blackbolt rocketed over to her, drove its shoulder into her ribs, and knocked her to the ground as well. Chagon had just rolled back over onto her stomach when Blackbolt darted over to her, picked her up over its head, and then tossed her a half a mile away from where it was standing.

Leviathan managed to return to a sitting position when he saw a black mass moving toward him. He then felt a metal fist connect with his jaw at a velocity near the speed of sound. The blow sent Leviathan falling onto his back once more.

The instant that Chagon hit the ground from where she was thrown to, she began burrowing first into the earth and then along it. When she burrowed the complete length of her body, she started moving back toward the surface. As she made her way back above ground, she wrapped her body around every large rock and root that she could find. When her head and the top of her neck popped back above ground, she saw the quick-moving Blackbolt glide across the ground and then deliver a crushing blow to Bearadon's skull that knocked her back to the ground.

Chagon shook her head and hissed at Blackbolt, drawing its attention to her. The swift-moving robot turned toward her, and when it did so, Chagon tightened her grip around the rocks and roots that her body was wrapped around. A second later, Chagon felt Blackbolt grab her by the throat and pull her forward with the momentum of its directional boosters. Chagon wriggled her neck around the robot's wrist to secure a grip on it. She then felt her body being stretched to its limits, and for a brief second, she thought that she was going to be torn in half. She then felt her body snap back like a giant rubber band as Blackbolt was slammed into the ground face first. Chagon had torn several muscles inside of her body, but she had at least managed to temporarily ground Blackbolt and hold it in place.

Blackbolt looked over at Chagon then it stood. The mech began pulling on Chagon's neck and head in an attempt to free itself from her grip by either yanking her out of the ground or by tearing off her head. Once again, Chagon felt her body being stretched beyond its limits, and she hissed in agony, but she refused to release her grip on the robot.

Leviathan stood to see Chagon risking her life to keep Blackbolt in one spot and he ran over to help her. The saurian kaiju slammed into Blackbolt's back and tackled the mech to the ground face first, allowing Chagon to release her grip and slither back below ground. With the robot pinned beneath him, Leviathan unleashed a wave of flames onto the back of the robot's arms. While his flames were not powerful enough to damage the mech's TR-3B outer hull, they were more than hot enough to melt and sear shut the robot's thruster exhaust ports. Using some of the freestyle wrestling moves that the Horsemen had taught him, Leviathan spun around and directed his flames at the thrusters on the robot's legs, sealing them shut as well. Leviathan was about to start pounding on the mech when Blackbolt's fist struck him in the back of the head and knocked the kaiju off its body.

Leviathan rolled away from the robot then they both stood. Leviathan was facing Blackbolt while Bearadon had regained her feet and was now standing behind the robot. The ground to the left of the mech started to rumble, and then it exploded into the air as Chagon returned to the surface. When Chagon emerged from below ground, Leviathan shifted slightly to his left and Bearadon slightly to her right so that the three kaiju formed a triangle around the super robot.

The Kaiju Corps had taken away Blackbolt's ability to fly and to attack them at high speed. With the robot now trapped between them, they sought to not only win a battle that could shift the outcome of the war but also to avenge their fallen leader. Leviathan roared giving then signal to attack, then all three kaiju charged the mech. Despite being outnumbered and without his two greatest advantages, Blackbolt was still far from an easy target. The mech delivered a sidekick to Leviathan's stomach that doubled the kaiju over. It then threw its elbow back to strike Bearadon in the face and stop her dead in her tracks.

Chagon had managed to wrap her injured body around the mech's left leg, and Blackbolt responded by bending down and landing a crushing chop to the dragon beast's spine. The blow rocked Chagon's body, but the monster ignored the pain and forced her body to maintain its hold on the robot's leg.

With Blackbolt's foot restrained by Chagon, Leviathan sprang forward and hit the robot with a roundhouse punch to the face that knocked the mech off balance and into Bearadon's waiting arms. The mammalian kaiju wrapped her arms around the mech and then bit down into its shoulder. Blackbolt reached under Bearadon's right arm with its left hand and then it shifted its body and free leg into her as well. Blackbolt then pulled forward and hip-tossed Bearadon directly into Leviathan, sending both kaiju sprawling to the ground.

Blackbolt then reached down and wrapped both of its hands around Chagon. It was starting to squeeze her when Bearadon's spiked tail swung around and smashed through Blackbolt's right hand above the wrist. Leviathan then sprang up and delivered an uppercut to Blackbolt's head that forced its body back into an upright position. Bearadon then pounced on the robot's right hip and started tearing into it with her teeth and claws. Leviathan roared as he delivered another punch to the mech's body that knocked it to the ground. Leviathan then jumped on top of the fallen robot where he began slamming his fists into the robot's chest.

With the Blackbolt on the ground and unable to resist her, Chagon continued to increase the pressure on the mech's leg until she felt it crumble beneath her. Bearadon dug her claws into the back of the mech's damaged right leg then she pulled it up and towards the mech's body until it tore off at the hip she was mauling. Leviathan continued to pound on the crippled mech's chest until he punched clear through its body and was striking the ground beneath it. When Blackbolt was completely destroyed, Leviathan stood and roared and Bearadon and Chagon joined him in a victory call.

Leviathan then looked toward the launch site to see dozens of small machines working to prepare another ship to carry the frozen remains of countless people into deep space. Leviathan looked at Chagon and Bearadon who both nodded at him. The three kaiju then made their way to the launch site and razed it to the ground.

After the destruction of the launch site, the remaining members of the Kaiju Corps walked back to the body of their fallen leader. The three monsters then sat down to rest and look at Garudasaurus. As they waited for their bodies to heal, they said their last goodbyes to their fallen friend.

Russia

Captain Okafur landed in Russia then he and Thomas pulled the last of their warheads out into the wilds of northern Russia. They attached the deflated weather balloon and detonator to the warhead then they walked back to the TR-3B for warmth. When they were sitting inside the craft, Okafur looked at Thomas, "How long do we wait?"

Thomas looked at his watch. "Williams and Brian have one hour to reach the last drop point in India."

India

Williams, Brian, and the rest of their team had managed to make the drop and move on to India with fifteen minutes to spare before the designated launch time. Brian quickly prepped the balloon, warhead, and detonator for launch then he looked over at Williams. "Everything is ready to go. Now we just wait." The exhausted Williams simply nodded as he leaned against his TR-3B. Brian watched as the seconds ticked by, and when his watch hit zero, he filled up the balloon and let it go. He watched as it rose into the air.

Williams yelled out to him, "Are we safe out here?"

Brian nodded. "We should be fine. The explosion will take place so high above the Earth that we should be safe from any fallout." Brian shifted his eyes to the ground. "I would avoid looking directly at the explosion though."

Both men cast their eyes to ground, and then a few seconds later, a bright flash of light appeared overhead. Brian waited for the light to dissipate. "We did it. If everyone else was successful, there will be no new robots created from this point on. Now to backtrack on our journey and see if the others were successful with their launches."

The two men climbed back into their TR-3B and started backtracking their journey halfway around the world.

EPILOGUE

Chicago – Six weeks after the Battle of Cape Canaveral and the execution of Program 437

Clarissa stood at the head of the table where she had previously led the discussion on initiating Program 437 and freeing the major cities along the US East Coast from robot occupation. Seated at the table with here were Nick, Miki, Michelle, Captains Okafur, Granderson, and Williams, as well as Thomas, Brian, and Susan. Clarissa took a deep breath before addressing everyone. "I want to thank you all for your exemplary service to mankind over the past two months. As you know, the execution of Project 437 was a success. We have stopped the production of giant robots across the planet and as far as we know severely hampered the robots' ability to send resources into space. Captains Okafur and Williams were also able to retrieve every volunteer who set off one of the warheads and bring them back here to basecamp."

She unrolled a map of the US across the table. "We have also secured the areas along the Great Lakes and the United States eastern seaboard. Susan and Thomas have been working tirelessly to set up food production, medical, and water purification systems in these areas. With winter approaching, we expect to lose a good deal of the population over the next few months, but we will do all that we can to help keep these losses to a minimum. The other good news regarding our two settlements is that Brian and a small team of electricians and mechanics he has put together are constructing a telegraph system that we can use to communicate between the two camps and that the robots will not be able to hack."

Clarissa pointed to three dots she had marked in the Midwestern US. "Surveillance from our two remaining TR-3Bs suggest that the three dots indicated here represent the human farms that we thought the robots might construct. These farms will be the next targets for the Kaiju Corps. If we can destroy the farms in these spots, we can liberate the people within them and add them to our numbers. The Kaiju Corps will attack them in teams of two with one TR-3B for transportation and support. The other TR-3B and Kaiju Corp member will stay back at one of the two basecamps to serve as protection against a potential attack. Once we free these three farms, we will continue to attack farms in North America, and eventually, the rest of the planet. Utilizing this beachhead attack on the farms across the planet will take a long time to prove to be completely successful. Our latest estimates are that there are still over two thousand robots active across the planet."

Miki raised her hand. "If the robots are still holding people in the farms, does that mean that they still feel that they have a way to launch them into space and send them back to where the Signal originated from?"

Clarissa shrugged. "We honestly do not know. It is possible that the robots who were programmed to carry out specific duties on the farms are simply following their programming. We are, however, having our TR-3B pilots make periodic flights over known launches sites around the world to see if it looks likes the already-existing robots are trying to construct new deep-space transportation vehicles. If we find a launch site that appears to be active, we will send in the Kaiju Corps to destroy it." She looked around the room. "Is there anything else that we need to cover with the group?"

Nick stood up. "I just want everyone to know that Garudasaurus's body has been buried and that Miki, Michelle, and I have constructed a memorial above it. The area is currently secure so that if anyone wishes to visit to pay their respects to Jerome, they can do so."

Clarissa nodded. "Thank you, Nick."

Michelle quietly stood and reached into her pocket. "I have never been good at saying things like this, but there will be another way to remember Jerome as well." She pulled out a pregnancy test and placed it on the table. Miki was the first person to see that the test was positive. She jumped out of her seat, wrapped her arms Michelle, and hugged her.

Everyone at the table knew that they were still fighting a war that would take lifetimes to win. They all knew that the world would never be the same. Despite all of this, they also knew that there were still people in the world worth fighting for.

THE END

 **SEVERED**PRESS

facebook.com/severedpress

twitter.com/severedpress

CHECK OUT OTHER GREAT KAIJU NOVELS

KAIJU WINTER
by Jake Bible

The Yellowstone super volcano has begun to erupt, sending North America into chaos and the rest of the world into panic. People are dangerous and desperate to escape the oncoming mega-eruption, knowing it will plunge the continent, and the world, into a perpetual ashen winter. But no matter how ready humanity is, nothing can prepare them for what comes out of the ash: Kaiju!

RAIJU
by K.H. Koehler

His home destroyed by a rampaging kaiju, Kevin Takahashi and his father relocate to New York City where Kevin hopes the nightmare is over. Soon after his arrival in the Big Apple, a new kaiju emerges. Qilin is so powerful that even the U.S. Military may be unable to contain or destroy the monster. But Kevin is more than a ragged refugee from the now defunct city of San Francisco. He's also a Keeper who can summon ancient, demonic god-beasts to do battle for him, and his creature to call is Raiju, the oldest of the ancient Kami. Kevin has only a short time to save the city of New York. Because Raiju and Qilin are about to clash, and after the dust settles, there may be no home left for any of them!

CHECK OUT OTHER GREAT KAIJU NOVELS

MURDER WORLD | KAIJU DAWN
by Jason Cordova
& Eric S Brown

Captain Vincente Huerta and the crew of the Fancy have been hired to retrieve a valuable item from a downed research vessel at the edge of the enemy's space.
It was going to be an easy payday.
But what Captain Huerta and the men, women and alien under his command didn't know was that they were being sent to the most dangerous planet in the galaxy.
Something large, ancient and most assuredly evil resides on the planet of Gorgon IV. Something so terrifying that man could barely fathom it with his puny mind. Captain Huerta must use every trick in the book, and possibly write an entirely new one, if he wants to escape Murder World.

KAIJU ARMAGEDDON
by Eric S. Brown

The attacks began without warning. Civilian and Military vessels alike simply vanished upon the waves. Crypto-zoologist Jerry Bryson found himself swept up into the chaos as the world discovered that the legendary beasts known as Kaiju are very real. Armies of the great beasts arose from the oceans and burrowed their way free of the Earth to declare war upon mankind. Now Dr. Bryson may be the human race's last hope in stopping the Kaiju from bringing civilization to its knees.
This is not some far distant future. This is not some alien world. This is the Earth, here and now, as we know it today, faced with the greatest threat its ever known. The Kaiju Armageddon has begun.

SEVEREDPRESS

 facebook.com/severedpress
 twitter.com/severedpress

CHECK OUT OTHER GREAT KAIJU NOVELS

KAIJU SPAWN
by David Robbins
& Eric S Brown

Wally didn't believe it was really the end of the world until he saw the Kaiju with his own eyes. The great beasts rose from the Earth's oceans, laying waste to civilization. Now Wally must fight his way across the Kaiju ravaged wasteland of modern day America in search of his daughter. He is the only hope she has left . . . and the clock is ticking.

From authors David Robbins (Endworld) and Eric S Brown (Kaiju Apocalypse), Kaiju Spawn is an action packed, horror tale of desperate determination and the battle to overcome impossible odds.

KUA MAU
by Mark Onspaugh

The Spider Islands. A mysterious ship has completed a treacherous journey to this hidden island chain. Their mission: to capture the legendary monster, Kua'Mau. Thinking they are successful, they sail back to the United States, where the terrifying creature will be displayed at a new luxury casino in Las Vegas. But the crew has made a horrible mistake - they did not trap Kua'Mau, they took her offspring. Now hot on their heels comes a living nightmare, a two hundred foot, one hundred ton tentacled horror, Kua'Mau, Kaiju Mother of Wrath, who will stop at nothing to safeguard her young. As she tears across California heading towards Vegas, she leaves a monumental body-count in her wake, and not even the U. S. military or private black ops can stop this city-crushing, havoc-wreaking monstrous mother of all Kaiju as she seeks her revenge.

CHECK OUT OTHER GREAT KAIJU NOVELS

ATOMIC REX
by Matthew Dennion

The war is over, humanity has lost, and the Kaiju rule the earth.

Three years have passed since the US government attempted to use giant mechs to fight off an incursion of kaiju. The eight most powerful kaiju have carved up North America into their respective territories and their mutant offspring also roam the continent. The remnants of humanity are gathered in a remote settlement with Steel Samurai, the last of the remaining mechs, as their only protection. The mech is piloted by Captain Chris Myers who realizes that humanity will not survive if they stay at the settlement. In order to preserve the human race, he leaves the settlement unprotected as he engages on a desperate plan to draw the eight kaiju into each other's territories. His hope is that the kaiju will destroy each other. Chris will encounter horrors including the amorphous Amebos, Tortiraus the Giant turtle , and the nuclear powered mutant dinosaur Atomic Rex!

KAIJU DEADFALL
by JE Gurley

Death from space. The first meteor landed in the Pacific Ocean near San Francisco, causing an earthquake and a tsunami. The second wiped out a small Indiana city. The third struck the deserts of Nevada. When gigantic monsters- Ishom, Girra, and Nusku- emerge from the impact craters, the world faces a threat unlike any it had ever known - Kaiju . NASA catastrophist Gate Rutherford and Special Ops Captain Aiden Walker must find a way to stop the creatures before they destroy every major city in America..

www.ingramcontent.com/pod-product-compliance
Lightning Source LLC
Chambersburg PA
CBHW032001170626
46807CB00006B/2598